Praise for the Wood...

Contradi...

"Tiffany King pours her soul into each book. She captures the hearts and minds of her characters perfectly, weaving tales of angst, hope, and redemption." —M. Leighton, *New York Times* bestselling author

Misunderstandings

"A beautifully woven story of a love that can withstand anything."
—Molly McAdams, *New York Times* bestselling author

"Funny, real, moving, and passionate, *Misunderstandings* is a MUST-READ for New Adult contemporary romance fans."
—Samantha Young, *New York Times* bestselling author

"Sweet and sexy! Great characters and an intriguing romance . . . So good!" —Cora Carmack, *New York Times* bestselling author

"I was completely captivated and caught up in this story. I haven't had a book make me laugh, swoon, or cry as much as *Misunderstandings* did in a while." —*Fresh Fiction*

No Attachments

"Allow me to summarize *No Attachments*: Great story. Amazing characters. Awesome read." —*Book Freak Book Reviews*

continued . . .

"Readers will spend the first half of this story on the edge of their seats and the last half hugging a box of tissues."

—Priscilla Glenn, bestselling author

"Sweet, beautiful, funny, and heartbreaking all rolled into one amazing story." —Tara Sivec, *USA Today* bestselling author

"Super sweet and swoon-worthy!"

—Jennifer L. Armentrout, #1 *New York Times* bestselling author

"The story itself is heartwarming, which really is a characteristic of a Tiffany King book. Her stories always turn struggles into strength and her characters always find the good. That's one of the reasons I love to read her books. They're real. They're emotional."

—*Stuck in Books*

"*No Attachments* will leave you more than a little attached to Ashton and Nathan." —*Book Angel Booktopia*

"Absolutely heartbreakingly beautiful." —*Once Upon a Twilight*

"Anyone who loves a great contemporary should check out this title. You'll laugh, you'll swoon, and you'll love these two characters just like I have." —*A Life Bound by Books*

a shattered moment

TIFFANY KING

BERKLEY BOOKS, NEW YORK

BERKLEY

An imprint of Penguin Random House LLC
375 Hudson Street, New York, New York 10014

Library of Congress Cataloging-in-Publication Data

King, Tiffany.
A shattered moment / Tiffany King. — Berkley trade paperback edition.
pages ; cm. — (A fractured lives novel ; 1)
ISBN 978-0-425-27950-2 (softcover)
1. Life change events—Fiction. 2. Traffic accident victims—Fiction.
3. Women college students—Fiction. I. Title.
PS3611.I5863S53 2015
813'.6—dc23
2014046513

PUBLISHING HISTORY
Berkley trade paperback edition / May 2015

PRINTED IN THE UNITED STATES OF AMERICA

10 9 8 7 6 5 4 3 2 1

Cover photo: Flowers by Vilor/Shutterstock.
Cover design by Lesley Worrell.
Interior text design by Kelly Lipovich.

Penguin
Random
House

To Valerie, Shana, and Rob. Thank you for your support during my ride on this amazing crazy train.

a shattered moment

prologue

graduation night 2013

The breeze blowing through the open windows of the SUV was hot and sticky thanks to the blanket of humidity that was normal for this time of year. Not that my friends and I cared. Even with sweat running down our backs and our hair plastered to the napes of our necks. We were too amped-up to worry about something as pesky as the weather. Today we were free. This was the moment we had discussed at length. The moment we had planned for and dreamed about. We didn't need drugs or alcohol to experience our current state of euphoria. We were high on life and the anticipation of what the future held.

Laughter filled the interior of the Suburban, drowning out

the roar from the oversized off-road tires as we cruised down the highway. It was the sound of exhilaration and triumph fifteen years in the making. Fifteen years of friendship that had stood the test of time. Through the muck of adolescent squabbles, preteen dramas, and the turbulent years of high school, we had made it to the other side of graduation. Our friendship was unbreakable. We made a pact many years ago over mud pies and juice boxes. We swore we would always be friends. No matter what the obstacles, we managed to stay inseparable. Our parents, who had also become close over the years, had coined us the "Brat Pack." They would laugh every time they said it, like it was some inside joke only they were privy to. I guess you had to be older than forty to get it.

I swept my eyes around the vehicle, listening to the loud music blaring from the radio as the wind played with my hair. With the exception of my family, anyone who had ever meant anything to me was here.

Zach was always our driver. His parents gave him the keys to the Suburban when he turned sixteen, knowing it was the perfect vehicle for our group. We were used to doing everything together, so it only made sense that the first of us to obtain a coveted driver's license would receive a vehicle big enough to carry everyone. The Suburban was a year older than we were and had its fair share of dings and rust spots, but it was trusty and reliable.

If he minded becoming our designated chauffeur, he never complained. That was Zach in a nutshell. He was the guy everyone liked, and for good reason. He was the first to lend a hand or volunteer his services, or even listen if you needed someone to talk to. He had been the captain of the football team and class president junior and senior year. Zach was a born leader, which is why he was bound for FSU in the fall on full scholarship. He had also always been my stand-in boyfriend. It was an on-again/off-again routine we had fallen into. I knew I could always count on him. My plan was to avoid a serious relationship before college. Zach had provided the perfect buffer. All along we had planned to spend this final summer together before we headed off to separate schools. If Zach promised, I knew I could bank on it, or so I thought.

I pulled my thoughts away from their current path. There was no reason to muck up the evening we'd been planning forever. Instead, I moved my eyes to Dan and Kathleen sitting in the third row with their heads pressed together. They had been a thing since we were kids. Not a thing like Zach and me, but a real couple. Their love had been forged over shared cookies and building sandcastles. It had always been Dan and Kat/Kat and Dan. In the beginning, their parents tried to rein in their kids' feelings for each other, but that was like telling the sun not to shine. They were the image of soul mates. The pending separation of our group would be hardest on them. Kat's parents insisted on the idea of her and Dan attending separate colleges, at least for the first couple of years. They wanted her to be sure that Dan would be more than a childhood romance. Kat confided to us that she only planned on giving it a year, if that long. This is why I'd always kept things casual. As close as we all were as friends, the idea of planning your college career around a guy seemed extreme to me.

"Class of 2013, bitches!" Jessica yelled from the second row, where she sat with my best friend, Tracey. Filled with exuberance and more adventurous than the rest of our Brat Pack, they were usually also the loudest. They were ready to take on the world and would stretch their wings wider than any of the rest of us in the group. I actually felt a little jealous, wishing I had an ounce of their fearlessness. Tracey's eyes met mine briefly before darting away. I grimaced without saying a word. Nothing would mar today. That is the vow I made to myself. Tomorrow would be soon enough to analyze what I had discovered.

I shifted back around in my seat as Zach drove over the causeway. We all whooped with our hands in the air as we reached the top. In the remaining light of dusk, we could see the dark never-ending expansion of water in the distance. We were close to our first destination of the evening.

Zach slowed to a crawl; maneuvering the Suburban around an old Lincoln Towncar going twenty-five miles per hour, even though the speed limit was almost double that. I had respect for my elders, but anyone who says teenagers are the worst drivers has obviously never lived in Florida.

Of course, Zach didn't mind. He was patient and cautious, even after jerking the wheel to avoid a moped that darted in front of us. The bikini-clad girl perched on the back didn't even bother looking at us as she flipped us off.

"Stupid asses, huh?" Zach laughed, shooting me a smile I

thought I returned until I saw his face fall slightly before he looked back to the road. Sighing, I turned my head to look out my window. Of all the days for me to discover what had probably been going on under my nose for some time, why did it have to be today?

Seeing Zach's smile drop, I realized I wasn't fooling anyone. I could put on a facade that everything was okay, but deep down, three of us in this vehicle knew differently.

Minutes later we arrived at the public parking lot at New Smyrna Beach. We piled out of the Suburban, breathing in the salty sea air. Kat linked her arms with mine and Tracey's while Jessica linked my other arm. Our human chain was complete when the guys bookended us on either side and we raced down the grassy slope to the long expansion of sand. We kicked our shoes off the instant our feet touched the sand, which had already started to cool now that the sun had gone down.

Laughter rang through the air as we raced toward the dark water without slowing. Our graduation robes flared out behind us like capes. With the wind whipping them around, we almost felt like we could fly as we splashed into the incoming waves. Nothing could hold us back. We were invincible.

We never made it to our second destination that night. Sadly, we weren't invincible.

I would later be asked countless times what happened, forced to recall what I remembered about the accident that changed everything. Clarity of the events was never an issue. I breathed it—had nightmares about it. It would haunt me for the rest of my life.

Zach had just merged onto the interstate, heading toward Orlando. Everything happened so quickly and unexpectedly. My mind was still focused on what had transpired as we left the beach. Not on the careless driver on the highway who acted like we were never there.

It was Jessica screaming after the semitruck slammed into the side of the Suburban that will be forever burned into my mind like a bad song that refused to go away. The oversized advertisement for fresh strawberries that ran the length of the trailer was the last thing that appeared upright after Zach jerked the wheel to avoid another collision. I would later learn that our momentum combined with the impact from the trailer were the culprits for what happened next.

With the horrific grinding sound of metal against metal and the sickening smell of burning rubber, the wheels on the right side of the Suburban left the road, sending us airborne. I had heard once that when you're in an accident, everything passes in a blur of slow motion. That is total bullshit. It's instant chaos. Fast and scary are more accurate—and loud. So loud you feel like your ears will burst. So hectic you can't tell where sounds are coming from. It's a jumbled mess of groaning metal beat out of its original shape, shattering glass, blaring horns, and worst of all, screams of pain from your friends. And yet, through it all, I remember every detail with painstaking lucidity.

"How could you possibly know how many times the vehicle rolled?" That is always the first question asked when I recount the series of events for someone. It was a question that haunted me as well. It was as if I was being cosmically punished for some wrong I had committed. If I knew what it was, I would take it all back. I would trade places with any of my friends over being forever tormented by vivid memories that I could never escape. Each roll of the vehicle was significant by what it did to my friends. The first roll sent Tracey's head against her window with a thud. The second roll abruptly silenced Dan, who had been swearing from the moment Jessica started screaming. Kat shrieked Dan's name in anguish, overpowering Jessica's screams during the third bone-crunching roll of the vehicle. On the fourth roll, Jessica's screams stopped like someone had flipped a switch. I panicked, believing at any moment my last breath would be snuffed out like the flame of a candle.

We stopped on the fifth roll, finally coming to a rest mid-turn, leaving us upside down. The bench seat Zach and I shared tore away from the metal bolts that attached it to the floorboard and tumbled forward, pinning me to the dashboard. My head exploded with pain as it bounced off the windshield. I vaguely remember wondering why an airbag hadn't opened. It turns out the old Suburban that Zach had been given by his parents was a year away from that upgrade. A steady hum filled my ears. It was as if I had been swaddled in a cocoon of cotton. I felt absolutely nothing.

one

Mac

one year later

"No, Mom, not this weekend," I said, rolling my eyes at the phone even though she couldn't see me. "I have a big test next week in sociology. I have to stay and study." I sank down on the dorm room bed, which was adjusted to the perfect height for my bum leg.

"But, Mackenzie, you haven't been home in ages."

"Mac," I corrected automatically.

She sighed, but didn't comment on my correction. I had decided to change my name over a year ago, after the accident. For a while, she protested, which led to the same argument so many times, I could recite it word for word. I think she assumed I would eventually get sick of the shortened version or that if she ignored it and continued to call me by my full name, I would concede and "come to my senses," as she would say. I could have told her not to hold her breath, but that would be like telling her I was fine, which was pointless because my mom had selective hearing. She didn't understand what I had endured and probably never would.

I only half listened as she rattled out all the reasons I should come home for the weekend. My eyes drifted to the other side of the room that belonged to my dorm mate, Trina. I noticed her belongings were slowly beginning to disappear. It was no secret she was unhappy living with me. She had certain expectations for a college roommate, like occasional conversation, some exchanged pleasantries, maybe even a friendly smile once in a while. What she got instead was mostly silence mixed with shrugs, an occasional grunt, and a half-darkened room because I usually turned off my lamp at 9 p.m. each night and pretended to be asleep, even if I wasn't really tired. She put up with it for a while, but eventually gave up trying to coax me out of my shell.

None of it was her fault, of course. I just wasn't ready to be anyone's friend. That was my mistake when I convinced my parents I would be better off living in the dorms than making the forty-five-minute commute from home for classes each day like I had done freshman year. I thought I was ready to interact, but I couldn't have been more wrong. I wished I could find the words to explain myself to Trina, but I couldn't seem to muster up enough emotion to care.

Mom broke through my thoughts when she switched the conversation to where it inevitably always ended up—the accident. I wondered if we would ever have a normal conversation again. She droned on about the letter that had come in from the law firm that was handling everything for the victims. That's how we were referred to now—*the victims*. A full year had passed and the insurance companies were still dragging their feet, not allowing anyone involved to move on. They had proven to be complete scumbags. I couldn't care less about the money or who was suing who. All I wanted was to be able to have a conversation with my parents without the words "victims" or "lawyers" or "insurance claims."

I waited until she took a breath in between sentences. "Mom, I can't talk about this now, okay? I'll come home in a couple weeks. I really do need to study for my test."

"Maybe your father and I can drive up to take you to dinner."

This time it was my turn to sigh. I understood why she pushed so hard. Hell, for a long time after everything that happened, I needed her. I had become afraid of the dark. Closing my eyes meant reliving images that were too painful to remember. Mom spent many nights during my recovery sleeping in my hospital room in a backbreaking chair that converted into a narrow bed. Through it all she never complained. She was my rock. It was only after I left the hospital that I began to resent the constraints of having her around. At that point, everything was dictated for me. Therapy for my leg, follow-up visits with doctors, and weekly appointments with the psychiatrist were all scheduled for me. I had no say in anything. I knew my parents were only trying to help, but I felt smothered.

"Honey, are you listening?" Mom's voice broke through my reverie.

"Yeah, Mom," I lied. I didn't have a clue what she had said.

"Okay, so we'll pick you up tomorrow evening at five for Olive Garden, and then maybe afterward we can even see a movie. There's that new romantic comedy with the guy from that Disney show you used to like."

"You mean the show I haven't watched since I was twelve? You do know I'm an adult now, right, Mom?" I pulled the phone away from my ear and silently screamed at it. "Look, my test is really important and—"

"I know, honey, but you have to eat, and taking two hours to relax while you watch a movie should be allowed. I realize you wanted to live on campus for some space, but it's still just college, not jail."

"Isn't that supposed to be my argument?" I asked dryly. "A little space."

I used the cane I had developed a love-hate relationship with, to rise from my bed. I absolutely hated being dependent on it, but I couldn't deny its necessity. The hard truth was I would probably need it for the rest of my life. The surgeons had done everything in their power to fix my leg. In the end, despite having more hardware than the Bionic Woman, it was still a mess.

"How's the leg?" Mom asked like she was hot-wired into my brain.

"Fine." We all knew it wasn't anywhere close to fine, but when she asked, what else was I going to say? At least I could walk. I was lucky in comparison to my friends. I jerked my thoughts back before they could stroll down that agony-filled path again. "Look, Mom, I've gotta go. I'll see you tomorrow for dinner."

"And a movie," she persisted before I could hang up.

"We'll see," I said reluctantly. "I love you."

"Love you, too, sweets."

Glad to have my daily interrogation out of the way, I placed my cell phone into the side pocket of my backpack for easy access. Gone were the days of carrying a purse. The backpack I used was lightweight and completely functional, keeping my hands free— one for my cane, and the other hand ready to catch myself on the rare occasion when my leg would not cooperate while walking on uneven ground. I had learned that painfully embarrassing lesson one time in front of the campus bookstore, falling flat on my ass when a seemingly innocuous crack tripped me up.

I gathered the rest of my belongings and headed for the library, leaving my newly constructed dorm building that resembled condominiums in size and amenities. My dad had complained when we toured the university during my senior year in high school that the campus was too "new looking." Of course, he was an alumnus of Florida State University, which, he liked to brag, was steeped in tradition and character. Over the years, we had gone to several FSU football games, and to me, there was a fine line between history and just old. I personally preferred UCF's modern architecture and facilities over aged vine-covered brick buildings. Of course, I had to keep my opinions to myself when I chose UCF since Dad would have a coronary if he heard me criticizing his old stomping grounds.

It was a long walk from my dorm to the library, and my leg had a tendency to lag about halfway there. I slowed my pace, hoping today it would give me a break until I could pass the lawn in front of the Student Academic Resource Center, where everyone liked to hang out. As I approached the popular hot spot, I tried to hide my limp as I passed a group of guys playing a game of Frisbee on the lush green lawn.

I remember the first brochure I opened for the school, before I had even decided to apply. I was immediately enthralled by the pictures of carefree students playing touch football and hanging out studying on heavy quilts lying in this plush expansion of grass. Everyone looked hip and happy. I remember thinking it reminded me of one of the Old Navy commercials on TV. I used to imagine myself in those pictures, spending time with the new friends I was sure to make. That memory was almost laughable now. I had no friends, and wouldn't even think of trying to play Frisbee. Even something as simple as getting up from a sitting position on the ground required crawling and rocking back and forth as I tried to get my leg to cooperate.

My only goal, as it was every day, was to get to the library without anyone noticing me. Once I rounded the corner and was out of sight, my steps became nothing more than a shuffle the closer I got to my destination. Sweat beaded on my forehead while a steady stream ran down my back. There was no such thing as mild autumn temperatures in central Florida. Even in October, it was still eighty-five degrees and humid. I had exerted a fair amount of energy crossing the campus. My good leg was beginning to shake from shouldering the brunt of the work, while the handle of my cane became slick from the sweat of my palm. I knew I should stop and wipe it off, but I ignored it. I just needed to get to my safe place.

That was what the library had become for me. It was a sanctuary, an easy place to hide among the books and computers. Avoiding conversation was easy since talking in the library wasn't encouraged. Being there made me feel normal—the way I wanted my normal to be—which was why I would trek halfway across campus every day after classes. Jake, my physical therapist, whom I still saw twice a month, was always riding me about pushing myself too hard, but the walk was better than the alternative of spending evenings at my dorm.

Not that I would ever admit that fact to Mom or Dad. They would press me to move back home again, but that would be the easy way out. All that did was keep me dependent on my parents. It was a struggle living on campus, but I had to keep trying. It didn't help that no one seemed to respect private space and that every night felt like a giant sleepover. The first couple days of the semester, people barged into my room, looking for Trina, not even bothering to knock. By the end of the first weekend, I grew tired of it and started locking the door, forcing Trina to use her key anytime she entered. She was never quiet with her grumblings, making a point to tell me I was becoming the hermit of our dorm building. Ironically, I discovered the seclusion of the library around the same time that Trina started spending more time away from our room. I should have told her I was rarely there during the day anyway, but that would have required initiating a conversation.

I stopped just outside the library to let out a pent-up breath—taking a moment to wipe the perspiration from the handle of my cane.

A cool blast of air welcomed me as I pulled open the heavy door. Giving my eyes a chance to adjust to the dim interior, I glanced around the large room, grimacing at the crowds of people scattered about. Midterms for the first nine weeks were approaching, making my hideout a popular spot during the past week.

Trying to be discreet, I headed for my normal seat in the far corner of the room. My cane clicked loudly on the floor, echoing through the open space with each step. I kept my head down, trying to make myself invisible, but I could feel everyone's eyes upon me. Their stares were heavy and smothering. It didn't help that I was still overexerted from my trek across campus. My breath came out in slight wheezing gasps. I needed to sit. I made the final surge to my secluded seat, stumbling slightly from the floor's transition from hard tile to carpet. Luckily, my cane helped keep me upright.

Relieved to be able to rest, I sank into the comfortable leather wing chair that I'd discovered weeks ago. If I had my way, I'd hang a sign from it, declaring this spot as mine alone. I closed my eyes, dropping my head into my hands as I waited for my lungs to start breathing evenly again. Maybe Jake had a point. It was possible my brisk pace to get past the crowded scene at the Student Resource Center wasn't the smartest thing for me to do. My leg ached badly, and I felt slightly nauseous. I fumbled blindly through my backpack for a water bottle I knew I had packed, jumping at the sound of a male voice over my shoulder.

"Are you okay?"

"I'm fine," I answered, keeping my eyes closed while I gripped the arm of the chair. I could feel the presence of the person beside me, invading my personal space. I counted to ten in my head, waiting for him to leave.

"Do you mind?" My voice dripped like a leaky faucet with sarcasm after stopping at six in frustration.

"Not at all," the stranger responded without budging.

"This seat is taken."

He barked out a laugh. "I know. By me."

Great. Just what I needed—a smart-ass. Dropping my hands, I glared up at the douche bag who couldn't take a hint. I was just about ready to tear him a new one until his face came into focus.

I knew him, or at least, I remembered him. The one time I had gotten a good look at him would be forever branded into my mind.

graduation night 2013

A male face peered at me through the broken window, shining a small penlight into my eyes. "Do you know where you are?"

I started to nod my head, forgetting it was pinned against the dashboard. I grimaced from the resulting stab of pain. "Yes," I answered.

"Try not to move," he instructed. "Can you tell me what your name is?"

"Mackenzie Robinson."

"Good, very good. Do you know what day it is?" He swept the light through the rest of the vehicle assessing the damage.

"Graduation."

"Huh?" he responded, returning the light back to me.

"Today was graduation. May twenty-eighth."

His face was difficult to make out in the dim light, but he was definitely younger with a boyish look. I couldn't help wondering if he was even old enough to be here. No offense to him, but the last thing I wanted was someone who was new to the job.

He continued to ask me questions while he took my vitals. After assuring me they would have me out soon, he turned to Zach, who was not in my line of vision.

"Is he dead?" My voice was thick as I braced myself to hear the words I assumed to be true. The EMT didn't answer, which made it much worse. Tears fell hot and fast from my eyes. I was stuck in a coffin with all of my friends. Why was this happening?

two

Mac

"You sorta stole my seat," he chuckled, pointing to the backpack I had missed that was resting beside the chair. Judging by the array of papers spread out on the table, he'd been hard at work.

"Oh shit, I'm sorry." Heat crept up my neck to my face as I fumbled around to locate my cane, which had slipped to the ground. After finding it, I struggled to get to my feet with my right leg still quivering. I couldn't tell if he recognized me. The last time he'd seen my face, it was bruised and battered. I wasn't even sure why I cared, to tell you the truth. I shook my head to clear the sudden cobwebs that had muddled my thoughts.

He gently pushed me back into the seat. "It's no biggie. I can move to another chair," he said, reaching for his backpack.

"I don't mind moving," I mumbled even though my legs were begging me to stay put.

"Please. I'm serious. You stay. This is my first time trying to study in the library, but I've discovered I'm easily distracted."

I nodded my head, not sure what the appropriate answer would be. I looked away, hoping that would be the end of our exchange and he would move on. Hearing his voice again was stirring up the demons I worked hard to keep at bay.

I exhaled gratefully when he began to gather his papers.

"So, how have you been?" he asked.

Crap balls. That answered my question. Of course he recognized me. My friends and I had been splashed across the news for weeks after the accident. The media decided to make us the faces of No Texting While Driving campaigns.

Not that we were the culprits. My friends and I were the victims of a crime that was as illegal as drinking and driving, yet everyone seemed to do it. Everyone except Zach, who refused even to talk on his phone while he was driving. Even after all of us pitched in and bought him a Bluetooth earpiece for his phone, he refused to use it. That was the ironic thing about our accident. I couldn't help wondering what had been so important that the truck driver felt the need to text while he was driving a big rig. Was he telling his wife he'd be home late, or maybe reminding his kids to finish their homework, or was he texting a buddy about going out? Did he regret that text now? Did he even realize or care about the lives he had shattered into a million pieces? There were so many questions, but no real answers.

"I, uh—" I tried to answer his question, but the tall bookshelves surrounding us began to close in on me. I was in no shape to flee, but I could feel the all too familiar signs of a panic attack approaching.

Panic attacks had become my body's way of dealing with any uncomfortable situation since the accident. They were sneaky bastards, creeping in when I least wanted them to. Like the time Mom and Dad helped me get into a car for the first time after the accident, or when I drove by the scene of an accident six months after I was released from the hospital. I had become an expert at knowing when it was happening. My breathing would become labored, I would sweat profusely, and it was as if there was a voice in my head telling me to run or hide. Consequently, it had been nearly six months since my last attack and I had naïvely convinced myself they were gone for good.

Trying to get a handle on myself before things got too embarrassing, I moved my eyes past the EMT, finding a focal point on the wall just over his shoulder. Joan, my therapist, had given me tips and advice on how to avoid a full-blown attack before it sank its claws into me. It was all about focusing on something you could control. For me, it worked to count for as long as it took to calm down. I had reached twenty when I could feel the stranglehold of the attack slowly releasing me.

"You okay?" the EMT asked, stepping directly into my field of vision. It felt like déjà vu. My eyes became fixated by the soft comforting brown of his pupils. My breathing returned to normal as I took in the genuine concern on his face. This was the second time he had calmed me from a near-panicked state.

"Fine—I'm fine." I wasn't sure which of us I was trying to convince. I looked down to find the water bottle I had been searching for sitting in my hand.

He perched on the corner of the table he'd just cleared off. "Sorry. It's a hazard of the job. I'm always overstepping boundaries by being too helpful. My mom says I've been trying to save things since I was four years old when I tried to reattach a lizard's tail with superglue. I'd say she was exaggerating, but the picture she snapped of me with the lizard superglued to my finger speaks for itself." He laughed, flashing a dimpled smile.

I surprised myself by returning his smile.

"You have a beautiful smile."

My mouth dropped, as did my stomach. He was a liar.

I didn't need his pity. I knew my smile was anything but attractive now. The shattered glass from the windshield had made sure of that, leaving a thin scar from the corner of my lip and down my chin. It had whitened a bit over the past year, but was still noticeable.

"Gee, thanks," I said sarcastically as I grabbed my bag.

He sat watching me with fascination, which only added to my aggravation. In my haste to stand up to leave, I forgot about the water bottle, which dropped from my hand and rolled away, coming to a rest beneath the table. I blurted out a string of swear words that would have made a biker blush, gaining me several disapproving looks from everyone except the EMT, who only chuckled. Shouldering my bag, I gripped my cane and limped away, leaving my water bottle and the EMT behind.

My leg complained bitterly as I hobbled toward another

seating area on the far side of the room. The chairs were situated near a high-traffic area, making it less desirable, but it would have to do.

Mr. Persistent followed me, handing over the water bottle I had dropped. "Hey, you didn't have to leave because of me."

I bit back a groan. Seriously, this guy needed to get a clue. "I just need a little peace, so I can study." My words were rude, and the tone was harsh.

"Right. Well, like I said, I'm not very good at this whole library studying thing. I'm Bentley, by the way. Bentley James."

"Mac," I returned shortly.

"So, what are you studying?"

"Listen, Bentley. It was cool seeing you again. I'm, uh, just not very good around people right now, you know?" I hated being this way, but I wasn't much of a conversationalist anymore.

"Oh, hey, I get it. I'll leave you to it then. It's time I got back to the old grindstone anyway," he said, holding up an anatomy book that was easily three times as thick as a regular textbook. Oddly, he still didn't walk away.

An awkward silence stretched between us until finally, after a few seconds that felt like an eternity, he spoke up again. "Okay, I guess I better get busy." He flashed another smile before walking off.

My eyes followed him now that his back was turned. It was actually the first time I had noticed any of his features below the shoulders. He was taller than me, which wasn't saying much, but I guessed him to be at least six feet tall. His broad shoulders made him appear even bigger. His face was boyishly cute with warm brown eyes that sparkled like he was keeping a secret he couldn't wait to share. On the night he rescued me, he had been serious and focused, while today he was laid-back and carefree. Regardless of his mood, he was definitely handsome.

Tracey would say he was hunk-worthy. My breath hitched at the errant thought that had slipped into my mind. My heart thumped erratically in my chest. I clasped my hand against it, trying to ease the ache that was quickly spreading down to my clenching stomach. Pulling my eyes away from Bentley, I forced my mind to go blank. As long as I didn't think about them, I could make it through another minute, another hour, and maybe another day.

As I worked to pull my thoughts from entering what I called my *dark zone*, I kept my eyes away from Bentley, blaming him for taking me there in the first place. The idea was irrational, I realized. It's not like it was his fault we had run into each other on campus. He had as much right to be here as I did. How ironic that in a city with millions of people, I would run into the EMT who had helped save my life.

graduation night 2013

"Hey, hey, it's okay," the EMT said, moving to my side as the machines I was hooked to responded to my distress. "You need to calm down." He adjusted the oxygen mask on my face. "Breathe in slowly," he coaxed, leaning over to make sure the mask was snug against my cheeks. The panic dispersed slightly

as oxygen entered my airway. My lungs inhaled deeply while I looked into my rescuer's eyes.

"It's going to be okay, I promise." His hand gently stroked my head. If the tape on my forehead wasn't restricting my movement, I would have shaken my head in protest. It would never be okay.

"Trust me," he murmured, seeing the doubt in my eyes. He continued to stroke my head. His touch worked better at soothing me than the oxygen now pouring into my lungs. I could also feel my head beginning to clear.

With one last sudden jerk of the wheel, the ambulance pulled into the brightly lit emergency bay at Halifax Medical Center. I lost sight of my rescuer after several medical personnel surrounded my stretcher, which was cautiously lifted from the vehicle. I wanted to call out to him. I couldn't do this by myself.

I glanced back toward the table to see if he was looking at me. He wasn't, of course, and I couldn't blame him. I was pretty much a bitch. After everything he had done for me, I couldn't muster a thank-you, or any other way to show my appreciation. Instead, I'd basically told him off.

I was unsure of how long Bentley stuck around because I couldn't bring myself to peek in his direction again. To show any kind of interest would be a misrepresentation of my intentions. I was incapable of functioning as a normal person. Not because of my limp, or even my less-than-perfect smile, but because I was nothing but a shell. Everything inside me died more than a year ago.

The serenity of the library had been replaced by a blanket of painful reminders. As the afternoon bled into evening and the light outside dimmed from twilight to nighttime, the library began to empty. I never looked up as each set of footsteps passed. My headphones and iPad gave the illusion that I was too busy to care. Finally able to breathe normally again, I packed up my bag. Tomorrow, the library would be my sanctuary again. Bentley had mentioned that studying in the library wasn't his thing. Hopefully, today had been a fluke, and I wouldn't run into him again.

three

Bentley

I slammed my anatomy book closed a little louder than necessary, earning a curious glance from a long-legged redhead
who had been eye flirting with me since she sat down. For a
solid hour, I'd been staring at the same damn page in my book
without comprehending a single word. My focus was for shit
today. I could blame it on trying to study at the library rather
than my apartment, but truthfully, the reason for my distraction
was sitting in a chair across the room. Not the redhead who
was practically begging for me to notice her, but the five-foot-
something, sharp-tongued cutie who had basically told me to
take a flying leap. She'd introduced herself as Mac. I remembered
her name being Mackenzie, but Mac was better. It suited her.

I recognized her the instant she sat in my chair. How could
I not? For days following the accident, the media had a field

day splashing her and her friends' faces on every news channel. Maybe that was the reason I found myself so captivated with her at the moment. It definitely wasn't her winning personality, since she practically had a *no trespassing* sign hanging from her neck. Being shot down might have bruised my ego any other time, but her "fuck off" attitude intrigued me.

She was not only my first rescue, but now the first person I'd rescued and then bumped into in a normal setting. I remember that night clearly. The guys at the station called me "The Green Pea" because I was new to the job. I was so nervous when the dispatch alarm went off that I launched myself from the chair I was sitting in like I had just heard the starting gun for a hundred-meter dash. The worst part was I tripped over my own feet and fell face-first into my supervisor's ass. Steve was the lead paramedic and luckily a patient dude. Newbie or not, when we arrived at the scene of the accident, I was thrown right into the thick of things.

The images of their crushed Suburban have stayed with me to this day. When our rescue crew arrived on the scene, I remember assuming there was no way anyone could survive an accident of that magnitude. The one point Steve had hammered into my head that first day was that not everyone can be saved. It was a tough pill all first responders were forced to swallow. I stood like a deer in headlights, staring at the mangled heap of twisted metal. After all my anxiousness for my first call, I suddenly panicked that I wouldn't be able to hack it as an EMT, let alone continue my education to become a certified paramedic.

"James, get your ass over to the passenger side and check

for signs of any survivors!" Steve had yelled, snapping me into action. After that, it was Mac who reminded me of why I'd chosen to become an EMT. That night she needed me. Even with my limited responsibilities, I felt I had helped her that night.

The redhead working for my attention jerked my thoughts back to the present. She stood up, making a show of stretching out a kink while her tight black Hollister T-shirt rode upward, exposing a taut tanned stomach that she was obviously proud of. She eyed me appraisingly for a moment before sashaying in my direction.

"Hey, you want to get some coffee or maybe a drink?" Her voice had a female huskiness that was sexy and inviting.

I contemplated her words. She was smoking hot, and judging from the way she was eyeing me, she liked what she saw. I glanced over toward Mac. Her head was down like it had been all afternoon since our exchange earlier. Her hair cascaded over her face, hiding it from view. By the way she was feverishly typing on her iPad, it was obvious I was the farthest thing from her mind. Her indifference should have turned me off. I might not be a chiseled Greek god, but I'd never had much trouble in the girl department. As evidenced by Red standing in front of me, asking me out. I didn't need to chase after someone who clearly wasn't interested, but that was the problem. I swear I'd caught a hint of interest from Mac before I commented on her smile. I'm not sure why, but after that she clammed up. I guess

I came on too strong. Some girls don't like that. Regardless, I may have struck out, but I wasn't ready to throw in the towel.

"Can't. I have a bitch of a test coming up in anatomy," I answered, dragging my eyes away from Mac and back to the redhead. She seemed put out that she didn't have my full attention.

"Come on, everyone deserves a break, right?" She placed a manicured hand on my bicep, sliding her fingers up to my shoulder and back down.

"Believe me, I wish I could, but I need to hit this hard tonight." I held up my book for evidence.

"You sure that's what you want to hit tonight? You have no idea what you're missing," she purred, still softly running her hand along my arm, leaving no doubt as to what she wanted. Her words had the opposite effect of what she had hoped, like a bucket of cold water being dumped on my head. I knew her type. Hell, freshman and sophomore year I'd seen more ass than a proctologist. My roommates and I had been in hog heaven after realizing many college girls were much more prone to jump into bed than they were in high school. It was as if they'd left their inhibitions back home and were now embracing their inner bad girl.

Eventually, it hit me that my friends and I couldn't be the only guys on campus getting lucky with some of these girls. One night at a party, I walked in on Lisa, a girl I was starting to fall for, while she was going down on some douche. Needless to say, I slowed down in the chick department after that. My roommates like to tease me now and call me a monk, but I'm not dumb enough to get burned twice.

"No thanks," I replied, gently extracting her fingers from my arm.

Apparently, rejection was new to her, because she looked baffled. "You sure?" Her lips pouted as a last-ditch attempt to be cute.

My eyes zeroed in on her puckered lips. Despite myself, I had to admit, I was turned on. What could I say? I'm still a guy. "Yeah. My test won't pass itself." I exhaled. My words had far less conviction than I was displaying on the outside.

"Maybe some other time?" she asked.

"Uh, sure. Maybe I'll run into you again sometime." The final cardinal sin I committed was not asking for her phone number. My roommates would definitely kick my ass and call me a pussy if they heard about this one.

She continued to look perplexed as she shrugged her shoulders and walked off without another word.

My eyes followed one of the finest rear ends I had ever seen, and for a moment, I felt like maybe my ass did need to be kicked.

The guy sitting in the chair to my right looked at me like I had turned down a million-dollar lottery ticket. "Dude, I can't believe you just said no to that." He was voicing my own sentiments, practically drooling as she pushed through the exit door. "Did you see how fucking long her legs were? Legs like that were made to wrap around your waist while you see if you can bottom out. You know what I mean?" he said, thrusting his hips in and out. "You gotta be crazy, dude. Or high."

"Crazy" pretty much fit. Feeling a bit like a chump, I shoved my book and papers into my backpack. Studying at the library had proven to be too much of a challenge. I needed space to spread out and access to food and drinks to fuel my brain. Not to mention, the library was too quiet. Apparently, I needed Michael's tunes blasting from his room and the sound of my best friend, Chad, playing Halo at full blast to get any studying done.

Shouldering my backpack, I nodded at the guy who thought I was a total dick for not taking up Red on her offer and headed for the door. I was tempted to stop and talk to Mac one last time, but I decided to play it cool and give her a little space. I'd be seeing her again. I would make sure of that.

The sun had already set, but the air was still thick with humidity when I pushed the library door open to leave. I barely noticed, setting off purposefully toward my apartment on the edge of campus. I was used to heat, having been born in south Florida. Cold weather was a completely different story. My parents took me skiing in Aspen when I turned eighteen, and I was a total pansy. I thought my balls would never recover from the frigid temperatures. Give me heat and humidity any day.

It looked like every light was on in the apartment I shared with Chad, my high school best friend, and Michael, a guy I had met from work. I could hear the sound of Master Chief's voice from Halo through the front door as I twisted the knob.

"Where you been all day?" Chad greeted me without looking away from the game on our fifty-inch TV.

"Studying. Weren't you playing when I left this morning?"
I sank down on the couch, reaching for a slice of pizza from
the box on the coffee table.

"Mom, is that you?" he asked, shooting an alien. "No, not
you, Slick. I was talking to B. He just walked in," Chad said
into the microphone of the headset he was wearing, speaking
to one of his online teammates.

"Like I'd claim a douche like you as my kid. And tell Slick
I said what's up." Chad responded by throwing pizza crust at
my head. I snatched it from the air before it could hit the ground,
and shoved it into my mouth.

"Want to play?" He tossed one of the spare controllers my
direction.

"Nah, I can only beat your guys' asses so many times." I
placed the controller on the table and ducked when he threw
an empty beer can at my head.

"You wish, bitch. I'm a Halo god."

"Riiight," I teased. "I need to shower anyway."

"I thought I smelled something foul."

"Shit, that's your upper lip, bro." I pulled off my T-shirt as
I stood up and headed toward the bathroom.

"You'll have to get Sherman out of the shower," he called
after me.

"Fantastic." Sherman and I had a hate-hate relationship. He
liked to show his distaste for me by spitting and hissing. As far
as I was concerned, he deserved a shallow grave.

Opening the bathroom door, I kicked a pile of Chad's and
Michael's clothes out of the way to get to the shower. I couldn't

complain. None of us were the best housekeepers. The only time it was ever really clean was when we knew one of our moms would be in town. We'd learned that lesson the hard way sophomore year when Chad's mom almost had a coronary when she walked through the front door.

Plucking a towel off the floor, I sniffed it to see if it was clean. It still had a faint scent of detergent, so I figured I was safe. I tossed it on the counter and approached the shower with trepidation. I should have told Chad to come get Sherman himself, but that would earn me the title of Total Pussy for a solid week.

I groaned, glaring down at the fluorescent green demon that was hanging out in an inch of water in our tub. "Don't be an asshole, Sherman." He responded to my words by hissing at me—ungrateful reptile. He obviously didn't give a shit who the shower belonged to. Reaching a hand down cautiously, I tried to extract the iguana, which was more than a foot long. That wasn't even counting his tail, which was almost as long. His tail whipped against the ceramic tub with a thud. I jerked my hand out of harm's way, but not before he grazed it. The little fucker, he did that on purpose. I swear the green monster had it in for me. After a few more failed attempts at grabbing him, I finally wrapped my hands around his leathery body and deposited him into his aquarium in Chad's room. Several welts decorated the back of my hand for my trouble. He was lucky I didn't feed him to the German shepherd next door. Sherman would make an excellent chew toy.

Twenty minutes later, I was showered and had another slice of pizza in my iguana tail–whipped hand. I shoved a pile of discarded clothes off my bed and sat down in front of my laptop, clicking the Google icon. I'd be up half the night studying, but that didn't stop me from investigating what had been occupying my mind all afternoon. It didn't take a lot of searching to find a list of articles about Mac and her friends. I clicked on the first website and a full picture of Mac and the others filled the screen. I'd seen this image dozens of times. It was the one the news stations loved to show viewers because of the poignant feel of lost youth. In the picture, Mac and her friends were decked out in graduation robes with their arms slung around each other's shoulders. They all looked so damn happy. Apparently, it was their last picture together. Little did they know that hours later their lives would never be the same.

I was beginning to feel like a stalker, but I enlarged the image so I could see Mac's face more clearly. She was laughing and seemed so carefree. Her eyes sparkled with excitement and her full lips were stretched into a wide smile. The girl I saw today was a far cry from the one smiling out at me on my computer screen. Her eyes no longer gleamed. They were flat and dull like an old stone.

four

Mac

Friday morning I still felt a little out of sorts over my encounter with Bentley, so I decided to take the cowardly approach and give up the sanctuary of the library for the weekend. With any luck, he would find another study spot and my world could return to normal on Monday. Since I had no Friday classes, I spent the day reading in bed and mentally preparing myself for the impending dinner with my parents that I had grudgingly agreed to. Trina never made an appearance, which wasn't surprising. I had no idea where she had gone, but she hadn't slept in her bed in days. She obviously still came and went from our dorm room when I wasn't here, because occasionally I would return to find some of her clothes freshly folded on her bed. I guess she was using our room for nothing more than her closet at this point.

Later that afternoon, I sat in a booth with my parents at Olive Garden, engaged in the customary small talk about school and how I was feeling. Inevitably, the conversation shifted to "the case." Every time the subject came up, it felt like I was watching a scene in a movie. I could almost hear the dramatic soundtrack of *dun-dun-duunn* as Mom's and Dad's normal faces would shift on cue to hardened expressions of concern. Over the past year and a half I'd gotten used to their transformation from loving, gentle-minded parents to unforgiving, hard-as-granite protectors whenever they discussed the accident. They were prepared to fight the insurance company and the trucking company for as long as it took until reparations were satisfied. I was not looking for a battle, though. The longer the fight dragged on, the more the memories of losing my friends gnawed at me. At times I felt like a dead carcass being devoured by wild animals.

Eventually we exhausted the subject, only to move to my second least favorite topic—Tracey's mom.

"She misses you. She feels like she not only lost Tracey, but you, too," Mom implored when I shook my head at her suggestion that I give her a call. I had always been closer to Tracey's mom, Patricia, than any of my other friends' parents. She looked younger than her actual age. Tracey had physically favored her so much that quite often people mistook them for sisters. It was a fun game we played throughout high school. Tracey and her mom would even go so far as to call me their sister when anyone would ask. "You spent as much time growing up at Tracey's house as you did at your own home. The twins miss you," my mom added.

"They don't miss me. They miss their sister," I mumbled. My bite of food lodged in my throat, making it difficult to swallow.

"Sweetie, they miss *you*, too. You haven't seen them since . . ." Her voice trailed off as she worked to compose herself before her emotions got the best of her. As steadfast as my parents were in their quest for justice, Mom had a hard time saying the word *accident*. It had become a tainted word. She didn't have to say any more for me to understand. The last time I had seen Tracey's twin brothers was when I hugged them after the graduation ceremony on that fateful night. Before my life changed so radically that I couldn't remember who I was.

Patricia had come to see me in the hospital two days after the accident. More than anyone else, I felt I owed her an explanation, but between the grief and the painkillers that had turned my thoughts into a jumbled mess, I couldn't put two coherent words together. I wished badly that I could go back now and wipe the slate clean. To tell her everything I wanted to say.

graduation night 2013

The beach was just what I needed to mellow me out. I was still trying to process what I had seen between Zach and Tracey. It didn't mean I wasn't hurt, but somewhere between splashing in the water with my friends beneath the stars and plucking up a few seashells to commemorate our night, I decided I would not allow this to cause a rift in our group. Tomorrow would be soon enough to talk about it.

After rinsing away the remaining tiny grains of sand from our feet at the outdoor showers, we began to pile into the Suburban. My foot hesitated on the running board as my hand gripped the handle I used to propel myself into my usual seat. Over the last two and a half years since Zach got his license, I had always ridden shotgun. Everyone assumed the front seat belonged to me. For the first time ever, it no longer felt like mine. Zach watched me with curiosity. I could tell he saw my indecisiveness. My eyes flickered to Tracey, who was watching us both intently. She looked apologetic, ready to throw herself on the mercy of the group. My eyes moved to the rest of our friends, who were oblivious to what was going on. If I moved to the second row, giving Tracey the front seat, it would be like posting one of those giant theme park billboards over our heads. Then we would have to spend the rest of the night explaining who knew what and when and how I felt. I wasn't ready to spend an evening discussing it. Seeing no diplomatic way to handle the situation, I finally climbed into the front seat, feeling like a complete fraud.

My hesitation that night still festered like an open wound, leaving me to forever deal with *if only*. Two words that should be stricken from the English language. *If only* we would have stayed at the beach a little longer, or *if only* we would have left just a few seconds earlier. *If only* I would have climbed into the Suburban without pause. Worst of all, *if only* I would have traded spots with Tracey. The thought of it keeps me up at night in a cold sweat, haunted by the rattling chains of guilt that bind me. If I would have switched seats, Tracey would be here and I wouldn't. I didn't want to be the person who said I was glad to be alive. Admitting that would be the same as accepting my friends' fates. How could I explain that to Tracey's mom or to her brothers? I was ashamed that I was glad to be alive. What kind of person did that make me?

Dad saved the day by finally changing the subject to something I could participate in, and by the end of our dinner I no longer felt the urge to stab myself in the eye with a fork. I considered that a success.

My parents refused to take no for an answer regarding the movie, threatening to follow me back to my dorm room to sit and chat for the next two hours as my only other option. Since the theater shared the same parking lot as the Olive Garden, we didn't bother to move the car. The surrounding area of different shopping complexes and restaurants was littered with people, mostly students because of the close proximity to campus. Usually I avoided this area like it was a breeding ground for some epic disease. Navigating through crowds with my leg was never fun, and I got enough stares from my peers while walking back and forth to classes every day. Before the accident I never gave much thought to people who were different. Dragging a bum leg around with a cane had opened my eyes to a new level of understanding. People couldn't seem to help looking. Not that anyone ever had an unkind word to say, but the pity in their eyes made me want to scream.

Walking bookended by my parents toward the theater, it occurred to me that it was the first time I had gone to the movies since the accident. Subconsciously, I think I realized it earlier, which was one of the reasons why I protested going. My thoughts transported me back to my adolescent years when Mom and Dad would take a turn at chaperoning my friends and me.

Over the years, all of our parents would take chaperoning duty on occasion to give the other parents a date night. My parents always liked taking us to the movies, saying it was an easy way to keep us corralled for a couple of hours. They would allow us to sit in our own row so we could feel like we didn't actually have parents looking over our shoulders.

That was how my life was now defined—before the accident, and after the accident. A simple movie with my parents today had become a significant moment in my life because everything I did that used to involve my friends would now be a *first*. I hated all the firsts, absolutely loathed them. They would sneak up on me in the form of inconsequential everyday occurrences to bite me in the ass.

In all the sessions during the past year with my therapist, Tanya, she had neglected to tell me how to deal with firsts. Like the first time I picked up my phone without thinking about it to text Tracey or Jessica, and forgetting neither of them would be there to answer, or how I would feel two months after the accident when our graduation pictures arrived in the mail. That day was tough to remember. Anger had rippled through my body until I shook so severely I could barely focus. My computer had suffered the wrath of my pain as I hurled it with all my might against the wall, leaving nothing but broken pieces.

That was the curse of surviving. You're left to pick up the pieces of your broken, shattered, decimated life. I couldn't remember what it felt like to be whole.

I managed to make it into the lobby without either of my parents catching a hint of what I was feeling inside. They lightly bickered over what size popcorn to get, while I shoved my pain deep down like I did all my feelings these days.

It was only after we entered the theater and faced the steep incline of the stadium-style seating that we remembered the stairs. In the past we had always preferred to sit in the top row. A row which now sat at the top of a mountain of mockery as yet another example of something that would never be the same again. Refusing to concede, I gripped the railing, preparing myself for the grueling task of making it to the top.

Mom made a move toward the first row. "Honey, let's sit down here."

Dad nodded his head. "This works for me," he said with a forced jovial cheerfulness.

I ignored them, mostly out of frustration, wondering briefly if this would be the moment that Mount Mac the volcano would make an appearance again and erupt all over the theater. Since the graduation picture episode, which led to the demise of my laptop, I'd managed to hide my feelings. I was convinced that if anyone caught a glimpse of the darkness that now resided inside me, they would lock me away.

I turned back toward the stairs, done with letting another simple task make me the victim again. With painstaking care, I climbed the first two steps, using my cane and the railing for support. Neither of my parents spoke as they trailed patiently behind me. The entire theater could have been staring at me at that point, but I didn't notice and, frankly, didn't care. My resolve, or perhaps stubbornness was a better way to say it, was set in stone. I made it up ten steps with a thin trail of sweat trickling down my back. My hand shook slightly on my cane from exertion. Dad offered me his hand when he saw me wavering on the fourteenth step, but I brushed it away. I had to do this on my own.

Shallow and erratic breaths wheezed from my lungs and black dots speckled across my vision. My hair clung to the nape of my neck from perspiration. I sounded and most likely looked like a wreck. Judging by the painful rhythmic throbbing, my leg had suffered the heaviest consequences, but I still made it to the top step.

The last task was getting to the seats Mom and Dad preferred. "Excuse me," I said to two couples who stood as I approached.

They began gathering their belongings. "Here, we'll move down."

"No," I answered abruptly as I shuffled awkwardly around them to get down the row. I heard my dad thank them as I sank down into my seat just as the lights in the theater dimmed. Grateful for the shield of darkness, I wiped a stray tear from my cheek as I tried to massage the pain from my leg.

Mom reached over without saying a word and handed me a couple of pain relievers and my drink. I kept my eyes glued to the screen, not daring to look at her. The last thing I wanted was some sort of merciful look from my own mother. My new-found streak of obstinacy had caused a fair amount of friction in our family over the past year. The old me would never have ignored my parents and climbed the steps. I would have gone with the flow and meekly followed Mom and Dad to the first-row crappiest seats in the house. Even with a kink in my neck from looking up at the screen, I would have remained sitting there, saying nothing because that was what I did. Before the accident I was the good girl—the one who didn't buck the system. Since then, everything my friends and I had endured made me reconsider the necessity of compliance for the sake of conformity.

I swallowed the pain pills, hoping the throbbing in my leg would subside soon. Most of the theater barked with laughter over a preview for some Christmas spoof movie coming out in November. It wasn't that I didn't think it was funny, but the pain in my leg had monopolized my focus. Thankfully, the pills worked their magic and the throbbing in my leg eased to a dull ache. I sat with a small measure of pride in the pit of my stomach. Six months ago those stairs would have been impossible. Today I wouldn't say I made them my bitch, but I definitely proved they couldn't beat me down.

For a brief moment in the darkened theater, I felt more alive than I had in a long time.

five

Bentley

Friday was a complete bust in one respect, but a surprising windfall in another. I headed to the library under the bullshit pretense of studying, hoping to see Mac again. I was banking on being able to coax her out of her shell a bit. It was a total Hail Mary pass considering the way she shot me down yesterday, but I couldn't help being intrigued.

I would have thought the library would be as busy as yesterday, but it was dead as a cemetery. The only people I saw were a couple dudes sitting at a table arguing in loud whispers about some card game they were playing. I looped the entire library, expecting to find Mac hiding in one of the far corners. Coming up empty, I sank down in the same chair as the day before to wait her out. I pulled out a book so I would at least look like I was studying when she came in.

Eventually boredom took over and I figured if I was going to sit here, I might as well at least attempt to get a little work done, so I pulled my laptop from my backpack. As it turned out, I was able to find my zone, roughing an outline for a paper that was due Monday. Mac still hadn't turned up, and I debated packing my bag and heading out. I stood up and stretched, looking over at the table of card players that had now increased to six people. It was some kind of fantasy nerdfest game, but they seemed to be taking it seriously.

"Fuck it," I said quietly as I sat back down to start my paper. I had it completely drafted out anyway, and it wasn't like I had anything going on at home.

Three hours later my neck was one big freaking knot from leaning over my laptop, but my paper was done. Rubbing a hand over my neck, I looked at my computer screen with satisfaction. It had been a while since I'd kicked out an assignment so flawlessly. Maybe there was something to using the library to study after all.

Looking around as I packed my bag, I could see I was the last person to leave. Even the fantasy geeks were gone. I glanced at my phone, knowing the library closed early on Fridays. "Sorry about that," I said to the librarian as she switched off the lights. I couldn't help noticing she had it going on a little bit. She was older—mid-thirties maybe, but she fit comfortably in the MILF category.

"That's okay. I had a few things to take care of. I was going to tell you when I was ready. Did you finish?" She nodded at my backpack.

I flashed my dimpled grin that I knew was my winning smile. "I did. Thanks."

She blushed slightly. "No problem." I couldn't help grinning. I hesitated for a moment. This was a once-in-a-lifetime, hot-for-teacher-fantasy kind of moment. After what I'd passed on yesterday, it was like karma was giving me a second chance to keep my man card.

"Was there something else you wanted?" she asked.

Fuck. It was like I had been transported back in time into an old Van Halen video. "Uh, nah," I answered as my thoughts drifted to Mac. I turned and got the hell out of there before my little head could make up my mind for me.

I slept in the next morning since I'd gotten my paper done. After leaving the library yesterday, I chilled out at home and went to sleep earlier than usual. Once I got out of bed, I made a halfhearted attempt to clear a path across my room so I was at least able to walk to the shower without tripping over dirty clothes and discarded shoes and textbooks. I grabbed my work uniform off the back of my desk chair where I'd draped it after washing it the week before. Mom would have my ass if she saw it there. I could just picture her yelling I had a closet for a reason. "This place would probably give her a stroke," I muttered to myself as I spotted an empty pizza box peeking out from under my bed. At least, I thought it was empty. Honestly, I couldn't even remember when it was from.

I should have probably cleaned up, but I dismissed the idea

before it could fully come to fruition. It wasn't all that bad, and I knew where everything was, so it wasn't like I was living in total filth.

My eyes drifted again to the pizza box. Okay, maybe a little filth. Tomorrow I would clean it.

Chad was playing Halo as usual when I left the bathroom a half an hour later with a cloud of steam following me. "Where you going?" His eyes looked milky and bloodshot and his hair was matted on one side while the rest stood on end.

"Work. You know that thing some of us have to do when we're not sucking off the parental tit."

"Don't be jealous, bro. We all can't live the high life." He stretched his arms around the area where he was sitting. Empty cans and dishes littered every square inch of the coffee table. Xbox games and their empty cases were scattered across the couch cushions and the floor.

"Dude, you're a fucking mess."

Chad ran a hand through the matted side of his hair, making it stand on end to match the other side. He looked like he'd gone mad. "What are you talking about?"

"You look like something a cat would hack up. You smell like it, too."

"Like hell I do," he said, grimacing when he lifted his arm and sniffed it.

"And you wonder why no chicks will come over here," I pointed out, heading to the kitchen, which was separated from the living room space by a high counter.

"Psh, I get pussy anytime I want, unlike some people I know."

I flipped him off. "By choice, man. And by *pussy*, I don't mean stray cats, motherfucker," I joked as he chucked an empty can at me.

"Fuck you, bitch. That pussy loved me," he retorted, laughing at his own joke. "How about throwing me another Red Bull?" He slouched back against the couch, picking up his game controller from a dirty plate on the coffee table.

I shook my head, pulling a Red Bull out of the refrigerator along with a nearly empty jug of milk. Tossing Chad his drink, I opened the milk and sniffed it apprehensively. It smelled okay even though according to the date on the side, it had expired two days ago. My stomach growled loudly, so I was willing to take the risk. Opening the cabinet, I pulled out the cereal I wanted while trying to keep the rest of the boxes that were crammed inside from falling out. Cereal, milk, and Red Bull were the three staple items that we all seemed to live on. We bought all three in bulk using Chad's parents' warehouse store card. Judging by the barren state of the refrigerator and the Red Bull cans everywhere, we'd be putting another dent on that card soon.

I was standing at the counter eating my breakfast/lunch when Michael stumbled out of his room looking worse than Chad.

"Hey, is that my Fruity Pebbles?" he asked, swiping the box off the counter.

I quickly snatched the box back. "No, they're my Fruity Pebbles. Next time get your own box."

"Don't be a douche. You can share."

"Okay, you can have some," I offered, grinning as I tossed the box to him before he headed around the counter.

"What did you do, spit in it?" he asked suspiciously.

"Dude? Like I'd do something like that. It'd be unholy to defile a box of Fruity Pebbles."

He looked in the box apprehensively before pouring himself a serving. He eyed the cereal skeptically as it filled the bowl.

I was already chuckling by the time he opened the refrigerator and discovered I used the last of the milk. "You're an asshole," he grumbled, grabbing a spoon from the sink. He rinsed it off before digging into his dry cereal.

"You can always use one of Chad's Red Bulls." To rub it in further, I tipped my bowl up to my lips to drink the last of the fruity-flavored milk.

Michael retaliated by flicking a spoonful of the brightly colored cereal my way. The small pieces flew in every direction except at me, which made me laugh again.

"You flick like a bitch," I mocked him, placing my bowl in the overflowing sink. "By the way, motherfuckers, tomorrow we're cleaning up this place."

Chad flipped me off as he continued to play his game.

"At least I know you heard me, asshole."

"You riding in with me?" I asked Michael as he finished the last of his dry cereal. He and I had met six months ago on the job. He was a cool guy and easy to work with, which was how he ended up moving in with Chad and me at the beginning of term.

"Hell yes."

"Well, then, get your ass in gear. I'm not going to be late because you're dicking around."

"Keep your panties on, Nancy. It'll only take me a few minutes to change."

"You've got ten."

"Relax. You nag more than my mom."

"That's what she told me last night."

"Yeah, well, I couldn't understand what your mom was saying 'cause she was too busy swallowing," he returned, grabbing his crotch.

"Want me to show you the mark on the wall from your mom's head banging against it?"

"Is that the same mark where your mom—"

"Shut up!" Chad yelled from the living room. "You fuckers are sick. Go to work already."

Thirteen-and-a-half minutes later, we headed out the door.

We made it to work with ten minutes to spare, and I was immediately called out. Michael and I rarely went out on calls together since we were both EMTs and were usually paired with a paramedic.

Living in Florida, we got the majority of our calls from retirement facilities. When I decided I wanted to be a paramedic, it was for one reason. I wanted to save lives. I was eight when Dad had clutched his chest one evening, complaining of pains. By the time the ambulance arrived at our house with lights flashing, he had stopped breathing. The entire time the para-medics worked over his body, I was convinced he was going to die. They administrated CPR and were able to get him breath-ing again before transporting him immediately to the hospital, where he underwent triple bypass surgery.

Those rescuers became my heroes when he pulled through. I knew one day I would do the same thing. I wanted to save people, too, and be the difference in some kid's life.

What I had never considered were the instances where I would be unable to make a difference. Sometimes there were circum-stances beyond our control—unexpected injuries or internal damage that was just too severe. In my naïve idea of the job, losing people was not something I had banked on. I guess I'd always assumed I'd be a superhero without the cool outfit.

Our first call of the day was to an elderly couple's house. The husband greeted us in the driveway, waving his frail hands.

"It's my wife," he said as we climbed from the ambu-lance. "She lost her balance stepping down off the stepstool and broke her ankle. I tried to help carry her to the car, but I just couldn't . . ." His voice trailed off.

Steve, the paramedic on call with me, patted him on the back reassuringly. "Don't worry, sir. That's why we're here. You wouldn't want to put us out of a job, right?" he asked, guiding the elderly gentleman back into the house. "What's your name?"

"Edmund Mazur."

"Polish?" Steve asked conversationally as we made our way through the door.

"Yes. My father and mother came to the United States when

I was a wee tike. Young folks nowadays don't put much stock into where they come from."

"Well, sir, my mother would have my head if I did that. Her surname was Wozniak."

"Ah, a strong Polish name," Mr. Mazur said, sounding less distressed.

Steve was good at his job. He knew having an upset spouse on our hands would only make the situation more difficult. Mr. Mazur's body language and his statements when we arrived indicated he was upset that he was unable to help his wife. He was a proud man. We'd seen this time and time again—husbands who'd spent years taking care of their families until, eventually, age got the better of them and their bodies simply couldn't do what their minds still believed possible, like in this case.

We found Mrs. Mazur on the kitchen floor next to a step-stool that was lying on its side. Mr. Mazur had obviously tried to make his wife as comfortable as possible. She had a pillow tucked under her head and a blanket similar to what my grams would crochet draped over her. Judging by the look on her face, she was in pain.

Steve and I made quick work of assessing her. While I was taking her vitals and asking questions to see how coherent she was, Steve checked her ankle and prepped her for transport. Before long, we had her loaded up on the stretcher and into the ambulance. After several handshakes and much appreciation from Mr. and Mrs. Mazur, we left them at the hospital in the hands of the capable ER staff. That was my favorite part of the job. We weren't superheroes like in the comic books, but in Mr.

Mazur's eyes, we had saved the day. It was a heady experience and made me feel invincible. I loved my job.

"I need some serious grub. You want to grab something to eat before we get called out again?" Steve asked as we both climbed into the ambulance. "I'm so hungry I could eat my own hand."

"As long as it's not Mexican food. I thought I was going to die from gas asphyxiation last week after you ate at that one taco truck."

"No doubt. That shit tore me up. I'm steering clear of all beans for a while. It put a serious dent in my social agenda with the wife."

"I told you not to eat a double deluxe burrito when you had a date that night. That's like rule number one in the marriage guidebook." My sentiments were interrupted by an incoming call coming on the radio. "Looks like you'll have to gnaw on your hand for a while," I said as Steve hit the sirens. "Domestic abuse, too. Wonderful."

I hated going out on these calls, especially when there were children involved. We got sketchy details from the dispatcher that a Caucasian male in his mid-thirties had been using his wife as a punching bag and she was barely breathing. A neighbor hysterically called it in. Steve and I exchanged looks as he weaved in and out of traffic.

The house was located in one of the older, less desirable parts of the city. The flashing lights from several police cars illuminated a yard that looked like a trash heap. A broken-down car and moldy couch pretty much took up the entire driveway.

The small patch of grass that hadn't been dug up by the large barking dog chained to a nearby tree was dead and littered with empty beer cans and various other items.

Climbing from the ambulance, Steve and I both wrinkled our noses from the smell of dog shit. As we unloaded the gurney from the back of our rig, three officers escorted a man with a pockmarked face and wearing a wife-beater tank from the house. He was three sheets to the wind and even in handcuffs wasn't making their job any easier as he fought against them, yelling slurred obscenities and spitting at anyone in his direction.

"You have no fucking right to pull me from my house. A man has a right to treat his bitch any way he sees fit!" He hollered at everyone, trying to head-butt the officer who was shoving him into the backseat of the cruiser. "I'm going to fucking shit in the back of your car and smear it all over you," he called out as the officer slammed the door in his face.

"Go ahead, asshole. I'll just hose it off." The officer shot Steve and me a grim look as we wheeled the stretcher down the sidewalk. "It's not pretty in there," he warned us.

His words couldn't have been more of an understatement. Stepping into the house, Steve and I both swore at the sight in front of us. There wasn't anything that didn't look like it hadn't been thrown and broken. Glass shards and broken pieces of wood covered every square inch of the floor. Furniture was overturned and tossed around. There were even a couple of chairs protruding from the walls of the small house like the dude had tried to bust through them or something.

Ignoring the mess, Steve and I approached the area where a

couple of officers were standing. It was obvious by the looks on their faces that we were too late. Despite that fact, we still had to check to make sure. It was all part of the job. The worst part, which shriveled up a small section of my soul every time we had to do it.

The coroner had arrived as Steve and I were loading the empty stretcher back into the ambulance. Neighbors stood on their front lawns pointing and gossiping as news station vans cluttered the scene, setting up to report the incident. We slowly pulled away from the broken-down house, feeling grim. No matter how many times you face the no-win scenario, it never gets any easier. So much for feeling like a superhero.

six

Mac

I walked into the library on Monday and spotted Bentley perched on the chair next to where I normally sat. Admittedly, I was surprised to see him again, despite the interest he'd shown in me last Thursday, which I'd basically chalked up to idle chitchat because he had recognized me. I debated turning around and finding a new place on campus to hide out, but frankly, I wasn't sure I wanted to give up the library. After my minor triumph over the steps at the theater on Friday, I'd reached a new level of resolve, promising myself that I would make more of an effort to step out of my comfort zone. Of course, the euphoric high had since worn off, and facing Bentley now had me second-guessing my newly established determination.

I glanced back over my shoulder at the door. It was mere steps away. I could escape unnoticed—no harm, no foul. My body turned halfway around when the stubborn inner voice that had challenged me at the theater reemerged. *Is this really how I want to continue existing in my life? Some guy talks to me and I run away with my tail between my legs and never come back?*

My mind seemed to make the decision for me because I found myself heading toward my chair without giving it another thought. I kept my eyes locked on my destination so the chair was the only thing I could see. My hope was that I could sit down without Bentley noticing. Of course, that was assuming he would even care. He really could be here to study, and all of this nonsense in my head was for nothing.

Making it to my seat, I made an effort to look busy by pulling out my iPad and a notebook from my backpack.

"Hey, Mac," Bentley said over my shoulder.

I looked up to meet his warm brown eyes, which were as inviting as the smile on his face. Despite my qualms over him invading my space, I nodded and returned my version of a smile. It felt brittle and forced, but it was there nonetheless. I didn't speak, though. I could get used to him being here, and could even tolerate an occasional smile, but I didn't want to encourage more conversation if I could help it. He continued studying me intently like he was deep in thought. If I didn't know any better, I would think he was trying to read my mind. That or he was expecting me to say something. If that was the case, he would be in for a long wait. Although part of me was curious as to what he saw looking at me. There had to be some reason for his apparent fascination. It felt different than the normal stares of pity I received. Finally, he looked back to his laptop, breaking our momentary connection. I was free to look away as well, but my eyes remained on him for a few seconds longer before dropping blindly to my iPad. I felt as shaky as I had after I climbed all twenty-nine steps at the movie theater.

The afternoon bled into early evening without another word being said between us. The seats around us emptied and refilled the entire time, and every so often Bentley would engage in conversation with whoever sat next to us, but never made an effort to include me. I pretended to be hard at work, but found myself unable to truly focus while he talked. His voice wasn't as painful to hear as it had been on Thursday when the initial shock of seeing him stirred up the demons I wasn't prepared to face. This time he was intriguing and easy to listen to. He had a bit of a Southern drawl, typical for Florida good old boys. Sometimes the accent became more prevalent, depending on how animated he got. He was easygoing and had a wicked sense of humor, which every so often made my lips quirk before I could stop them.

Eventually the chairs emptied for good, leaving the two of us alone, and I found myself missing the sound of his voice. I could have looked up, even asked a question that would have started a conversation, but I couldn't bring myself to do it. Mackenzie may have never had problems talking with people she just met, but I wasn't that girl anymore.

As usual, at seven on the nose, I loaded up my stuff and used my cane to get to my feet. Bentley also stood, like it was the signal he'd been waiting for. My pulse quickened as he followed

me out of the library without saying a word. The tentative ca-
maraderie I'd felt earlier turned into creepiness, putting me on
edge. I gripped my cane tightly, feeling apprehensive as I pushed
through the door and stepped outside. Feeling his hand reach
for my elbow, I nearly lost my balance as I whirled around with
my cane up, ready to crack him in the head.

He looked unfazed, smiling as warmly as he had earlier.
"Night, Mac," he said before turning and walking off in the
opposite direction of my dorm before I could fully process what
had just transpired.

An unexpected giggle bubbled up my throat. Not only do I
not talk to him when he says anything, but now he's Jack the
Ripper because he leaves when I do? It wasn't exactly the step
forward my therapist Tanya was looking for. Not that I would
tell her. That bit of paranoia would be better kept to myself.
She'd want to put me on anti-anxiety meds again. That was
some powerful shit that got me through for a while, but they
doped me up too much. I couldn't handle the loss of control.

Bentley was long gone by the time I turned toward the direction of the dorms, but thoughts of him clouded my walk the
entire time. Judging by the conversations I'd shamelessly eaves-
dropped on throughout the afternoon, it was pretty clear he
was a likable guy. He had the same quick-witted humor that
Dan has—*had*. It was *had* now. Dan would have liked him. For
that matter, my whole crew would have liked him.

I picked up my pace as much as my leg would allow, finding
my dorm building buzzing with activity like always, although
it didn't feel as jarring as other days. Keeping my eyes on the

tile floor in front of me, I made my way past the worst part of our building—the common area. The acoustics of the closed-in space only accentuated the laughter and boisterous activity. No one spoke to me as I made my way toward the hallway that led to my room.

I'd been given a ground floor room for obvious reasons. The only problem was I had to walk through the common living space to get there, which psychologically had become my own long walk of shame. In the beginning, I was worried someone would try to talk to me. Now I wondered what they said about me once I was out of earshot.

Just a few more steps once I reached my hallway and I would be home free and able to recoup from my overload of inter-action. Pushing my door open, I was surprised to find Trina inside our room. I stood awkwardly in the doorway. It had been a few weeks since I'd last seen her, and the tension between us rippled in the air like heat on a summer day.

"Oh, hey."

She looked at me incredulously, surprised that I had spoken to her. I felt bad. It wasn't like Trina was a hard person to live with. It was me who was the issue. Unfortunately, the right words to tell her where I was coming from failed to surface. My silence led to our initial discomfort then moved to near hostil-ity the more distant I became.

"Hey," she finally answered, zipping up the duffel bag she had stuffed with clothes. I moved to the side as she headed to-ward the door. The words to tell her she didn't need to keep sleeping somewhere else were on the tip of my tongue, refusing to cooperate. I stood by as she swept past me with one last look of uncertainty. The door closed softly behind her, leaving me standing in the center of my room alone.

Ordinarily I thrived on solitude. The privacy and the lack of staring from others gave me the only opportunity I had to feel free to be me. Tonight the silence felt heavy. I would fill the void the way I always did with either music or a show on my iPad, but tonight that seemed like a poor substitution for human interaction. It was as if listening to Bentley all afternoon had opened a small window into my soul. The interaction may not have been directed at me, but it felt nice to listen to conversations that had nothing to do with the accident. I realized I wanted more of that. If I was honest with myself, what I really wanted was more Bentley.

Shrugging it off, I changed into my robe and grabbed my caddy before heading to the showers. Communal showers in the dorm weren't the ideal situation for me, but I had no other choice. I tried to go at obscure times when they would be less crowded, but there always seemed to be at least one or two people there. I did what I had to do and got out of there as quickly as possible.

Fifteen minutes later I sat on my bed with damp hair balancing a plastic bowl of Easy Mac on my leg while I searched my iPad for something to watch.

There were plenty of places to dine on and off campus, but going to any of them was always out of the question. Mom and Dad would probably freak when they found out I was pretty much living on ramen noodles and macaroni and cheese rather than the meal plan ticket they bought me when I enrolled. The card was still sitting in my wallet brand spanking new. I figured eventually the shit would hit the fan, but I'd already made it two full months without them catching on.

After several minutes of scrolling listlessly through the selection of available shows, I clicked out of the Netflix app and tossed my iPad to the side. I stared pensively at nothing as I finished the last of my dinner. The loneliness I'd been fighting crept in like a stalker. I wanted to talk to someone. I debated calling Mom, but inevitably that conversation wouldn't go the way I wanted it to.

I picked up my iPad again and glared apprehensively at the e-mail icon, unsure of what I wanted to do as I gnawed at the corner of my thumbnail. Clicking it would most likely lead to disappointment. If I was smart, I would just put it away. As if I ever did anything smart anymore, I proceeded to scroll through a short list of e-mails searching for one particular response that I knew wouldn't be there. Only two legit e-mails remained after I dumped the spam. The first was from UCF about registration for spring semester, and the second from the lawyer handling the accident case, informing me that a court day had finally been scheduled. I was surprised Mom hadn't called me on that one, but then I remembered my phone was still on silent from when I was at the library.

Digging through my bag, I pulled out my phone, and sure enough, I had missed three calls from her. At least it was too late to call her back tonight. Nothing like dodging that bullet.

Closing out the message from the lawyer, I looked at my

now empty in-box and swallowed the lump of hurt in my throat. You'd think by now I would have gotten used to the fact that my e-mails were being unanswered, but each time it was like a punch in the gut. I clicked my sent folder and opened the last attempt I had sent, as if reading it again would somehow help.

Kat,

I miss you. I need to talk to you. I know you're hurting, but I am, too. You don't have to call me, but please send me back an e-mail. I know you're back home. We need each other. Please, Kat.

Brat Pack Member for Life,
Mac

I'd sent the e-mail more than three months ago after trying continuously to reach Kat for an entire year. She was the only one of us who'd come out of the accident relatively uninjured. Understandably, she took Dan's death extremely hard. She shut down completely, refusing to come to the hospital to visit me. It wasn't until I was released from the hospital that my mom told me Kat's parents had allowed her to spend the year studying overseas. It all happened so quickly I was shocked. Not that I couldn't relate to her need to get away, but when she came home over the summer, I truly believed she would finally be ready to reach out to me. I needed her, and yet my e-mails continued to go unanswered. When I moved away from home, I was angry to the point that I vowed never to send her another e-mail again, but there was no way I could stand by that. We'd known each other our entire lives. We were more than friends.

graduation night 2013

An avalanche of sensations with more pain than the mind can process at once flooded my body. My legs, pinned beneath my seat, which now rested on the roof of the vehicle, felt like they were being gnawed by wild animals. Every subtle muscle twitch and movement hurt. I tried lifting my throbbing left arm to get a better look at it, but the resulting ache prevented me from moving it more than a hair. As if excruciating agony wasn't bad enough, the dashboard made it impossible to turn my head. I was claustrophobic to begin with. Every instinct in me fought to stand up and move. Bile began to rise in my throat, and I felt the stirrings of dizziness tugging me from every direction.

I slammed my eyes closed, hoping to combat the nausea. Our steak dinner from earlier sat in my stomach like a ton of bricks. I swallowed hard, willing it to stay down. I would not vomit. I tried to force myself to concentrate on something else—the ringing in my ears, Zach, anything.

A strange mewling sound broke through my haze of pain. Opening my eyes, I focused my attention to where the noise was coming from. I couldn't turn my head, but I had a direct view of the back of the vehicle. I could vaguely see Kat in the third row. She wasn't moving. Neither was Tracey. Her body lay limp with her head resting at an odd angle where Zach's side of our seat had been. I surveyed the damage to the Suburban that had always felt so large, but now resembled a crushed tin can. The fact that I couldn't move was a curse. The distorted view of my friends was too painful to watch. Even if I closed my eyes, the images were already burned into my memory. I wanted to be anywhere but here.

The mewling sound grabbed my attention again. It was Kat.

"Kat? Are you okay?" My voice was raspy and dry. She continued her faint crying noise that sounded like a wounded animal. "Kat, are you okay?" I repeated, clearing my throat in an attempt to speak louder. Focusing on her was disorienting since we were both dangling upside down. I repeated my question a third time, trying to break through her stupor. It was difficult to see in the dark, but it looked like her head turned toward me.

"Can you hear me? What about Jessica, can you see her?"

"No-o-o," she sobbed. Her voice was thick with tears. "He's dead. They're all dead. We're all going to die." The words rang through the vehicle in a wail that pierced my tender head. I wanted to cover my ears or yell at her to stop, but I couldn't do either. Fear and grief were living, breathing beasts in an emergency situation, feeding off panic and threatening to consume you.

Kat may have lost the love of her life that night, but in the end we had all suffered.

seven

Bentley

"Night, Mac," I repeated to myself. That was my big fucking move. Are you kidding me? I spend half the day in the library and that was the best I could come up with? My plan to play it cool by giving her the brush-off didn't exactly come together the way I had intended. Giving chicks the silent treatment and letting them come to me had always worked in the past. The way she whipped around with that cane like a samurai ready to take my head off, she must think I'm a total dick bag. I don't know what the fuck I was thinking sneaking up on her like that. It surprised me that I had scared the shit out of her so much that I froze rather than ask her out for coffee like I had intended. And then for the icing on the cake, I practically run away like someone was stealing my car or some shit.

Her reaction reminded me of when I was a kid and we found

a stray cat huddled under Dad's truck. He was no bigger than my hand, but man, did he puff up and hiss and spit when we reached down to pick him up. It was all for show, and we ended up keeping him and calling him Gizmo. Not that I was comparing Mac to our cat. I'm sure that would go over about as well as things did today. I just meant I needed to figure out how to get her to trust me.

My Tuesday afternoon class had me getting to the library later the following day. Mac was already there when I arrived, which was what I was banking on. She didn't look up when I sank down in the seat next to her. Not that I expected her to, but I did notice that she stopped typing on her iPad.

"How can you type on that without a keyboard?" I asked, taking my opportunity to break the ice.

She looked at me, confused, almost like she didn't understand the question.

I pointed to her lap. "Your iPad. Isn't it hard to type on it without a keyboard?"

For a moment I thought she was going to flat-out ignore my question when her eyes followed where I had pointed. The guy across from me gave me a sympathetic grin that clearly indicated he thought I was striking out.

Mac surprised us both though by answering. "It's no different than texting." Her voice cracked slightly, but it was a start.

"Yeah, but I'm not the best at texting. My fingers are too fat," I said, wagging my fingers at her.

"They're not fat, just large." She blushed slightly before looking back down.

The guy across from us smirked again, but I ignored him. "Still makes it hard. My fingers need more space. I've had some seriously embarrassing autocorrect moments."

"My friend Za—I mean, a guy I knew had the same problem," she answered, tripping over her words.

"See what I mean? At least it's not just me. How about you? Are you a good texter?" I wanted to smack myself over the weak-ass line of questions, but I was desperate to keep her talking.

Her eyes, which had been looking everywhere but at me, finally focused on mine. "I used to be," she answered quietly before looking back down. Her body language made it clear she was done talking.

It was a step in the right direction, but I was starting to figure out that with this girl I needed to pick my moments, so I took the hint and gave her a little space.

We didn't talk again the rest of the afternoon. A couple of times I swore I felt her eyes on me while I chatted with Brian, a guy I shared a couple of classes with. He was studying to become a nurse, so some of our classes overlapped. Anytime I'd glance over to see if I was right about Mac, I would find her head buried in her textbook. Finally, just like clockwork, when seven rolled around, she packed up her stuff. This time I waited until she was gone before I even thought about gathering my own shit.

By the time I made it outside, I could barely see her as she disappeared into the darkness. "You'd think she'd be more concerned about walking at night," I said.

"Were you talking to me?" I hadn't noticed a guy leaning against the wall in the shadows smoking a cigarette.

"Nah, man, just thinking out loud," I answered.

The protective vibe over Mac came out of nowhere. It really wasn't my business, but for whatever reason, it was becoming important to me to know she was okay.

The following day, I hoped the headway I'd made yesterday would get Mac to open up a little more. She was already there when I arrived, and even looked over at me when I sat down. I was about ready to slide my chair closer when she looked back down at her notes without so much as a hello. Slightly frustrated, I pulled out my laptop, reminding myself I needed to be patient. As each hour ticked by, though, I began to second-guess the whole idea. Not talking was something she was obviously good at, but I was beginning to question my sanity for continuing to pursue a chick who clearly wasn't interested.

Thursday I decided to go for broke. I had basically reached my all-or-nothing point. I greeted Mac as soon as I sat down. Her cheeks turned a pretty shade of light pink, but she returned my greeting. Pleased that I at least had her attention, I pulled out my anatomy book and the body chart I had printed earlier. Shooting her one last smile, I pored over my chart using my book for reference as I began to label my paper. "You know, if I would have known the human body was this complicated, I never would have gotten into this racket."

"That's kind of your job, isn't it?" Mac's soft voice answered, giving me the opportunity I was waiting for.

"True, but I always figured I could skate by with just

knowing the general stuff. You know, arm, leg, head, but scapula bone, carpal bones, malleus—I mean, come on." She looked at me like I had two heads. "You know I'm kidding, right?"

"I figured as much."

"See, that's why I could also never be a comedian. I can't even tell a knock-knock joke without screwing it up," I answered, hoping to keep our momentum going. Glancing around, I noticed the library had emptied out somewhat and our corner was empty except for the two of us.

She smiled at my words. "I used to wish I had a photographic memory when I was younger. That way I would never have to study."

"I used to wish I was Batman."

Her smile that normally didn't reach her eyes grew. "Batman?"

"Sure. If I was Batman, I could save the day, plus have all the cool gadgets. I'd be a hero by day and stud by night."

Her smile dropped slightly. "And you like being a hero?" she asked quietly, studying me intently.

"It's all I wanted to be growing up. Only, there's an obvious difference between comic books and real life, but mostly I enjoy what I do."

"What don't you like about it?"

"That sometimes we arrive on the scene and realize there is nothing we can do to help." In my haste to keep our conversation flowing, I spit out the answer without thinking about how she might react.

"No, sometimes it's too late," she whispered. She looked back down at her textbook and I figured we had traveled into the land of no return again.

"What about you? What would you have done if you had a photographic memory?" I asked, hoping she'd keep talking.

"Definitely something worthwhile like cure cancer or end global warming."

"That's cool."

"I'm actually kidding. I wish I could say I'd use it for something that noble, but I'd probably use it to win *Jeopardy!* or something like that."

"Hey, at least you're honest. You know what I always wondered? Is everyone with a photographic memory a genius, or are there some poor bastards out there who can answer like any question in the world, but still can't figure out how to change the clock on their microwave?"

"I guess I never considered that," she answered after actually giggling slightly.

"See, I wonder about these things. Regardless, if nothing else, you could have gone to Vegas and cleaned up counting cards."

"What exactly is counting cards?"

"Like in blackjack. If you had a photographic memory, you could memorize the cards that were dealt, and you would have a better chance at knowing how many high cards were left in the deck to either bet high or hold back."

"Sounds like a subject you know quite well. Maybe you've done a little card counting."

"I wish. Imagine being able to pay for school in cash. I'll be paying off my student loans forever, even with having some scholarship money."

She shrugged. "I'm not sure that will be an issue with me."

"Trust fund baby?"

"No." She thumped her bad leg. "My lawyer thinks this will earn me a pretty penny."

"Right." I couldn't seem to stop dragging the conversation back to the topic she obviously wanted to avoid.

"It's okay. It's all my parents talk about," she said, pulling the thoughts from my head. "Not the money, I mean, but the accident. They're not overly happy it's dragged out so long."

"Can't say I blame them. It's been a year, right?"

"It'll be a year and a half next month."

I let out a low whistle. "That's seriously fucked-up."

She laughed at my words. It was the first time I'd heard her laugh that way. I liked it. If anything, she was even more beautiful. "I think my dad would agree with you. He's not taking the delay that well. I'm just ready for it to be over."

"I can understand that. Why the delay?"

"It's a lot of blah-blah-blah, but it all boils down to the blame game. Thankfully, the insurance company finally smartened up and stopped trying to blame us."

"Why would they blame you guys?"

"Because it's easy to blame the teenagers. We had to be doing something wrong, right? They figured it out, though, by talking to eyewitnesses and checking the truck driver's phone records."

I mulled over her words, not sure what to say. After a few awkward moments, we both returned to studying. I wanted to ask more questions. Everything about her intrigued me. Originally I thought it was because of the accident and the part I played in the situation, like I had some kind of vested interest in her life now, but that wasn't it. Something about the way she talked made me want to listen. That was the only way I could describe it.

We never really spoke again until she packed up her belongings at seven o'clock on the dot. I followed suit, debating whether I should ask her out for coffee. I tried to get a read on her body language, but it was hard to decipher. One thing was for sure, I didn't want to make the same mistake as the other night and scare the shit out of her, or take a whack in the head with a cane, for that matter.

Stepping outside, I smiled with satisfaction from the light breeze. A mild front had moved in earlier that day, dropping the temperature to a tolerable level. Now that October was nearly over, we might actually have highs that didn't reach almost ninety.

"It feels nice out," I said conversationally.

"We're getting close to my favorite time of year," she answered, zipping up her light hoodie. She adjusted her cane to balance her weight and gave me a look of dissatisfaction when she noticed me watching her. "Catch you later," she muttered, heading down the sidewalk.

"Hey, wait, I'll walk you to your dorm," I called out, jogging up to her.

"That's okay."

"No, I insist."

"So, un-insist. I'd rather you didn't." She turned and moved on without giving me a second glance.

eight

Mac

I was an asshole. Seriously. I should be locked away so society wouldn't have to deal with me. The look on Bentley's face when I told him I didn't want him to walk me home stayed with me all night, keeping me up. When he wasn't at the library the next afternoon, it was pretty clear I'd screwed up. He was the first person in a long time I'd felt comfortable enough to talk to, and I managed to blow it. For no real reason except that he looked at my cane. How could I possibly want to move on like I keep telling myself if I continued to push people away?

I couldn't get any studying done since all I could think about was how to fix the situation if the opportunity arose. Hopefully it would be as simple as biting the bullet and apologizing for my asinine behavior if he showed up, and of course hoping he accepted. I waited throughout the afternoon, looking up every time the library doors opened. Eventually, I resigned myself to the fact that just like I had done with my roommate, Trina, I had caused someone else to seek life elsewhere. Really, I couldn't blame him. I wouldn't want to be around me either. If he ever showed up again, I could still at least apologize so that he would know it wasn't because of him that I was such a bitch.

The library was typically dead on Fridays anyway, but given that it was Halloween, the place was a cemetery. No pun intended. I felt like a double loser, sitting there hoping some guy would show up while everyone else was getting ready to go out and party. Normally, I would have basked in the joy of having the place to myself, but after a week of being around Bentley, I suddenly missed the interaction. Frustrated over having branded myself the picture of pathetic, I was in no mood to study, and decided to pack my bag and head out.

I had just left the library and was rounding the corner toward my dorm when a couple of guys dressed in togas approached me. Judging by their loud obnoxious behavior and the beers in their hands, they had started partying early. They were being pretty ballsy walking around campus with open liquor bottles, but I wasn't about to tell them that. One of them turned and whistled as I passed. "Nice costume. You're like the Planters peanut guy," he slurred. His friend laughed as he pretended to prop himself up with an imaginary cane.

"That's so clever," I said sarcastically as I kept moving.

"Dude, I don't think that was her costume."

I pretended not to hear them, but the red on my cheeks told a different story. If it were the middle of the day, I could stop and say something, but being dark outside, and the fact that there weren't many people around who I could see, I would be an idiot to stand up for myself now. Not that I would be much braver around a packed courtyard of students.

"Hey, wait, don't go away mad. Here, stop and have a drink with us." I could hear their footsteps approaching from behind, and I began to panic. There was no way I could run and get away.

"Please just leave me alone. I'm just trying to get to my dorm," I stated as they jumped in front of me to stop my progress.

"What's the matter? You too good to party?"

"No, it's just—"

"Is there a problem?" Bentley interrupted as he forced his way between me and the two idiots. He towered over both of them and with his chest puffed up looked even more intimidating.

"Uh, sorry, dude. I guess she's with you?" one of them asked, taking a step backward. "We were just trying to invite her to the party we're headed to. You guys can both come if you want."

"Fuck yourself," Bentley answered, taking another step forward to make his point.

"It's cool, bro." One of them held up his hands. "We'll just head this way. It's all good."

Bentley made sure they were well on their way before he turned around. Judging by their quickened pace, they had no interest in coming back.

"Who called in the asshole brigade?" he asked, walking back

toward me. I lifted my eyes from the sidewalk with a relieved smile on my face.

"Were you being a creeper and following me, or did you just happen to be walking by?" The words slipped out, surprising us both. I could feel the red return to my cheeks. That wasn't what I had in mind when I promised myself I would apologize to him.

Thankfully, he responded to my teasing by laughing.

"Would I be a total dick if I said yes?"

"That depends. Yes to which part?"

"Ah, in that case, I plead the fifth," he countered. "Wait, let me just add that I'm glad I was here to intervene. How about that?"

"Well, I do appreciate it. They were obviously drunk, and I'm used to being teased. This makes being inconspicuous pretty hard," I said, holding up my cane. The words to apologize about last night were on the tip of my tongue, but he seemed to have forgotten about it.

His eyes hardened as he glared over my shoulder. "You shouldn't have to be used to it. Besides, those dipshits had something else in mind. So, are you done studying?" His expression instantly changed to a crooked smile like someone had flipped a switch.

His question threw me off and took me a few seconds to process. "What?"

"I asked if you were done studying tonight." He grinned.

"Um—why?"

"Because it's a holiday, and I thought maybe we could go do something."

"I'm not sure that's the best idea."

"Why not? Do you have other plans for the holiday?"

My eyes narrowed. Was he mocking me? It was hard to tell since he was still grinning. "I'm not sure Halloween is technically considered a holiday."

"Sure it is. Check the calendar. It's on there. I think that makes it a law that it has to be observed, recognized, and celebrated."

A smile tugged at my lips. "Well, Presidents' Day is on the calendar, too. What about that one?"

"Absolutely. We exchange political presents for that one."

"What, like a year of Obamacare?" I teased.

"Exactly." He winked at me. "So, what do you say? Want to blow this Cracker Jack box and have some fun?"

"I probably shouldn't," I answered, thinking of the safe haven of my dorm room. It may be lonely, but it would keep me veiled in obscurity.

"Come on. We're friends, right?"

"We are?" The claim was new to me. Besides, it had been so long since I had made a new friend.

"Please. Of course we are. How about it, then?" he asked like a child begging to open presents on Christmas morning.

"What did you have in mind?" I could feel the butterflies taking flight in my stomach.

"My roommates said there's a Halloween party going on at our building."

"Oh." My stomach dropped. "I don't do parties."

"Like at all, ever?"

My throat became as dry as the Sahara. "No, not ever." It was a lie. There was a time when I would have gone to my share of parties, but my crew was always with me. We hung out together in our own little bubble. People would filter in and out, talking and joking, but in the end, they were outsiders. We didn't do it intentionally. It was just the way it had always been.

"That's cool. We can do something else. How about going to a haunted house? I heard the Petrified Forest is killer this year."

I shook my head as the first stirrings of despair began to claw their way through me. Walking through a crowded haunted house with my leg wasn't the best idea anyway, but the Petrified Forest was outside, which would be nearly impossible. My leg wasn't ready for unpaved terrain.

"Wait. I got it! Do you like chocolate?"

"Love it," I answered, wondering if he was going to suggest trick-or-treating. I hated to shoot down another suggestion.

"Excellent," he said, rubbing his hands together like a kid before reaching for my backpack. "Okay, well, let's hit it."

"Where are we going?" I asked apprehensively as he shouldered my backpack. I had no idea how I'd suddenly gone from wishing for the sanctity of my dorm room to going who knows where to do who knows what.

"You'll have to wait and see." He reached for my hand.

"You know trick-or-treating is probably out, too," I said, looking down at our linked hands. Whether I was reading more into it than he intended, I wasn't sure, but I pulled away. It was a little presumptuous of him to think I would jump immediately from talking in the library to becoming the type of friends who held hands.

"Come on, this way." He continued as if he hadn't even noticed my reluctance.

His legs were easily a foot longer than mine, but he matched my pace so I wouldn't fall behind. It was hard not to feel self-conscious about it, even though Bentley didn't seem to care. He kept me entertained with a running commentary about his roommates. I had discovered in my eavesdropping earlier that week at the library that Bentley was a good storyteller. He knew how to use words to paint a picture. By now I had a pretty good visual of Sherman, the iguana, who apparently had it out for him, and Chad, his best friend, the gamer. I couldn't help smiling at how animated Bentley became in his descriptions. It had been a long time since I'd felt so carefree. I wondered if that was his intention or just a coincidence of his charm. The nice thing was not once did the conversation go to my leg, my friends, or anything else about the accident.

Wherever Bentley's surprise destination was, the walk was longer than I was used to. I began to worry about my leg tiring, but he kept the pace slow, and for the time being I was holding up fairly well. Finally, we had made it off campus on the opposite side of the property from where my dorm building was. He seemed to be guiding me toward an apartment complex. I thought I had made it clear a party was out.

"You okay?" he asked when I paused in the middle of the

sidewalk. He looked down at my leg, clearly concerned. "Do you need to sit down for a minute?"

"Where are you taking me?" My tone was completely bitchy, but I didn't care. I was not relishing a long hike all the way back to my dorm because he'd decided to ignore my wishes.

"My apartment." He looked surprisingly confused at my sudden mood swing. "Oh, shit. My bad. Look, I was just trying to be charmingly mysterious, but it's not what you think. I promise."

"So, why else would we go to your apartment? I told you I didn't want to go to a party." My stomach began to clench. This is what I got for letting my guard down around people.

"I know. Trust me. We're not going to a party. I have something else planned."

"In your apartment?"

"I swear these hands will come nowhere near you if that's what you're worried about," he said, shoving his hands into his pockets for emphasis. He began walking backward while coaxing me to follow him with a nod of his head.

I stood in place, waiting for my legs to make the one-hundred-eighty-degree turn to walk back to campus. I felt like a child who couldn't make up her mind. I just didn't want him to think he could force me to do something I didn't want to do. This was ridiculous. One way or another, I had to make up my mind.

"Come on," Bentley continued to tease me. "You know you want to."

"Gah, fine. Just so you know, I'm going because I want to, not because you're forcing me to."

"I would never. I know how to respect the wishes of a lady," he said in a mocking tone.

"Not funny, jerk."

"I'm sorry, I'm sorry. So, you're good with this?"

"I still don't know what *this* is," I said, waving my cane toward the apartment building.

"Come on and I'll show you." He grabbed my hand and led me toward the apartment complex. This guy didn't know how to take a hint. His grip was strong, but not like he was trying to pull me anywhere against my will. Evidently, I was going with the flow, and tonight would be another *first*.

The feeling was a bit liberating. It wasn't that often anymore that I left caution to the wind like I had tonight. Then I noticed the concrete set of stairs. "Oh, please no," I mouthed to myself. I guess it was too much to ask the cosmos for Bentley to suddenly turn toward an apartment on the ground floor. There was no way I'd be able to climb them, not after the long walk it took to get here.

I ran several scenarios through my head on how to get out of making a fool of myself with the stairs. I could claim to be sick. Tell him I changed my mind and didn't feel comfortable going to a guy's apartment who I barely knew. That seemed like the more reasonable excuse. Of course, it didn't feel like that with Bentley. I felt like I'd known him forever. A week was far from forever. I was smart enough to realize that, but he had also been there to help me during the worst night of my life.

Before I could shoot down another one of his ideas, he'd

already taken matters into his own hands—literally. One minute both my feet were firmly on the ground, the next they were dangling over his shoulder. "What the hell are you doing?"

"Killing two birds with one stone. I need to keep in shape for work. What better way than carrying a pretty lady up a flight of stairs. It's the least I can do after dragging you all the way across campus."

"Put me down." I tried to sound stern, but I couldn't help laughing as I bounced up and down with each step he took.

"Trust me, ma'am. I'm a trained professional," he answered as I continued to laugh. Damn him. Why did he have to be so sweet? As we reached the midpoint between floors, he stopped and gently moved me from his shoulder to where I was cradled in his arms. He held me like I weighed next to nothing, pulling me snugly against his chest. His breathing was smooth and effortless. I held myself stiff in his arms, although the urge to relax and nestle closer was strong as my heart raced. I felt safe, which was a problem. That feeling frightened the ever-living daylights out of me.

Bentley chatted away as he climbed the stairs, just like he had done during the walk to the apartment complex. He talked so much I never noticed that his apartment was only on the second floor, and even though we were no longer on the stairs, he was still carrying me.

"You know. You broke your promise."

"What do you mean?"

"You said your hands would come nowhere near me," I reminded him.

"Oh, yeah. You sure you don't have a photographic memory?"

"I know a player when I see one."

"What? You overestimate me. I'm just a servant of the people."

"Yeah, right. I think I can manage now, by the way." I began to squirm so he would put me down.

"Oh, sorry. Yeah, I guess you can walk the rest of the way, huh?"

"Obviously. Lead the way." I straightened my clothes before bumping into his backside.

"Here we are," he said after taking one step forward.

"You shit." I slapped him on the arm for good measure.

He unlocked the door and I smirked, stepping into his apartment. It looked fairly nice, but glancing around, I could tell it was what you would call "guy" clean. One of the cushions on the couch was slightly askew, hinting that there might be something beneath it. The entertainment center looked like a half-hearted attempt had been made at dusting, judging by the leftover trail of grime that was visible. Still, I had to admit I liked it.

"See, not too shabby, right?" Bentley asked, shoving a stray sock out of sight that was poking out from under the couch.

"What are you doing there?"

"Fixing the carpet," he lied, smoothing a hand over the spot where the sock had just been.

"Won't you forget that's under there?"

He grinned at me, flashing a pair of dimples. "Nah, besides, my mom gives me novelty socks for every holiday." He laughed, lifting the pant leg of his jeans to reveal a black sock covered in white skeletons.

"Wow, you weren't lying about celebrating every holiday."

He shrugged his shoulders. "Told you. We take our holidays seriously. My mom was bumped from one foster home to another growing up. Needless to say, birthdays and Christmas were pretty much nonexistent for her. When Dad asked her to marry him, he vowed to make every holiday special. I guess you could say my sister and I reaped the benefits."

"You have a sister?"

"Oh yeah, but actually she's not into the holiday thing anymore. She's younger than me, but thinks she knows everything."

"That's cool. Holidays used to be a big deal with us, too . . ." My voice trailed off. I shouldn't have been surprised that we had ended up here. This was why I avoided talking to anyone. It was hard to get personal without the subject of family coming up at some point. Tanya told me it was part of the healing process, but I had no idea how that was possible when everything seemed to remind me of my friends.

Bentley looked at me like he was trying to get a read on what I was thinking. I'm sure he was asking himself how he'd gotten stuck with such a dud.

"So, are you ready to do some celebrating?" he asked, rubbing his hands together.

He had a way of lightening the mood, I'd give him that. It

was nice to be with someone who was able to let things roll off his back. Doom and gloom just didn't seem to be in his DNA. "You did promise me chocolate."

"And chocolate I will deliver," he said, heading toward the kitchen. I trailed behind him and watched as he pulled a large box of brownie mix from the cabinet.

"You're making brownies?"

"Correction: we're making brownies. Will you get the eggs out of the fridge?"

"Oh, *we're* making them?" I opened the fridge, nearly laughing out loud at the contents. There was an entire shelf dedicated to Red Bull and beer, while another held about a half-dozen jugs of milk. Squeezed in the space of the final shelf was a pizza box with a leftover Chinese food container and a carton of eggs perched on top. I would have expected nothing less from an apartment of guys. "You have a calcium fetish or something?" I asked, closing the door.

"More like a cereal fetish." He opened one of the cabinets to show me what looked like more than a dozen boxes of cereal crammed inside.

"Holy crap. That's a lot of cereal."

"It's cheap. Well, for us it's sorta free."

"Free?"

"Yeah. Chad's parents gave him their BJ's Warehouse credit card to buy a few things for the apartment. He just neglected to give it back."

"Oh Lord. Isn't he afraid what they'll say when they see the bill?"

"Nah. His parents spoil him. I doubt they'll say anything. His mom's not quite ready to cut the cord, if you know what I mean."

"Is he a freshman?" I assumed he must be by the way Bentley was describing him.

Bentley laughed at my question as he dumped the contents of the box into a pot instead of a mixing bowl. "Hell no. He's a junior like me. He turned twenty-one a couple months ago. She just treats him like he's still a baby. He doesn't care, though. He likes being coddled. The asshole is twenty-one and has never held down a job." His words were harsh, but his tone was affectionate.

"I'm not much better. I worked at an ice cream stand not far from my house the summer I was seventeen, but the hours were a bit of a joke."

"Hey, you get an A for effort," he said, cracking some eggs and depositing the contents into the pot.

"You know you'll need a different pan to cook them in, right?" I wasn't the best baker, but watching Dad, who was the cook in our house, I'd picked up a few things. I definitely knew a stockpot was not the best choice to bake brownies.

"Are you sure?" He winked at me. "Kidding." He pulled a baking pan from the drawer at the bottom of the stove. "We bought this when we got the brownies. We just forgot a mixing bowl. This worked, though."

After a moment of vigorous stirring, he handed me the spoon to lick, which I accepted happily. Brownie mix was even better than cookie dough. Mom always thought it was gross that Dad and I licked the bowl after making brownies or cookies, but we considered it a perk.

I flushed slightly, finding Bentley watching me. I licked my lips, trying to erase the last traces of the brownie mix. His eyes flickered and he raised his hand toward me. My body immediately tensed in anticipation.

He moved slowly, gently swiping his thumb over the corner of my mouth. "You missed a little," he said before licking his thumb clean. Instant heat coursed through my body with a desire like I'd never felt. I hadn't realized it was possible. It definitely had never happened with Zach.

fall 2012

"Dude, I counted like twelve scouts in the stands. You're a star, brother," Dan said, clapping Zach on the back when he left the locker room with his hair still wet from the shower.

Zach's face went slack at Dan's words. "You're yanking my chain, right? Dad said two at the most would be showing up for this game."

"I'm serious, brother. You're a hot commodity." Dan held out his closed fist so they could bump.

I was surprised it took Zach a moment to respond, and when he did, it was halfhearted at best. "What's wrong?" I asked, sidling up to him and dragging Tracey, who seemed reluctant to follow, behind me.

He answered, running a hand through his wet locks. "Nothing. I just wish I would have played better."

"Played better? You threw three touchdowns. It would have been four if Butterfinger Bradley wouldn't have dropped that last pass."

"Yeah, but I got sacked twice and threw an interception before halftime."

"Which translated to nothing."

Zach shrugged, and I could still see he was bothered by it. "You played great, Zach." I gave him a quick peck on the lips. He smiled at me, but I noticed it didn't quite make it to his eyes. I wasn't sure what to say to make him feel better, and in the end it was Tracey who seemed to center him with her comment.

"You only care about FSU anyway, and they already want you, right?" she reasoned. "Who cares about any of the rest?"

"She's right, my friend," Dan added. "You were destined for FSU since you were a baby crapping in your diaper."

"Nice, Dan," Kat laughed, giving him a swat. He retaliated by pulling her into his arms and giving her a searing kiss. I looked away. Lately it seemed intrusive to watch them when they were affectionate with each other. Zach and I had shared our fair amount of kisses over the years, but even though they were pleasant and familiar, they were never as heated as what Dan and Kat shared.

Zach tugged my hand and held me back as the others headed toward his Suburban.

"You okay?" I asked as he turned me to face him. He answered by crushing his lips to mine. Caught unprepared, I gasped, which he responded to by shoving his tongue in my mouth. He backed me against the wall and pressed his body completely against mine. The contact was not new for us, but it had been a year since we'd gone all the way. It wasn't quite what I had been expecting and since then had kept things above the waist. If Zach wanted more, he'd never indicated it until now.

I maneuvered my hands up to his chest, pushing him back. "Zach, someone might see us." I felt inadequate when he kissed me like this. Where was the heat I always heard about?

Zach's eyes met mine briefly. They were filled with anguish that totally did not match his personality. "You're right," he agreed, shouldering his gym bag. He headed toward the parking lot while I watched from the shadows of the breezeway. I told myself his kiss had something to do with his feelings about the game, but deep down I suspected it meant something more. My insecurity that this was my fault always lingered. He would never utter the words, but I couldn't help wondering if he was sorry we stayed together. If I really cared about him, I would let him go. Let him find someone who could offer him what I was lacking. Selfishly, I pushed the thoughts away. It wasn't like he'd ever asked for an out. This would be our last year together anyway. Soon we'd be at different universities, and he could explore other relationships. Logically it made sense.

nine

Bentley

Is there anything hotter than watching a girl lick something? Not that I could tell Mac that, but damn. With any other girl I would have made a move. Mac was different, though. I knew I needed to take it slow with her. She always seemed to be on the verge of fleeing, and I didn't want to do anything to spook her. There was no rush. Though other parts of my body might disagree.

It was like Mac didn't realize how attractive she was. I'm sure it had something to do with her disability, but that was all in her mind. I guarantee no other guy would see her the way she obviously viewed herself. I know I didn't. It was a conversation I would love to have with her, but definitely at another time.

"Okay, now that the brownies are in the oven, it's time to

do some serious pumpkin carving." I plucked the remaining uncarved pumpkin off the counter.

"Should I ask what this is supposed to be?" she asked, turning Chad's pumpkin around.

"It's the Halo symbol. That's Chad's work. I told you he was a total slacker."

"And this one?" She turned another pumpkin around. "Is that supposed to be boobs?"

"That's Michael for you." I didn't mention that I was the one who sketched the outline on the pumpkin since he had totally effed it up.

"I'm sure you and Chad didn't have any input," she deadpanned before cracking a smile.

"We may have offered a little guidance."

"So, what are your plans for this one?" She patted my pumpkin, spinning it around.

"I'm more of a traditionalist. Triangle eyes and nose, a toothy grin. You know, classic. Do you want to work at the bar or the coffee table?" I asked, grabbing a knife from the drawer.

She eyed the counter and the high barstools before answering. "I think the coffee table works best."

"Good for me. I'll grab some newspaper and a marker. You can go grab a seat," I said, noticing she looked like she was dragging a little. I felt like a complete asshole making her stand so long. I should have offered her a chair while we made the brownies. She was obviously the suffer-in-silence type. It was easy to forget about her leg because she never harped on it.

"So, where's Sherman?" she asked, maneuvering around the

coffee table and sinking down on the couch. A pinched look crossed her face as she absentmindedly massaged her leg.

"Probably plotting my demise." I spread the newspaper across the coffee table.

"He can't be that bad. After all, he's nothing more than an overgrown lizard."

"Trust me. That green bastard has it out for me. He's lucky I haven't fed him to the neighbor's dog." I set the pumpkin on the coffee table and plopped down next to Mac. If my close proximity bothered her, she didn't let on. The same enticing smell of strawberries and vanilla that I had caught a whiff of when I carried her assaulted my senses. I was a fan of the fruity body sprays chicks liked to wear. It made exploring certain things more like a treat.

I spun the pumpkin around trying to find the best side to sketch out the face before we started carving. That damn body spray was distracting me. I had to be cool or I'd look like an idiot. It was all about mind over matter.

After a moment, my body finally started cooperating, allowing me to focus on the task at hand. "I figured we'd both contribute to the drawing," I said, sketching a pair of triangle eyes with the black Sharpie. I eyeballed them to make sure they were symmetrical.

"Are you sure? I might ruin it." She smirked at me. "It looks like you take your pumpkin carving seriously."

"I take pride in my work. Even if it is just carving a jack-o'-lantern. I trust that you understand the importance of superior pumpkin carving."

"I'll try not to let you down," she answered as I handed the pumpkin over.

She turned the pumpkin to face her, blocking it from my view. I smiled at the way her eyebrows came together in deep concentration as she studied it intently before starting to draw. I thought I took my pumpkin carving seriously, but Mac was all business the way she gnawed the corner of her lip as she worked. After a few minutes, she finally turned it around so I could see it.

I chuckled when I saw that she had painstakingly drawn eyebrows and eyelashes above the eyes. Obviously my pumpkin was going to be a she this year.

"You know that's going to be a bitch to carve out?"

"Surely not for a professional like yourself?"

"You're right. My turn again."

Taking her eyelashes as a challenge, I drew a curved nose versus the simple triangle I normally would have gone with before handing the pumpkin back to Mac. It took her a long time to draw the mouth, and I was more than a little curious. Finally, after several minutes, she handed the pumpkin back to me, looking quite pleased with herself.

This time we laughed together as we eyed the pumpkin. Instead of the toothy grin I would have drawn, she had given the pumpkin wide heart-shaped lips that curved up into a smile. It looked like the jack-o'-lantern version of Angelina Jolie.

I cut a hole in the top and together Mac and I cleared the pumpkin of all its slimy innards, placing them on the newspaper

I had laid out. Halfway through the messy process, I left Mac briefly to remove the brownies from the oven. Leaving them on the counter to cool, I grabbed a couple of waters from the fridge that were hidden behind the milk. I was satisfied to see her looking so relaxed while she separated the seeds from the slimy gunk we'd pulled from the pumpkin.

"Are you planning on planting your own pumpkin patch?" I teased, handing her one of the waters.

"Yep, right outside my dorm room window. No, really, I thought we could bake them and then eat them."

I shot her a skeptical look.

"I'm serious. My dad used to do it when I was little," she added when I still looked doubtful.

While Mac handled the pumpkin seeds, I started carving the mouth and eyes of the cleaned-out pumpkin. I was just finishing up by the time she was sliding the seeds into the oven. I handed the pumpkin to her when she sat back down so she could do the more delicate work. The nose, eyelashes, and eyebrows were too tricky for my big hands.

Once she was done, I dug around, looking for something to light it up since the guys and I had forgotten to get candles when we bought the pumpkins. I hit pay dirt, finding a mini flashlight in Michael's room. We turned off the lights to admire our handiwork as we munched on brownies. Mac, who was coming completely out of her shell, *oohed* and *awwed*. My eyes kept straying to her face as she gazed at the pumpkin. I didn't know her well, but I knew happiness when I saw it. If you would have told me a week ago that the standoffish girl I'd tried to talk to at the library would be standing in my apartment now, I would have thought you were high as a kite.

To make the evening complete, I turned on the TV and scrolled through the menu until I found a classic Halloween movie. Mac looked at the couch, and I could see the indecision on her face. With the only lights in the living room coming from the TV and the jack-o'-lantern, it wasn't hard to discern what she was thinking. Not wanting the evening to end, I sat down on the couch, acting oblivious to her dilemma. It took a few seconds, but with one last look at the door, she came over to the couch and sat next to me. She practically hugged the arm of the couch like it was a lifeline. I wanted to chuckle, but that would be like showing her the door. I was cool waiting. She was worth it.

ten

Mac

Spending the evening with Bentley was nothing like I would have expected. Of course, that wasn't saying much since my expectations were virtually nonexistent. I had no measuring stick to compare it to. My relationship with Zach throughout high school never reached the intensity of other couples like Dan and Kat. They acted like the sun would fail to rise if they skipped a day of seeing each other. Their dedication to one another had been unique and special. With college always in my sights, I'd found their relationship unsettling at times, especially when I worried that Zach would want the same from me. He and I had shared our moments, but there was never anything there that would take us to that next level.

With Bentley, it felt different already. The sensations he evoked in me when he removed the chocolate from my lips were unexpected, even foreign in a way. I wanted to write them off as a fluke, but as the evening wore on, the feelings would continue to surface. It was as if my body was ready to react every time we stood close or, worse yet, touched slightly, like when his hand found mine inside the pumpkin. I'd worked so hard over the past year and a half to avoid human contact that I now found myself unprepared for how to handle it.

It was only when Bentley turned the lights off and started the movie that I really questioned my sanity. I tried to put as much distance between us as possible by sitting on the opposite arm of the couch. It wasn't exactly subtle, but outside of sitting on one of the barstools behind him, which would have been truly awkward, it was the best I could do. I surreptitiously studied his profile when he was so into the movie that he wasn't paying attention. I'd been right on that first day. He really was handsome. Even without the dimples, he had the kind of face that called for a second look. At first glance, you might chalk him up as cute, but something would draw your attention back, making you realize he went beyond that. Maybe it was the constant gleam in his eyes and the subtle grin that never seemed to be far from the surface. Or maybe it just boiled down to the fact that I was so hard up for human interaction that a paper bag would look attractive.

Even with the gap between us on the couch, our hands were mere inches apart. I expected him to reach for mine, considering the way he had held my hand during our walk to get to his apartment. Of course, I had snatched it away. Maybe that had bothered him after all. I could have reached over and taken his hand, but there was no way I could muster the nerve. Basically, that was how the rest of the evening went. My mind was so preoccupied, I don't think I could tell you anything about the movie.

Later on, Bentley drove me home. I was grateful not to walk the distance again and had readily agreed. All the parking spots were taken when we arrived, so I had him drop me off at the front of my building. He seemed disappointed that he wouldn't be walking me to my door.

We sat in the car for several seconds of awkward silence. "So, thanks for the lift," I finally said, opening the car door. He hesitated before answering. I hoped he didn't think I was expecting him to kiss me or anything like that.

"No problem. Thanks for celebrating the holiday with me."

"That's what *friends* do, right?" I emphasized the *friend* part.

He looked serious for a moment before his sexy full lips stretched into a smile. I found his lips to be very distracting. They were enticing no matter what they were doing. The temptation to see if they were as soft as they looked was becoming hard to ignore.

He burst my bubble by agreeing with me. "Absolutely."

My heart dipped. That was my problem. I obviously didn't know what I wanted. One minute I'm worried he might kiss me, and the next I'm disappointed when he doesn't. I obviously had a problem with mixed signals. I couldn't help wondering if that had been what came between me and Zach.

graduation night 2013

We had all been herded together like a bunch of cattle inside the Ocean Center, waiting for the ceremony to start. I was searching for Tracey so she could help me reattach the opal hair clip my aunt had sent me for graduation. The clip was a beautiful soft shade of pink that complemented my light blond hair. The problem was my hair was too wispy and thin to keep it in place. Tracey had the magic touch when it came to fixing hair. I knew she could make it look beautiful like she had hundreds of times before.

I sidestepped Marcus and Kent, who were roughhousing in the middle of the room as Ms. Jenkins, one of the school administrators, tried to organize everyone into some semblance of a line. The ceremony start time was still forty-five minutes away. How she thought she could maintain order for that long was beyond me. Not wanting to be corralled, I darted around one of the black curtain dividers when I noticed Mr. Griffin, our assistant principal, jumping in to intervene with a determined look in his eyes. "Gentlemen, please. Let's try to act like adults." I smiled with satisfaction at my escape into the nearly empty space beyond the black drapes. Freedom, no matter how brief, was sweet.

Walking silently to the other side of the large room, I spotted Tracey and Zach standing together. I skipped in the wide-armed-swinging-and-exaggerated-stepping fashion Tracey and I had developed when we were six years old. Even as teenagers, Tracey would link her arm through mine and skip through the outdoor hallways of our school. I'd cringe every time she did it. I hated people staring at me and judging me. When Tracey did stuff like that, people would smile, responding to her enthusiasm. If I did it, I felt foolish and stupid. Like I was trying too hard to be something I wasn't. Today was different. It was easy to throw my insecurities to the side. We'd been talking about graduating for what felt like forever—having it finally upon us was exhilarating.

Tracey and Zach didn't notice me skipping toward them, and I suddenly realized I had stumbled upon a scene that wasn't meant for my eyes. I wasn't supposed to see the guy I had always relied on tuck another girl's hair behind her ear with such loving care. The act should have been innocent. We were all friends—best friends—but this was something more. Maybe it was the way his hand lingered as he gently cupped her ear. Had his hand ever lingered on me like that? Judging by the sheen in Tracey's crystal blue eyes, it was clear there was something more between them than Zach and I had ever shared. Indecision gripped me. Should I confront them or back away? I was torn. My emotions felt as if they had been thrown in a blender. I didn't know how I should feel about what I was seeing. How long had I missed this?

I began to move forward, but hesitated with my foot paused mid-step. Forward or backward? Somehow, everything seemed to hinge on what direction my foot would take. The moment felt heavy with significance. Retreat. That was the right move. My attempted getaway was thwarted when Tracey spotted me out of the corner of her eye. Any doubt that what I was seeing was only my imagination was clarified by the horrified look on her face. My best friend, who I had spent practically every Friday and Saturday night with for years, who shared a mutual crush on Troy Bolton from High School Musical, who squealed with me when my parents gave me Miley Cyrus tickets for my twelfth birthday, who held my hand when I had to get sixteen stitches after falling off the bed laughing—that same friend looked thunderstruck. A surge of anger swirled through me. I didn't know what they were expecting. We were surrounded by a thousand graduating seniors, and she was surprised someone had caught them in the act?

Without a word, I whirled around and stalked away. All the joy and excitement I felt just moments ago had dimmed. I walked blindly, searching for a buffer that used to be Zach. Obviously, he was no longer mine.

I pasted a smile on my face when I found Kat, Dan, and Jessica, who were animated with enthusiasm as they adjusted their caps and gowns.

"Ladies and gentlemen. Please take your places. We are about to begin." Mrs. Flores's voice crackled across a loudspeaker. Jessica, Kat, and I hugged each other before they scurried off to their places in line. I felt someone behind me move into place. I didn't need to turn around to know it was Tracey. Her signature body spray wafting toward me gave her away. Neither of us spoke. I could feel her breathing on the back of my neck. It was heavy and hinted at impending tears. Over the years, we had cried together many times, so I knew when she was about to break down. Tracey hated for anyone to see her cry, and right now she was gulping hard to fight back the tears. Most times it worked, but on the rare occasion when she felt overwhelmed, she would spew like a fountain. When that happened, no amount of tissues stood a chance.

I knew she was seconds away from the impending flood. The bitch side of me wanted it to happen to vindicate the fissure of betrayal of my now suffering heart. If we would have been anywhere but in this line, I would have remained stoic and let her suffer, but this was our graduation—our shared moment. Everything we'd planned since we walked through the doors as freshmen would crumble away: our matching outfits, our secret plan to stand together to have our picture taken after we received our diplomas. There would be no single shots. We wanted to graduate the same way we had done every other event in our lives—together. We declared ourselves best friends from the day we met and discovered we shared the same last name. We were convinced we were sisters separated at birth. From that day forward, we'd always been together. All our other friends envied us, and we bragged about it whenever the occasion arose.

Tracey's breathing behind me was now coming out in gasps. If I was going to fix this, I needed to do it now.

Forcing a painful smile on my face, I whirled around. Just as I expected, her eyes were swimming with tears. The situation felt surreal. Shouldn't it be me crying? I was the one who just found out the two people I trusted the most had betrayed me. What did it say about me that I wasn't the one whose eyes were filled with tears?

"It's fine," I told her, swallowing hard. A single tear escaped from the corner of her eye. She opened her mouth to answer, but it came out garbled. "It's fine," I repeated with more conviction. I wasn't sure which of us I was trying to convince.

I climbed out of Bentley's car, throwing him a good-bye as I shut the door. He thanked me again, flashing another one of his dimpled smiles. Even though I didn't turn around to look once I walked away, I could hear his car idling at the curb as I entered the front door of my building. He was just doing the friend thing, like I emphasized I wanted, by making sure I got in safely. How could I expect anything else? I seemed to be the one dictating things between us. He was only respecting my wishes.

The weekend dragged by. Even if I wanted to talk to Bentley, he was at work. Keeping up with my classes and homework was a nonissue since I had an abundance of time to study. As the hours slowly trickled on, I was almost sorry I didn't go home for the weekend. At least there I could have had something to occupy my mind.

By Sunday evening I was going stir-crazy. I was on the verge of doing something drastic like actually leave my dorm room when Trina showed up. I'm pretty sure my reaction to her arrival made her think I needed a padded room.

My greeting could only be described as a squeal gone wrong.

"Are you okay?" she asked, eyeing my cheesy smile with

skepticism. She kept her hand on the doorknob like she wasn't sure if she should flee while she had a chance.

"Yeah. The weekend's been a bit of a drag." I felt as stupid as I sounded.

"Right," she answered, still looking at me cautiously.

"Look, I know I've been a total asshole." My voice stalled slightly, but I plunged on. "I wasn't expecting dorm living to be . . ." I paused as I searched for the right words. I knew everyone thought I was a complete dud. How did I explain that it was more of a sensory overload issue?

Trina waited with one eyebrow raised for me to continue. I could tell she was curious to see where this was going.

"So much," I finished lamely, wishing she would at least sit down. It felt oddly intimidating to be sitting down while she remained standing. "I guess I knew there would be parties and hanging out. I just didn't know it would be like twenty-four/ seven, and always in here. I didn't mean to be such a bitch. After the accident and a month in the hospital, I learned to value my alone time. Everyone was always coddling me. I think I went overboard."

She moved to her bed, looking uncomfortable with my sudden openness. This was the first time I'd mentioned my leg or the accident since we moved in together. She perched on the edge of her bed. "It's mellowed out a lot," she said, smoothing out the wrinkles from her comforter.

"I know. I'm trying to get better."

She nodded, but didn't look up as she continued to slide her hand over her comforter. My confession had embarrassed her. I should have stopped talking so she could make her retreat without things getting even more awkward, if that was even possible.

"So, you were in the hospital?" she asked quietly. "Is that why you have the—you know?" She finally looked up toward my cane.

I briefly regretted mentioning it. I knew it was bound to open a can of worms. I found myself answering her anyway. "Yeah. I was in a car accident." My throat dried out halfway through the sentence, but I got the words out. It felt strange to have a conversation with someone who knew nothing about what had happened.

"Car accidents freak me out. My cousin died in an accident when I was twelve. He was a total dipshit. He was street racing with some friends and flipped his car. I remember seeing the pictures. It was crushed to smithereens."

"Accidents have a way of doing that," I answered, feeling like someone was pressing on my chest.

"Did your vehicle flip, too?"

"Yeah, it did."

My therapist would call this another milestone. She felt the more I talked about what happened, the easier it would eventually become. I'd come to the conclusion that she must be dipping into the meds she prescribed. It would never get easier.

eleven

Bentley

Mac was already at the library when I showed up on Monday. I took it as good sign that she smiled at me and removed her backpack from the chair next to her. Saving me a seat was definitely a positive sign.

"Hey," I greeted her, plopping down in the empty seat.

"Hey," she answered, looking right at me. "How was your weekend?" she asked, twisting the lid off her water.

"Not bad. You know, the work thing. How about you?"

"It was boring as hell."

I chuckled. "That's too bad. If I didn't have to work, we could have done something."

"Do you work every weekend?" I was totally digging the new eye contact thing. Obviously, Friday night had helped her open up. Now, if I could coax her to move beyond the "friends" thing.

"For the most part. I tried working shifts during the week, but it screwed up my school schedule completely. Staying up half the night going out on calls and then trying to get to class the next day was too hard. Especially when I fell asleep in class. Turns out college professors don't take too kindly to that."

"Very true." Her eyes twinkled with humor, and it was all I could do not to stand up and tell her how gorgeous she was. "What high school did you attend?"

My thoughts were still on her eyes, and it took me a moment to switch gears. "Uh, Mainland. Class of 2011."

"That's a nice school. I had a project there for the Volusia County Literacy Fair when I was a freshman in high school."

"Yeah. It's not where I was zoned for, but we got it switched because they had the Science and Medical Career Academy."

"So, you knew even before high school that you wanted to be an EMT?" she asked, chewing on the end of her pen.

"My ultimate goal was to become a paramedic, but I'm not sure if I have what it takes." I couldn't believe I'd voiced the thought. I hadn't admitted that to anyone, not even my parents. Being a paramedic had been my only career choice for so long, it freaked me out that all my hard work would go to waste if I changed my mind.

"How can you say that? You're great at what you do. You help people more than you might realize."

I ran my hand through my hair, trying to better articulate what I meant. "I know we help people. I'm just saying it's tougher than I thought it would be. Going in, I assumed I'd be making a difference. The bitch of it is—I'm not. Or not as much as I thought I would be." I was thinking specifically of the domestic violence call from last week. Despite our training, Steve and I had been powerless to help. We didn't even get the chance.

"Sometimes it may not seem like you're helping, but in reality, you're the difference between darkness and light," she said quietly. "You were for me." She lowered her head, studying the screen of her phone.

I mulled over her words. I would have expected her of all people to hold a grudge against first responders, considering the way things worked out with her and her friends.

We both sort of sat there silently for a few minutes, digesting the confessions each of us had admitted. I finally piped in, asking her if she'd like to get some dinner. At first I thought she was going to turn me down by the way she started to shake her head. She shocked me by suddenly agreeing.

Triumphantly, I helped her to her feet and shouldered both our backpacks. As I followed her out of the library, I couldn't help sneaking a few looks at her trim backside. I knew from carrying her up the stairs on Friday that she couldn't have weighed more than a buck-five, if that, but she had the right curves. Something about her made me want to go all *caveman* and keep her from harm. She'd probably assume it was because of her limp and take it as an insult if I told her. Mom claims I've been that way since I was a kid. She said it was in my DNA that I inherited from Dad's side of the family. They were always protective of the ones they loved. If Mac heard that shit, she'd really go running for the hills. I wouldn't have blamed her.

"Is there anything you don't like to eat?" I asked as she climbed into my car.

"Just seafood."

"Really? All seafood?" That still left lots of options. There were plenty of places to eat around the school, but they were always crowded and loud. I wanted to be able to talk to her without shouting over everyone.

"Yep, all of it. Especially lobster. The idea of cracking their shells open and devouring their bodies seriously creeps me out. Shrimp are the same way, and clams are just yuck. And don't even get me started on any fish that is served with its head still on."

I laughed at her description. "So, are you a vegan?"

"Vegan?" She laughed. "Heck no. I'm just not a fan of watching my food being boiled to death. I know it sounds funny, but as long as my food's not looking at me, I'm good to go."

"You do realize chicken, beef, and pork are all animals with eyes, too, right? And their faces are cuter than a fish's any day."

"Yeah, but they don't ever bring out a burger with the cow's head still attached. Are you a vegetarian or something?"

"I'm a nonpracticing vegetarian."

She snorted. "What does that even mean?"

"It means I wish I was a vegetarian, but I sorta don't like vegetables. It makes being a vegetarian awfully hard."

"What do you mean you don't like vegetables? Like all of them?"

"Unfortunately, yes. My parents tried to force me to eat them when I was little. They'd tell me I couldn't get up from the table until my plate was clean. They eventually gave up after I fell asleep at the table for like the hundredth time. Nothing like having green beans stuck to your face."

I noticed when I mentioned my parents that Mac shifted gears and began talking about food again. It seemed anytime the subjects of family and friends came up, she would say as little as possible. Not that I would embarrass her by probing the matter further. I had a feeling that would be like adding gas to a fire.

We spent the rest of the drive talking about what other foods neither of us liked. At least she seemed to be having a good time and was completely relaxed when I pulled into a hole-in-the-wall Mexican restaurant I'd been going to all my life. I could tell she approved when she breathed in deeply the moment we stepped into the restaurant. I couldn't blame her. The scent of spices and fresh tortillas hung heavily in the air.

"It smells like heaven on a stick in here," she commented as the hostess led us to a table.

"That's nothing. Wait till you try the food. I swear, every-thing they make here is delicious. The tortillas are the fucking bomb, though."

"Señor Bentley, your mouth." Ana approached our table with a frown on her face. Her accent was heavy, but easy to understand, especially after all the years I'd been coming here. "What would your poor momma say?"

"Ana, I was only expressing how delicious your homemade

tortillas are. You can't blame a guy for being enthusiastic about your cooking," I crooned, turning on the charm. Ana and her husband, Pedro, were practically family after the amount of time my family and I had spent at their restaurant over the years. Never having children of their own, they'd showered my sister and me with attention while I was growing up. Between Ana and my mom, I had two women who regularly chastised me for my language. I tried to tell them both I was an adult now, but my argument never seemed to stick.

"Don't think you can charm me with that smile of yours, mijo. I'll tell your momma if I catch vulgar language on that tongue again. *Comprende?*"

"Yes, ma'am," I answered as Mac smirked.

"And who is this pretty young lady?" Ana asked, studying Mac with her typical eagle eye.

"This is Mac." Mac shifted slightly now that the attention was on her.

"Mac? That is not a name suitable for such a lovely girl."

"Ana," I warned. Ana had an uncomfortable habit of saying whatever was on her mind.

"It's short for Mackenzie," Mac answered. Her gaze was unwavering, though her voice shook slightly. It pained me to see her uncomfortable. Her shyness was what had initially drawn me in and now I felt protective because of it.

"Mackenzie," Ana said aloud, like she was testing it out. "Now that is a beautiful name. I will call you Mackenzie. Mac is some disgusting hamburger you get at fake restaurants."

"Ana, fast-food restaurants are not fake. And Mackenzie prefers Mac."

"Don't you sass me. If I say they're fake, then they are. And if I want to call your new girl by her given name, I will." She placed her hands on her plump hips, daring Mac or me to argue. She took our drink orders and stomped off toward the kitchen to complain to Pedro.

"Sorry about that. Ana's pretty old-school. Arguing with her is about as much fun as letting seagulls poke your eyes out."

Mac flashed me a weak smile, but shrugged her shoulders. "That's fine. My mom still insists on calling me Mackenzie, too. She pretends it's because she forgets, but I know that's just her stubborn way of keeping me in my place."

"Can I ask why you changed it?" It seemed like a good opportunity to get a little insight into her family life.

She took a steadying breath before answering. "It was just easier after the accident. I don't know how to really explain it. Everything changed so drastically. I didn't feel like the same person anymore. I was so sick of the sadness and the depression. I wanted to shake it all off."

She paused while Ana placed our drinks and a basket of chips and a bowl of fresh salsa on the table. We gave her our dinner orders and I waited for Mac to continue. I dipped a chip in salsa, waiting for her to finish without pressuring her.

After a few moments, she continued, "Anyway, it got to the point that I wanted to shed everything from my old life. That's why I transferred to the dorms this year. While I was at home, I was the victim who had lost everything. I would go to classes and then come home every night to the same questions about how I was doing or how I was feeling. If it wasn't that, we were always talking about the case. I just needed a change. During the summer, I broke it to my parents that I wanted to live on campus, and shortened my name. Needless to say, neither made them happy. They tried to fight my decisions, but in the end I played the 'I'm an adult now' card." She sat back in her chair looking like she had just confessed to a crime.

"I can understand that," I told her, dunking another chip into the salsa. "I bet deep down your parents do, too."

"I think my dad does. He's always been the go-with-the-flow kind of guy. Mom, not so much. It's usually her way or the highway. She works as a business executive in a marketing firm, so she's used to getting her way. In the beginning, she tried to fix me like she does problems that arise at work, but she realized I'm unfixable."

"Mac, you're not broken." I reached across the table and placed my hand on top of hers.

She looked down at my hand, surprised to find it there. I half expected her to pull away, but she didn't. "That's where you're wrong. I am broken. I've been broken from the moment some asshole truck driver decided the text message he wanted to send was more important than keeping his eyes on the road. I am weak and broken because of it."

I waited until Ana set our food down and we had thanked her before answering Mac's ludicrous claim. I told her she was crazy if she thought she was broken. She was the strongest person I'd ever known. She looked at me skeptically, asking how I could know that when we'd only known each other less than a couple weeks.

"That's exactly how I know it. In less than a day I knew you were stronger than you'll ever give yourself credit for. You think you're weak because of your injury, but in reality that injury shows just how strong you are."

"Did Ana lace your food with drugs?" she asked, shaking off my proclamation.

"Let me ask you a question."

She lowered her fork, waiting for me to continue.

"Why do you think you're weak?"

"I don't think I'm weak. I know it. I'm too scared to face people in my dorm, so I hide out in the library every single night."

"Yeah, but that's where you're missing the point. Do you drive to the library or have campus security cart you across campus in their golf carts?"

"God no," she answered, shuddering at the thought.

"Why?"

"Because I don't need them carting me around like I'm some invalid. I can walk on my own. I might not be very fast, and it might not look all that elegant, but I know how to get from A to B."

"Exactly. You force yourself to trek across campus every single day in the heat. Campus security would have no problem giving you a ride, and you wouldn't even think of asking."

"Of course not, but that still doesn't mean I don't hide out every day." She picked up her fork and resumed eating.

I wanted to press the subject further, and argue with her until she saw how ridiculous her statement sounded. She had a distorted view of herself. The more time I spent with her, the more I wanted to show her how wrong she was.

twelve

Mac

The small amount of my food I ate was delicious. Unfortunately, the dinner conversation twisted my stomach into knots, and my appetite was pretty much shot after that. I was used to keeping my feelings bottled up, but Bentley had a way of getting me to talk. Between that and my heart-to-heart with Trina the night before, I was left raw and exposed.

Bentley had obviously sensed my grief, because he never commented on how little I ate. As we drove back to my dorm after dinner, I was sure this would be the last time he asked me out and the end of his interest.

"What's your least favorite class?" he asked out of the blue.

The question was so random, it caught me off guard. "Uh, probably humanities, but only because the professor is so boring."

"Boring how?"

"His voice is so monotone, and it never changes. Plus, he keeps the lights in the room dim. You want to Tase yourself to keep from falling asleep."

"That's funny. You know who that reminds me of? 'Bueller . . . Bueller.'" He lowered his voice, laughing as he waited for me to join in. I must have missed the joke. "You know, Ferris Bueller?" he added when I still looked confused.

"Is that another professor?"

"What! Are you telling me you've never seen *Ferris Bueller*?" He looked at me incredulously.

"I've never had him. What class does he teach?"

"No, it's a movie. An old movie from the eighties."

"Oh, well, obviously I've never seen it."

"Holy shit. I'm going to have to fix that. I'm a huge John Hughes fan. I've seen every Brat Pack movie like a hundred times."

"Brat Pack?" I asked, as understanding dawned on me after all these years. I guess that was where our parents had gotten the group's nickname.

"Yeah. This one has Matthew Broderick in it. Trust me, it's a classic. On Wednesday you can come over and watch it," he added smoothly.

"I thought you had class Wednesday evenings."

"Nope. I'm good. So, what do you think?" he asked, pulling in front of my building.

I hesitated before agreeing. I wasn't entirely sure what his definition of our forming relationship was. For the most part, he was sticking to our claim that we were just friends. Every once in a while he found excuses to touch me, or hold my hand, like he had while we were eating, making me wonder if he wanted something more. Of course, that could be me misinterpreting things.

Trina was in our room for the second night in a row when I arrived. I was startled to see she had moved all her stuff back in. She was busy hanging a poster above her bed of a hunky guy wearing nothing but boxer briefs. I took in the chiseled chest and defined six-pack with appreciation.

"Oh, hey." I had surprised her, causing her to drop the poster on the bed.

"Hey. How's it going?"

"Okay. I figured it would be nice to sleep in my own bed for a change," she said, explaining her appearance. She looked uncomfortable, like she expected me to object or something.

"It'll be nice to have some company," I responded, smiling. "In more ways than one," I added, looking at the poster she had picked up and smoothed onto the wall above her bed.

"I've been dying to hang him up since my friend from high school sent it to me last month. I figured he could be our inspiration."

"That works for me," I said, dropping my backpack on my bed. "Do you need any help?" She unrolled another poster and made a move to hang it over her desk.

"That would be great." She smiled gratefully as I held the poster while she taped the corners down.

As we spent the rest of the evening setting up Trina's side of the room, we discovered that we shared many of the same interests. It was a conversation we should have had two months ago, but we made up for lost time. We played music as we chatted, mocking popular songs that we secretly loved even though they had dumb lyrics.

"When I was younger, I thought one of Taylor Swift's songs had the line 'one-eyed jeans,'" I admitted as she started to giggle.

"What's the real line?"

"'Worn-out jeans.'" She chortled loudly. I couldn't help laughing with her. I gasped, clutching my side. "Sadly, I still say one-eyed jeans, even now."

"That's hilarious. We have to play it now," she said, clapping her hands as she bounced up and down on her bed.

Still laughing, I pulled the song up on my iPhone and plugged it into her stereo. We both sang it loudly before collapsing on my bed in laughter.

Eventually we wore ourselves out and turned off the lights under the pretense of going to sleep, but we ended up talking late into the night. It reminded me of my last sleepover with Tracey. As I lay in the dark after Trina conked out, I mulled over my feelings in my head. Deep down I realized the reason I'd kept everyone at arm's length since the accident was because I felt it would be the ultimate betrayal to my friends to allow myself to care about anyone else. Like I would be turning my back on all our memories.

I fell asleep before I could reach a true conclusion on how I felt about the recent changes in my life. My last coherent thought was that Tanya would have a field day when I saw her next week. She'd been waiting for this moment.

The next morning Trina dragged me down to the dining hall for breakfast. I tried to decline, but our newfound friendship made it hard to ignore her pleas. My normal paranoia over everyone staring at me had me shaking slightly as we entered the large room. Trina noticed my stress and linked her elbow with mine so we could walk together.

"If they're looking at you, it's because you're drop-dead gorgeous."

"You're high as a kite," I said, following her to the cereal bar.

"Don't be dense. And before you say anything else, if you try to spit out some line that you're not pretty, I'll have to throat-punch you. I hate when girls do that. If you're beautiful, own it."

Laughing at her threat, I grabbed a banana, a carton of milk, and a mini box of Frosted Flakes. "I'm not saying I'm ugly or anything, but you said I was 'drop-dead gorgeous.' That's so an exaggeration. Runway models are drop-dead gorgeous."

"Fine. You're prettier than a toad. Is that better?"

"Much," I said, handing my meal card to the cashier.

I waited close by for Trina before heading to a table. Everything in me wanted to slink off so I was no longer standing conspicuously out in the open. After what felt like an insane amount of time, she finally finished paying for her food and we headed off to find a table. Trina's name was called out several times as we wove our way through the maze of tables. She acknowledged each greeting, but didn't stop to talk, which I was grateful for. Being so exposed was making me tense and slowly sucking away the confidence I had just gained back the night before.

Thankfully, Trina picked a small table for two that was in a less-crowded area. I turned my chair so my back would face the majority of the room. Relieved to be at least sitting, I set my cane against the wall and off to the side so it wouldn't be in the way. I kept my eyes down, opening the small box of cereal to dump into my bowl. It was a struggle fighting the urge to look behind me to see how many people were staring. The voice in the back of my mind pleaded to return to the safety of my room. Obviously, I wasn't quite ready to jump into the whole social scene yet.

"Are you going to eat that or pulverize it?" Trina asked, jerking my attention back to my hand, which had mangled my poor banana.

"Uh, I eat it that way," I lied, looking up at her.

"Right, mushed is better," she teased, calling my bluff. "You know, you have nothing to worry about. So what if you need a cane to walk? You're not all that special." She winked.

I let out a startled laugh at her words. It was the first time someone had been so blunt with my condition. I liked it.

Her smile turned to a scowl as she took a bite of her quiche. "Great, a guy I went out with just walked in. He doesn't give up." She ducked down, using me as a shield.

Whipping my head around, I spotted a guy who looked vaguely familiar. It took me a second to place him. We'd had a class together the previous year. All I remembered about him was that he was obnoxiously loud.

"Really?" I asked, turning back around to face her.

"I know, right? Can you believe it? I swear I don't know what I was thinking. In my defense, I was pretty plastered when we met, and I thought he was funny. As soon as I sobered up, I saw the ass face for who he really was. We only went out a few times, but he was a total jerk-off when I tried to end it. He couldn't seem to take a hint."

"What do you mean?"

"Just the normal bullshit, like calling me constantly. When I ignored those, he sent me a million text messages. I had to have my parents switch my cell number." She peeked around me. "He manages to show up wherever I am. He's a total stalker."

"What a dick. Are you worried about him?" I asked as she picked at her quiche.

"Not really. I just wish he'd get the hint. It's getting old trying to avoid him. You'd think by the way he's acting we'd been in a relationship for months instead of a couple measly dates."

"Maybe you should report him or something," I said, placing my banana peel in my empty bowl.

"Nah, he's not worth the bother. I think he's relatively harmless, just slow. Eventually he's bound to get the hint," she said dismissively. "Okay, we can go. He left."

Trina changed the subject as we left the dining hall together, chatting until we got to the science building, where she had a class. We parted ways after making plans to grab a bite for dinner later. She was sneaky the way she hurriedly escaped into the building before I could come up with a plausible excuse not to go.

Between Bentley and Trina, my solitary lifestyle had come to a screeching halt. I had to be a glutton for punishment agreeing to go out to dinner two nights in a row. I reminded myself how lonely I'd been over the weekend. It wasn't like I could have it both ways.

Dinner that night turned out to be stressful at first. Trina seemed to know a lot of people, and she was an attention-getter. Our table at Chili's quickly became crowded as some of her friends dragged chairs over to join us. I felt like I was suffocating and needed to retreat. I mentally started my counting exercises to calm my nerves. I suspected Trina sensed my distress because she made a point to introduce me to everyone and included me in the conversations. It was awkward initially. One, because there were at least three different conversations happening simultaneously, and two, because I had issues making eye contact with people I didn't know. Eventually, as I realized everyone was nice and didn't appear the least bit interested in my cane, I mellowed out enough that I was able to participate. I'm not sure if I necessarily had fun, but at least I was out in a social setting.

Trina and I walked back to the dorms with the same group that had joined us at our table. I prepared myself for a barrage of questions about why I had the cane, and what was wrong with my leg, but they never came. I even had myself worried about slowing the group down until I realized no one seemed to be in a hurry. As a matter of fact, I had to hold up several times as they goofed off. College students really weren't much different than they were in high school. They still liked to screw around and mess with each other. It was comforting.

Bentley called me later that night after Trina and I got back to our room. She had headed off to the shower, so I had our room to myself when my phone buzzed.

"Hi," I answered, smiling like a total goober. "How was your class?"

"Not bad. If I can memorize about a hundred body parts, I should ace the exam next week."

"Maybe I can help you. I'm the queen of flash cards." I couldn't believe my own ears. Was that me who had offered to get together?

"Really? That would be awesome. I'd ask my roommates, but that would require Chad actually stepping away from the Xbox."

"Sure. When I come over tomorrow for the movie, I can help you," I suggested before giving myself a mental thrashing for sounding overeager.

"Oh no. Tomorrow night is all about Ferris. We'll have to study on Thursday and Friday. If you're not too busy, that is."

A relieved smile crossed my face. "Nope, that works for me."

"Great. I'll pick you up after your last class. Text me the details about where to meet you."

"Okay. Bye."

"What's that goofy smile for?" Trina asked when she entered our room wearing Victoria's Secret sweats and a T-shirt. She had her long curly hair wrapped in a towel.

"It's nothing," I answered. It wasn't necessarily a lie. I wasn't entirely sure myself.

"Liar," she said, pulling the towel off her head and tossing it at me. "Give me the deets. Someone put that sappy grin on your face." She plopped down on her bed, pulling a brush through her hair.

"It's just some guy I met at the library."

"Oh, very good, continue. Is he like geeky on the outside, but peel off the shirt and he's got the whole come-to-me-momma thing happening?"

"He's not a geek."

"Ooooh, I see then. But he is a hottie?"

I gnawed on my fingernail before answering. "He's cute," I answered lamely.

"Cute is good. How long have you two been seeing each other?"

"Oh, it's not that. We're just friends."

She chuckled at my words. "Not from where I'm sitting. You should see the look on your face, like you had the world's best piece of chocolate or something. That doesn't look like 'just friends' to me."

As much as I wanted to deny it, she had a point. I was seriously crushing on Bentley. I found my thoughts drifting to him throughout the day more times than I could count. Maybe he thought we were just friends, but I wanted more.

Trina continued to press me for details, but I clammed up. I was too embarrassed to admit that Bentley seemed to want to keep things platonic between us. We stayed up late talking again, but I changed the subject to something other than Bentley. I had an appointment tomorrow morning with Tanya anyway. I was still on the fence whether I wanted to mention Bentley in our session. She was sure to ask questions about him that I might not be ready to answer. Once Trina drifted off to sleep, I tossed and turned as her words played on an endless loop in my head.

The next morning I made sure I had everything I needed for school since I would have just enough time after therapy to make it back to campus for my first class. Whether or not I was a good driver depended on your definition. If you were the type who was good at weaving in and around traffic and getting to your destination quickly, then you definitely wouldn't want to ride with me. On the other hand, even a more conservative driver might get frustrated riding shotgun with me behind the wheel. Since the accident, I hadn't been the most comfortable in any vehicle, let alone driving. I basically only drove when I had absolutely no other choice, like in this case, to Tanya's office, which was on the other side of town. Before I moved from home to the dorms on campus, my commute back and forth to school had been two daily forty-minute torture sessions.

I had a bit of an OCD type of ritualistic checklist I went through each time I got into the car. I fastened my seat belt, checking it three times to make sure it locked, looked in both side mirrors and the rearview mirror, looked over both shoulders, and then looked again, let out three or four deep breaths, and finally, when all that was completed, I was ready to start my trip. Once out on the road, I merged over to the far right lane as soon as possible, and always kept my speed at least five miles below the actual speed limit. If you were expecting to speed up through an intersection to beat a yellow light changing to red, then you better not be behind me because it wasn't going to happen. I had to endure the occasional honk of a horn, or a road rage poster child flipping me off when they finally got the room to pass me, but at least I made it to my destination in one piece.

Tanya's office was located in a small building that housed various other medical practices. After a short elevator ride to the third floor, I walked into an empty waiting room. Her door was closed, meaning she was most likely still with another patient. There was a TV hanging on the wall, but it always remained on one of the cable news channels. No, thank you. She didn't have the most up-to-date magazines either, so I pulled out my iPad to read. It wasn't long before her door opened and a gangly-looking teenage boy walked out followed by Tanya, who was giving her good-byes.

"Hello, Mac. It's lovely to see you." Unlike my mom, Tanya had no qualms about my name preference. Especially since she had insisted from day one that calling her "Dr. Ziwiski" was far too formal for her taste. Not that I knew any other shrinks, but Tanya didn't seem to fit the typical mold of straitlaced, business-attired, or tacky sweater vest–wearing doctors I had seen on TV. She wore long skirts or sundresses with flowers in her hair, and if she even wore shoes in the office, they were usually flip-flops.

"Hi, Tanya." I walked toward her, bracing myself for the

inevitable hug I knew was coming. I didn't know if she did it as part of my therapy because she knew I hated hugs, or if she was that way with everyone, but I always got a hug before and after our sessions. The layout of her office was as informal as she was. The two chairs where we sat were separated by a small round coffee table, where she had a pitcher of ice-cold water and a plate of organic oatmeal chocolate chip cookies, which she claimed to have made herself.

I'd been coming to see Tanya for about a year now, and each of our sessions started the same way. She sat in silence, not asking any questions until I started talking first. "So, everything has been going pretty good," I offered. I knew when she continued to sit without commenting that she was expecting more than general statements. "Classes are fine. No problems there, so—"

"Have you met anyone yet?" Ugh, it was as if she could read my mind. I wanted to deny it, but I sucked at lying. She would know I was full of shit and would keep asking and asking.

"Sort of," I admitted, fidgeting uncomfortably in my chair.

"A guy?" I nodded my head, feeling like I had been tricked into admitting something I didn't want to. "Wonderful. Tell me about him."

"His name is Bentley. We met at school, in the library. Actually . . ." I paused, feeling strange about telling her that he had been the one who helped me during the accident. In her usual fashion, she sat, waiting for me to continue. "He's an EMT and well, actually, he was the one who saved me during the accident."

"And you recognized him? Is that how you met?" She surprised me. I guess I had expected something more from her. Some type of objection for my poor judgment. Maybe it was me who had the problem. What a shocker.

"Well, yes, but he approached me first. I think we're really just friends."

"New friends are a good thing. Is one of you under the impression that there is more to your relationship than that?" she asked. It was a fair question even though I had no good answer. Things were going okay between Bentley and me, but whether he was interested in more than just a friendship, I wasn't sure.

"I don't know. I mean, he's a great guy. Really cute, but, what I mean is, he might want more, but I'm not sure." I sounded like a twelve-year-old wondering if I should pass a note to a guy to see if he liked me.

"It sounds like you still have some things to work out."

"You could say that."

"Have you shared your feelings with him?"

"That's the problem. I'm not sure how I feel. I'm attracted to him, but I've never been in a real relationship like this. You know about Zach and me, but that was different. We were technically 'boyfriend' and 'girlfriend,' but there was never that kind of love. Does that make sense?" Looking back now, I realized I never gave much thought to my relationship with Zach while we were dating. At least not until graduation night when I found out I was the third wheel.

"You know, Mac, you don't have to be afraid to express

yourself. If you want something more from Bentley than friend-ship alone, tell him. You might be surprised."

For the rest of the session, we talked more about Bentley and how Trina and I had worked things out. Tanya seemed pleased that I was making some social progress in my life. I got my customary hug as I left, along with an offer to call her if I needed to talk more about my new budding relationship.

Bentley was waiting right where I told him to meet me when I left class that afternoon. "Hey." He pulled me in for a quick hug.

My breath swooshed out of me in a rush as his arms pulled me close. The hug was unexpected and left me feeling slightly disoriented, especially since he lifted me off my feet. It had been a long time since someone had hugged me so impulsively. His arms were strong and sure as they locked me against his chest. The cologne he wore swirled around me, clouding my senses. I didn't even know how to react. Before I knew it, he was already pulling away and plucking my backpack from my hands.

He trotted off toward the parking lot purposefully as I fol-lowed behind. I swear he had a way of constantly throwing me off guard. One time he wants to hold hands. Another time he swoops me up in his arms like he plans on ravishing me. Today he lifts me up and hugs me like he's wrestling a bear and then he strolls ahead of me like I'm no different than one of his roommates. Trailing behind him, I wondered if he really was oblivious to everything going on.

thirteen

Bentley

So I hugged her like a soldier coming home from deployment. Friends hugged. Well, not my friends and me per se, but chicks hugged each other a lot. Somehow I come up with these ideas with Mac that sound romantic in my head, but my execution keeps falling short. I get myself worked up and take it one step too far. Hence the way a gentle one-armed hug practically turned into an assault. I was lucky she didn't haul off and hit me. The only thing I could think of doing after that was to head for the car before she had a chance to ask what my problem was. Then I would have really sounded like an idiot because, quite frankly, my head was so fucked-up, I would've had nothing.

It was crazy how I kept telling myself not to be an asshole. To take it slow with Mac because she needed more time than any other girl I ever dated. I was cool with all that until I got around her. Then my nerves went to hell. I've been trained to stay calm under pressure and I still turn into a wuss around Mac.

By the time I reached the car, I had managed to pull myself together. Thankfully Mac had followed me, which for whatever dumb-ass reason, I had neglected to consider. Turning around, I could see she was trying her hardest to keep up. I definitely felt like the douche of the year after that.

"Shit, I'm sorry."

"For what?" she huffed out, trying to catch her breath. She genuinely looked confused.

"For making you chase after me," I answered, opening the car door for her. "You should have whacked me in the back of the head."

"I didn't mind," she confessed as she buckled her seat belt.

"Well, I mind. What kind of asshole does that? My mom would hit me with a club if she saw all her hard work of trying to make a gentleman out of me going down the tubes."

"It made me feel normal."

"What do you mean, it made you feel normal? You look pretty normal to me."

"You were walking like you normally do. I had to work to keep up with you, but it made me feel for the first time in forever that I wasn't holding someone back. It was nice. Like you forgot about this," she said, thumping her cane.

"That cane doesn't define you," I said, pulling up in front of my complex.

She snorted. "Of course it does. It's a glaring reminder of everything that happened and everything I'm no longer able to do. It's like I'm dragging along a ball and chain everywhere I go."

"Is it really that bad?" I wanted to understand, but how could I relate to those types of feelings?

She shrugged, but didn't answer.

I jumped out of the car after parking and helped her climb out before scooping her up in my arms.

"What are you doing?" she yelped.

"Isn't that obvious? I'm carrying you up the stairs."

"The stairs are all the way over there," she said dryly, even though I noticed she had marginally relaxed in my arms.

"I figured it was just as easy to pick you up here."

"Maybe you could at least ask before you keep picking me up. I'm beginning to think you went into the wrong profession. You sure you didn't want to be one of those pro wrestlers on TV?"

"Now there's an idea," I answered blandly, resisting the urge to bury my nose in her hair to see if it smelled as good as the last time I carried her.

She smirked at me, but snuggled even closer. I tightened my hold and slowed my pace. I was going to enjoy this moment for as long as I could.

"Am I too heavy?"

"Are you kidding? I've carried a stack of books that was heavier than you. I figure it's better to be cautious. It would suck if I fell backward, or for that matter, fell forward. I'd crush you." I was teasing, of course. It would be a cold day in hell before I let something like that happen.

"That would suck," she agreed.

Despite my attempt to prolong the moment, we eventually made it to my floor. I would have carried her all the way to my apartment like I had the other night, but I sensed that would be pushing it. Reluctantly, I set her back down.

"Thanks," she said, finding her footing. "Stairs are still my kryptonite."

"It's not a problem at all. You weigh less than a bag of cement."

"I'm sure there's a compliment in there somewhere."

I laughed. "Sorry. I worked at a building supply company when I was a teenager. It was the only comparison I could think of."

"That seems like a good job for a teenager."

"My uncle owns the company. I had to sling around bags of concrete and mulch in the heat all summer, but the pay was good. Everyone else I knew was making minimum wage working fast food or wherever and I was bringing home a cool ten bucks an hour."

I opened my apartment door and ushered her inside. Chad's boxers and jeans were draped over the arm of the couch. That freaking guy. He knew I was going to have company over. Obviously he'd decided to change in the living room, most likely while he played Xbox. Snatching his clothes off the couch, I carried them to his room and tossed them inside. Judging by the mess covering the majority of his floor, he'd never notice. I could see Sherman in his aquarium across the room staring at me with his beady black eyes. He was probably plotting how he was going to strangle me in my sleep with his tail.

"You guys feed pizza to your couch?" Mac asked when I joined her.

"What?" I asked, momentarily confused until I spotted a piece of crust poking up between the couch cushions. "Of course. Don't you?" I dug the half-eaten piece out and tossed it on the coffee table.

"Nah, our couch at home is a food snob. If it's not from a five-star restaurant, it wants no part of our cuisine."

"Too bad. Day-old sofa pizza isn't bad. You should try it."

"You know, I think I'll pass. We'll save it for Chad."

I was glad to see that her sense of humor ran along the same lines as mine. My jokes went completely over the head of the last girl I dated. On that note, just about everything I said went over her head. She was a knockout with a body that wouldn't quit, but by our second date, the wall in my apartment was more interesting to talk to. Now that I thought about it, that was way back in May. Chad was right. I was practically a monk.

"You sure you don't want to get a little studying done first?" Mac asked, sinking into the crust-free couch.

"No way. Unless you need to get some work done. I didn't even think to ask that."

"I'm good. I have plenty of time to get my studying in."

"Excellent," I said, rubbing my hands together. "Are you ready to Ferris your life?"

"Ferris my life?"

"Absolutely. Watching *Ferris Bueller* is a life-changing experience. You'll never be the same after this. For the rest of your life Ferris will find a way to influence the decisions you make," I said solemnly as I held up the DVD.

"Wow. I didn't realize it would be such a privilege."

"Have you not heard anything I've said? *Ferris Bueller's Day Off* is not an ordinary movie. It's special." I switched off the light after sliding the disc into Chad's Xbox. A little sunlight managed to sneak through the blinds, so it wasn't quite the same as a theater, but it would have to do.

"Well, now I feel honored." She smirked as I joined her on the couch. I sat within inches of her to gauge her reaction.

I'd given the seating for this occasion a lot of thought over the last few days. Probably more than any dude should. I'm sure if Chad or Michael knew, I'd wake up wearing the bra we kept around for when one of us was acting like a total pussy. Chad had been the last bra victim when we busted him bleaching the tips of his hair in the bathroom. That night Michael and I snuck in while he slept and hung the bra over his neck and snapped a few pictures.

Mac didn't seem to mind that I was sitting so close. At least she didn't flinch or anything. I'd never been this nervous with a girl. Hell, I'd done more in the first five minutes with other chicks. Mac and I were two weeks into our weird friendship/relationship, whatever this was, and I was being a total pansy-ass. I thought about getting the bra and strapping it on myself. I was acting like a chick anyway.

fourteen

Mac

The fine hairs on the back of my neck stood on end with awareness. We were thirty minutes into watching the movie and I'd been on edge the entire time. Bentley was a foot away and we both sat like statues. It was like we were playing chicken and the first one to move would lose. Each minute that ticked by felt like an eternity. I thought about what Tanya had said about telling Bentley how I felt, but outside the privacy of her office, that seemed like an impossible idea. I was as indecisive as ever. I couldn't deny the reaction he evoked from me when we were together. My pulse raced, making my breathing slightly heavier.

Feeling braver than I had in a long time, I moved my hand over until it was touching his. My eyes flickered away from the glowing TV screen to his face. His eyes remained on the movie, but I could see a small smile playing on his lips.

He surprised me by capturing my hand with his. Smiling, he turned my hand over and slowly traced the lines on my palm with the tip of his finger.

"We're not watching the movie," he said. Like I cared at that moment. I was more concerned with his finger tickling its way across the hypersensitive skin of my wrist.

"Yeah," I answered as he began gently massaging my forearm. He moved in slow lazy circles, giving me goose bumps. My blood felt as if it was reaching a boiling point. Bentley's touch was soft and tormenting, making me crazy with sensations I'd never experienced. I wanted him to tighten his hold, to stop the tingling of every nerve ending in my body. My free hand itched to grab his.

As I raised my head, I found his eyes locked with mine. He moved both his hands to my upper arms, tightening his hold in a way that made it clear he wanted more. It only served to set the fire in me to a roar, ready to blaze out of control.

My lips and throat completely dried out. I needed to tell him. I needed him to know what he was doing to me. "Bentley," I gasped.

"I know," he answered, pulling me closer. "We're just friends." His lips moved within an inch of mine.

I nodded my head in agreement, but I wanted more. He was so close, but still unattainable since he was holding me in place. His touch was rough, but in a demented sort of way that felt so good. "Bentley, please," I found myself pleading.

"Please what?" He teased my chin with the softness of his lips. The touch was foreign and erotic in a way that made me tremble from head to toe.

"Kiss me," I uttered with another spasm of desire shaking me. The intense response of my body was intoxicating. I wondered if he felt the same, or was I just like any other girl he had been with?

His lips halted any further words. They settled on mine so abruptly, so fiercely, they crushed every bit of anticipation that had built to that point. This time it was me who held him in place as my fingers wove into his short locks of hair. Bentley's tongue stroked against mine. Brazen and possessive, it felt so damn good, I pulled him closer. I opened up to him, giving him everything he sought and taking everything I needed. Nothing else mattered. His kisses somehow filled the emptiness I'd been feeling for so long. The empty shell that carried the ghosts of my past filled with an overflowing gamut of new emotion.

I was unsure how long we had kissed before we heard the jingling of keys. Bentley pulled away abruptly as the front door swung open. My fingertips moved to my lips, which felt swollen after the heat of passion.

A loud voice boomed behind me as the overhead light came on. "Dude, were you two sucking face?" There was no denying his statement considering I was still sitting with Bentley practically sprawled on top of me. He thought it was funny as he laughed at my feeble attempts at moving him off me. Bentley made it hard since he refused to let go of me.

"I thought you had class," Bentley said over my head as he moved to his own spot next to me on the couch.

"It ended like an hour ago, bro." His roommate bounced down on the couch where I had been sprawled. "I'm Chad," he greeted me, offering his hand.

"Mac," I returned, trying to maneuver around in Bentley's arms so I could shake his hand.

He grinned at me. "Mac? I like it. Like mac and cheese. I'm a huge fan."

"Chad," Bentley warned, helping me position myself so I was tucked against his side.

"What? I'm serious," Chad answered, holding his palms up. "So, what have you two wacky kids been up to sitting here in the dark?"

"Watching a movie," Bentley answered.

"Really? Looks like I just missed it." Chad looked pointedly at the TV, which was now displaying the movie's menu screen. "Methinks you two were playing spin the bottle without the bottle."

Bentley flicked him in the ear. "Don't be an asshole."

"Just being observant. I'm bummed I missed the movie, though. Ferris Bueller is my idol."

"We can watch it again," I offered since I'd missed about ninety percent of the movie.

"Ha, I knew you two were busy playing tonsil hockey," Chad said, making himself comfortable as he restarted the movie.

"Make yourself at home," Bentley drawled dryly.

"Why, thank you, my boy," Chad answered, picking up the pizza crust we had rescued from the couch earlier. He sniffed it before biting an end off.

I shook my head. Men had no standards at times.

He polished off the rest of the crust, looking around for a pizza box he may have missed. "I'm starving. We should order a pizza."

"You hungry?" Bentley asked me. My stomach grumbled, answering his question. I had skipped lunch since my stomach was tied in knots thinking about tonight.

We all laughed at my stomach's reaction. "The lady's belly has answered. Order us some grub, my good friend," Chad ordered.

Bentley chucked the remote at him, but rose from the couch to call the pizza place anyway. I sat sandwiched between the two of them while they provided a running commentary throughout the movie. They could practically quote every line word for word. The movie was funny, but the premise was a little too unrealistic for me. Not that I would confess to Bentley that it wasn't exactly the life-changing experience he had promised. I didn't want to hurt his feelings. Besides, by the time the movie ended, I had to hold my stomach from laughing so hard at his and Chad's impressions of the characters.

It was by far the most fun I'd had in a while. Chad was like a big kid, thrusting an Xbox controller in my hands because he insisted that I had to give Halo a try. He then proceeded to mock me as I fumbled around like a complete novice. Bentley offered helpful hints in between shooting his own aliens, but it became apparent that I wouldn't have a future as a pro gamer.

"Hey, has she met Sherman yet?" Chad asked as we cleaned up the pizza mess.

"No. Why would I let her meet that no-good future pair of boots?"

"Harsh, man." Chad looked at me, patting my hand. "He just doesn't understand Sherman. I'll be right back."

"Chad, come on," Bentley objected.

"No, it's cool. I want to see him," I piped in.

"See. Listen to your lady, bro," Chad added to rub it in.

He returned seconds later, holding the large reptile. It was the first time I'd seen an iguana in person. If I didn't know any better, I would have thought it was fake because Sherman never moved as Chad carried him. That is, until Bentley came close, at which time he hissed like he had seen a mortal enemy.

"Wow, he really doesn't like you, does he?" I asked.

"I told you," Bentley replied. "That fucker is the devil."

"You want to hold him, Mac?" Chad asked.

"Maybe next time," I said, hesitantly reaching a finger out to touch him. His skin felt rough and leathery. I almost lost my balance from jumping when he suddenly moved his tail with my finger on him.

"That's enough Sherman now," Bentley said, catching me to steady me on my feet.

"All right, come on, Shermi, say bye," Chad said, taking one of the iguana's menacingly clawed limbs and pretending to wave.

He returned moments later, shocking me by giving me a bear hug before I left, sending my cane clattering to the floor. He retrieved it for me after giving me a pat on the head. "Come back again soon," he said, sinking back down on the couch.

Bentley apologized a few times for Chad during the ride back to my dorm. "He has no social life," he explained, finding an empty parking spot in front of my building.

"I liked him. You could have just dropped me off."

"Friends drop each other off. Boyfriends walk their girlfriends inside."

"Whoa, did I miss the memo?"

He climbed from the car without answering, jogging around to the passenger side to open my door. Holding out his hand to help me, he pulled me from the seat and placed his hands on my waist to face him. "Do you have a problem with that?" he teased.

"Hmmm, I don't know. You're awfully presumptuous."

He quirked his eyebrow. "Maybe, but do you always kiss your friends like that?"

"Well, since I don't have any friends . . ." I regretted the words as soon as I said them. I'm not even sure where the statement came from. Bentley looked completely shocked, like he'd mistakenly said something wrong.

"Mac, I'm sorry. I wasn't saying—I mean. I wouldn't do that." He tripped over his own tongue, searching for an apology that wasn't even necessary.

"No, Bentley, don't. I'm the one who's sorry. That was a

bitch thing to say. I don't even know why I said it. I knew what you meant."

"Holy shit," he said, taking me in his arms and dropping his lips to the sensitive skin by my ear. My head dropped to the side to give him easy access. "So does this mean the boyfriend-girlfriend thing is a yes?"

"Well, let's not get ahead of ourselves here." I pulled away, taking a step backward. "You still have to admit, you were being pretty presumptuous."

"Meaning?" he returned, wondering where I was going with this.

"Well, a girl likes to be asked."

"Oh, of course. What was I thinking?" He got down on one knee as three people spilled out from the side door of the dorm that faced the parking lot. He took my hand. "Mac, will you be my girlfriend?"

"Say yes, say yes," the trio shouted in unison as they laughed their way to their car.

"Get up, you fool." I laughed, slapping Bentley on the arm.

"Not until you say yes."

"Fine, yes." Bentley rose to his feet and placed a long kiss on me that practically melted me from the inside out.

"Should I start doodling your name on my school folders?" I asked, my voice coming out as a croak as his mouth found my neck.

"I'd expect nothing less," he said as his lips captured mine again.

fifteen

Bentley

"Yo, Bentley, did you make sure the rig was stocked up?" Steve asked, entering the staff break room, where I was drinking a Coke while waiting for my shift to end. The weekend had dragged, and I was ready to clock out and be done. I hadn't seen Mac since Friday. We had texted and talked on the phone a few times, but it wasn't the same thing. I'd say I was completely pussy-whipped, but even Chad had complained about her absence when I arrived home late last night after working a sixteen-hour shift.

"Like six hours ago," I answered, looking at the clock on the wall, which seemed not to be moving. Today wouldn't have been so bad if we had been called out a couple times, but with the exception of responding to a 911 call that turned out to be false, Steve and I had been sitting around all night twiddling our thumbs. At least now that midnight had come and gone, we were on the down side of my shift. Three hours to go and I would be home free.

"That's right. Shit, I must be losing my mind. I swear these dead nights suck my brain cells." He sat down at the round table across from me. "How about some cards?" he asked, plucking a deck out of his shirt pocket.

"Sure, as long as you don't cheat this time."

"Whatever. If anyone cheats, it's you. No one can have the luck you have."

"Whatever helps you sleep at night. Speaking of which, how's Jacob?" I asked as he shuffled the deck.

"According to Molly, he actually slept through the night last night. Maybe I can get a full night's sleep in tonight."

"You mean you won't have to nudge Molly and tell her the baby needs her," I quipped, looking at my cards.

"I'm going to regret telling you that, aren't I?"

"Regret telling me that you make your poor exhausted wife get up every night with your baby? Most likely. You're lucky my mom isn't here to ream your ass. She'd have a field day with you. My dad can tell you stories about walking around all night holding me because I had colic or some shit like that when I was a baby. He and my mom both took turns."

"Hey, Molly likes getting up with Jacob. She's all about this mother thing."

"Right? Because she doesn't value her sleep as much as you do yours?"

"Damn, I'm starting to think you're my mother. Fine, I'll

get up tonight with him if he wakes up. Now, can we please stop gabbing like a bunch of chicks and play some cards?"

"Just waiting on you, old man," I ribbed him, looking at my cards.

"It's about time," he grumbled, looking at his own cards. "Do you have any eights?"

"Go fish."

He looked at me hard for a moment before grabbing a card off the pile. "Ha," he said, triumphantly holding up an eight he'd just drawn.

Rolling my eyes, I took my turn. We played a half-dozen hands of Go Fish, which was the only game of cards we ever played since Steve had struggled with gambling a few years ago. He quit cold turkey before he and Molly got married and she had given him an ultimatum: give up gambling or find someone else to warm his bed. He turned in his poker chips, but got to keep his lucky deck of cards as long as he promised never to use them for any game that involved betting.

The end of our shift couldn't have come quick enough. We left with me reminding him that he owed Molly a night of sleep. He grudgingly agreed before heading toward his mommy mini-van that Molly insisted they buy when Jacob arrived.

By the time I got home, I felt more exhausted than when we worked one of our busy shifts. I wanted to call Mac, but obviously she was sleeping. Instead, I sent her a text that she would see when she woke up.

The next day I slept in longer than I wanted to. I had only one class on Mondays, and it started in an hour. Mac had seen my text because I had a return message from her asking if we were still on for tonight. I had talked her into going to a UCF basketball game when I found out she hadn't been to one yet. She grudgingly agreed to go after I bribed her with chocolate-covered pretzels, which I had learned were her weakness.

Later that afternoon, I grabbed my keys to head to Mac's dorm, leaving a sour Chad at my apartment. He was grumbling that I couldn't hog Mac every night. "Stop sleeping around and get your own girlfriend, dickhead."

"Like that's even a legit argument. Come on, bro," he answered. Maybe he had a point, but it wasn't like I was asking him to throw his Xbox out the window and run it over. I just wanted my girl to myself. Michael, who caught the tail end of our exchange, laughed as he headed out for his evening class.

Mac was waiting on a bench outside her dorm when I showed up ten minutes later. The arena was halfway between my apartment and her dorm, so it made no sense to drive and deal with the parking mess.

"Hey," she said, looking a bit unsure as she stood up. She fidgeted with the thin strap of the small purse that crisscrossed her body. It was strange to see her without the typical backpack she normally carried everywhere. I liked it. The backpack always seemed to make her shoulders slump. I stopped in front of her.

"Hey, yourself." She bit her lip at my close proximity. I cupped her face with my hands, tilting her chin up so I could be the one biting her lip. She sighed against my lips the moment they touched hers. It made me consider saying hell with the game and taking her back to my apartment and kicking Chad to the curb, so she and I could pick up what we had started a few nights ago.

I nipped on her bottom lip one last time before reluctantly pulling back. A few seconds longer and she would feel on her leg what I was thinking. "Ready to cheer on some Knights?"

"Sure," she answered, still looking kiss-shocked.

I tucked her hand in the crook of my elbow so she could hold on to me. She asked me about my weekend as we walked. I found myself launching into a complete recap even though Steve and I had basically sat around. She was easy to talk to. The awkwardness that was inevitable in any new relationship was missing. With Mac, I didn't feel like I had to say anything to try and impress her.

She tightened her grip on my elbow as the sidewalk around us filled up with more people heading in the same direction. A few guys pushed past us, obviously not satisfied with our pace. I gritted my teeth when they jostled Mac, making her stumble slightly.

"Are you okay?" I asked, glaring at the backs of the total pricks who were oblivious to anyone but themselves. As a rule I didn't fight. It was my job to take care of people who were hurt, but at the moment, I wanted to shove my fist down their throats.

She looked at me questioningly and I realized I was clenching my fist. "I'm fine. It's nothing I'm not used to."

"What?" My voice was louder than usual and I noticed she

flinched. I forced myself to bring it down a notch. "You shouldn't have to be used to it," I said, clenching my jaw.

She patted my arm like she needed to pacify me. "Bentley, it's nothing to get worked up about. I move slower than the average person. Believe me, if I could walk normally and was in a hurry, I'd probably get frustrated walking behind someone as slow as me. No one likes to get behind the slowpoke." She sounded okay, but I detected a trace of regret beneath those words. I wanted to pound the assholes into the ground.

"It freaking rips me up that you somehow think it's your fault," I said, handing over our tickets at our gate into the arena.

"I'm just being realistic," she said as we took the programs handed to us.

I grumbled under my breath, but let the subject drop. Things didn't get much better when I realized our seats were higher up the rows than I'd anticipated. I was the asshole. I forgot to even think about that when I bought the tickets.

Mac eyed the shallow steps like they were serpents ready to snap at her feet. I could have swept her up in my arms like I did at my apartment complex, but I couldn't imagine her going for that.

"Let me see if I can get our seats switched," I said, making a move toward the exit.

"It's fine." She stopped me, looking at the stairs with determination. "It'll get me out of having to face the stair climber at physical therapy."

"You still go to therapy?" I asked, supporting her as we

climbed toward our row. A thin bead of sweat collected on her temple by the fifth step.

"Yep, a couple times a month. They'd like me to go more, but classes make it hard. We reached a compromise since I do so much walking around campus," she answered, somewhat out of breath.

"Do you need to stop for a second?" We reached the eighth step, but she looked determined to continue.

"No, I'm okay. Only six more to go," she said, counting along with the numbers on each row of seats.

The more she struggled, the more I felt like total pond scum. Mac was only putting herself through this because of me. I deserved a suitable punishment, like picking up Sherman and letting him pelt me in the face with his tail. Mac's face when we reached our row made me feel slightly better. She beamed in triumph, looking so damn happy I couldn't help placing a kiss on her smiling lips.

We found our seats, which were a pain to get to since they were in the middle of the row, which was hard for Mac because of her cane. I probably couldn't have picked worse seats if I had tried.

"At least we're in the middle," she rationalized once we managed to get seated.

I raised my eyebrows in confusion. As dates went, this would go down in history as the worst ever.

"No matter what, I won't have to stand up again. Anyone who has to go to the bathroom can go that way or that way," she said, using her thumbs to point in both directions.

"How about some grub?" I asked, smiling at her reasoning.

"Sure, you want me to get it?"

"That would be great. I'll take a couple dogs and some nachos."

"You're funny," she said, flipping open her program.

"What would you like?" I laughed, standing up.

"Couple dogs and nachos."

"Done." I started down our aisle.

"I'm kidding," she called after me. "I'll take one hot dog and a Coke," she added, holding up one finger.

The concession stand was pregame busy, causing me to miss tip-off by the time I made it back to our seats juggling the food. I handed Mac's hot dog to her and set her drink on the floor at our feet. Squeezing her knee reassuringly, I unwrapped my first dog while balancing a second on my lap, along with nachos and extra cheese.

"You sure that's enough?"

"At least till halftime." I downed half the first hot dog in one bite.

"I assume you know what to do if you start choking?"

"Sure. That's what the extra cheese is for. Just force it down my throat."

"That's gross," she said, wrinkling her nose.

By the fourth quarter it was clear she was having fun by the way she cheered and shouted at the refs when a call didn't go the Knights' way. She remained seated, of course, but that didn't stop her from being as loud as anyone else. It surprised me. It was the first time I'd seen her so animated.

"That was fun," Mac proclaimed when the game ended.

"I'm glad you liked it. I'm surprised we didn't get thrown out with all your colorful criticism of the refs." I nudged her as we waited for the crowd to thin before we attempted to leave.

"At least the Knights won, right? Besides, they'd look like total douches throwing a cripple out of a game."

"And you figure you had something to do with the outcome?"

"You can't prove I didn't."

"With that logic, how can I even think of arguing?" I said, shaking my head.

Our row was littered with discarded trash, so I used my foot to clear a path as Mac followed behind. Going down the stairs proved to be no less difficult, but she took more care by using me to balance herself. By the time we made our way outside, the charged-up crowd had clogged the entire surrounding area.

I held Mac's hand, pulling her as close to me as possible to avoid the crush of bodies. She took it all in stride, but I was beginning to fume again. It was like people lived in their own worlds, not noticing that maybe some of us needed the sidewalk for what it was actually intended for. I tried to remain calm, asking as nicely as possible to pass through, but a couple assholes had the nerve to look annoyed, like asking them to stop their conversation and take a step to the side was somehow an inconvenience. Mac could see that I was heating up because she placed her hand on my arm, telling me it was fine. I smiled at her, taking a deep breath. We were almost through the bulk of the crowd anyway.

Out of nowhere, a body slammed into Mac at full speed. Neither of us saw it coming and there was nothing I could do as the force of the collision sent Mac sprawling toward the ground.

Rage colored my vision red as I looked down at Mac, who had rolled over to find her jeans torn at the knees with blood already seeping through. Her hands were badly scraped from where she had hit the concrete. Some of the surrounding crowd rushed to Mac's side to make sure she was okay. As for the piece of shit who had knocked her down, whether or not he was attempting to apologize didn't matter to me at that moment.

I grabbed his arm and twirled him around just as my clenched fist smashed him squarely in the jaw. He staggered backward, falling on his ass.

"How's it feel, dickhead?" I growled, standing over him and ready to hit him again if he stood.

One of his friends jumped to his aid. "What the fuck, man?" He shoved me in the chest. I raised my hands, ready to throw down if he stepped forward. The crowd circled us, feeling the tension in the air. They watched eagerly, waiting to see who would be the next one to throw a punch. Nothing got a bunch of students hyped up like a fight.

Two guys in yellow security shirts pushed their way into the crowd, jumping between us to calm the situation. After a stare-off and some finger-pointing, the incident dissipated rather quickly, much to the dismay of some of the onlooking crowd. They expressed their disappointment that no further blows were exchanged. A few more security workers showed up and they assessed Mac's condition, asking if she needed medical help. I gave them my credentials, assuring them I could take care of her. After quietly telling me they would have reacted the same way, we all parted ways.

"Are you okay?" I asked Mac, kneeling beside her. Her eyes were as big as saucers.

"I can't believe you hit him." She looked shocked and angry with me like I'd done something wrong.

"Yeah, well, I can't believe he knocked you down. He was a total asshole."

"I get knocked into all the time. Maybe not like this by some drunken jockstrap who didn't even know what he was doing." She declined taking my hand to help her up, but realized quickly she had no choice. It was hard enough under normal conditions for her to stand from a sitting position. Scraped knees and hands definitely didn't help. I took her under the arm and she grudgingly accepted, wincing as we raised her to her feet. Her face was red, probably as much from anger at me as embarrassment. "You can't punch everyone who misses this," she added, holding up her cane with disgust.

"He was a prick, plain and simple. Maybe next time he'll be more considerate of people." I'd probably overreacted. Okay, I definitely overreacted. Seeing Mac lying in a bleeding heap on the sidewalk sent me over the edge. Especially since if I'd had a better hold of her, she may not have fallen so badly.

"So, now it's your job to protect me?" she huffed, heading down the sidewalk and leaving me behind. She looked like a wreck, but in her determination limped along with purpose.

"Mac, come on. I couldn't let him get away with it," I said through clenched teeth, catching up to her easily.

She whirled around in anger, catching me off guard. "Look, Bentley, in case you missed it, I don't like attention on me. This cane and my damn gimpy limp make it pretty hard to stay inconspicuous. Having some guy I'm dating punch out another guy is not inconspicuous."

Despite the circumstances, I felt the stirrings of desire. She was pissed as hell, but damn if she didn't look sexy. I don't know what kind of asshole that made me, but I couldn't help it.

"Why are you staring at me like that?" She paused in her tirade.

"Like what?" I asked, surprised. I guess I didn't have much of a poker face.

"Like I'm amusing you," she said with more aggravation.

"I can't help it. You're cute when you're mad."

sixteen

Mac

"Cute?" He seriously did not just call me cute. He punches a guy and then has the nerve to downplay my anger? I clenched my own fist, tempted to throw my own punch. Anything to knock the grin off his face.

"I would say *adorable*, but I'm guessing that would have been pushing it," he teased.

"Don't do that, okay? I'm pissed. Don't think you can get mad enough to hit someone and that's justified, but then dismiss my anger as cute. You don't seem to understand that makes me feel like you don't care about my feelings."

"Shit," he said, exhaling. "You're right. I'm sorry." His smile turned to a frown as he looked down at the dried blood covering my torn jeans. "Do you need to sit down?" he asked, indicating the low wall behind me.

"No, and I don't feel like standing in the middle of the sidewalk arguing about it with my knees throbbing. I just want to get to my dorm and then I'll take care of them," I said, limping forward.

"We're closer to my apartment. Let's go there and I'll clean them up."

I wanted to argue, especially since I was still mad, but he reasoned that he had everything we would need to clean me up, and was trained to do it. I grudgingly agreed. He was right that his apartment was closer. My embarrassment over the whole situation dissipated as we walked. My friends and I had always stuck up for each other, but no guy I'd ever known had punched someone to defend my honor. I was being completely mental, but I found it a bit flattering now that a large crowd of people wasn't looking at us. The fall itself had been mortifying. I know it wasn't my fault, but taking a dive in front of the guy you liked was not my idea of fun.

As usual, Bentley carried me up the stairs to his apartment. My knees, which had moved beyond throbbing to downright pain, nearly wept in relief when he scooped me up in his arms. When we reached his landing, he didn't pause to set me down. Instead, he continued to his apartment. I thought about complaining, but it felt so good to be off my feet.

Chad was playing Xbox when Bentley pushed the front door open, holding me in his arms. He looked up when we entered, cutting his greeting short at the sight of my knees.

"What the hell did you do to her?" He glared at Bentley as

he jumped off the couch. Despite my embarrassment, I couldn't help smiling at his reaction.

"I didn't do this, dumb-ass. Some jerk-off knocked her down in front of the arena," Bentley answered, depositing me on the couch carefully like I was delicate china.

"Are you kidding me? I hope you knocked his fucking lights out."

"See?" Bentley said, looking at me. "Maybe not his lights, but I think I might have loosened a couple teeth," Bentley answered, holding his fist up like a trophy.

"That's what I'm talking about, dude," Chad said, fist bumping Bentley.

"What else would I expect from a couple of cavemen?"

"Are you kidding? If some guy messes with our girl, it's our job to set him straight."

"Our girl?" I parroted, looking at Bentley.

"Bro, get your own girl," Bentley told him, nudging him out of the way so he could help me roll up my jeans. "Hand me my kit."

"I didn't mean we were both dating Mac. I just meant that as your friend, if I saw some asshat knock her down, I'd make sure he was also on the ground," Chad said, handing Bentley a first-aid kit that put any others I'd seen to shame.

"Trust me. He means well," Bentley said, working my jeans to midcalf. They refused to go any higher since they were skinny jeans. They happened to be my favorite pair, but at the moment I hated them. "This isn't working. You're going to have to take them off."

Chad, who had resumed his game, turned his head so suddenly to look at us, I was afraid he was going to get whiplash.

"I'm not taking my jeans off in front of you two."

"I won't peek," Chad piped in with a wolfish grin on his face.

"I didn't mean for you to strip down completely. Trust me, when that happens, Chad will not be with us. I was going to suggest you put on a pair of my sweats. That way I can get to your knees better."

"Okay. I guess I can do that."

Chad offered to help me with the sweats when Bentley came back out to the living room with them. Bentley glared at him. "Out," he said, pointing toward Chad's room.

"I'm not your fucking dog," Chad grumbled, picking up his Red Bull and heading for his room.

I smiled as he stomped away, leaving an awkward silence. I was perfectly capable of hobbling into the sweats, but Bentley wasn't making any movement to leave. This was not how I'd pictured taking my pants off in front of him. Not that I'd given it a lot of thought. Okay, I'd given it significant thought, but the scenario did not involve dried blood on both knees.

"I can do it," I said as Bentley kneeled on the floor in front of me and placed his hands on the hips of my jeans. I wasn't ready for him to see my leg. I knew if our relationship progressed, he was bound to see the numerous scars that ran from my knee all the way up to my thigh, but I wasn't quite ready for that yet.

He studied me intently, reading my face. "Trust me."

His finger found the snap of my jeans. I gripped his hand, terrified of what he would think when he saw my leg.

"Mac, it's okay. Trust me," he repeated. His words melted something inside me. The air around us felt like it had been sucked from the room like a vacuum. What shouldn't have been hot had suddenly become the most erotic experience of my life.

I sucked in a breath as his fingers grazed my lower stomach just above my panties. He popped my button open and carefully lowered my zipper. Luckily, he kept his head down because if he would have looked up, my eyes would have given away my secret yearning. As it was, my fingers itched to comb through his hair and pull him close to the sensitive skin that his fingers were currently tormenting. I balled my hands into fists, letting my nails dig into my palms. It was slightly embarrassing to be fantasizing about his mouth on my stomach when he was trying to help me. It was another kind of help I was looking for now.

He tugged slowly on my jeans. I was so wound up I wanted to shout at him to hurry. I closed my eyes, lifting my hips as he guided the hem of my jeans down until they rested at my feet. Every nerve in my body was at full charge as goose bumps covered my arms. The backs of his fingers stroked against my legs. I bit off a moan. All of this was so foreign. I felt almost sick from the scattered sensations shooting through me. Was this what arousal felt like?

I opened my eyes, expecting to still see his head down, but he was studying me intently. His eyes were dark as coal. My tongue wet my lips as my body felt ready and aware. My leg was now the farthest thing from my mind.

I watched him slide his hands lightly over my stomach, which tightened in response. The movement didn't go unnoticed as the tips of Bentley's fingers toyed with my panties, letting me know I only had to say the word and they would come off, too. I dragged my lip nervously into my mouth. My eyes flickered to his hands, which had set me on fire. I didn't have to ask what he was thinking. The intensity of his stare made it clear he was as hot as I was.

His lips lowered to my skin, kissing the soft barely visible peach fuzz on my stomach. A sigh that turned into a moan left my lips when his tongue glided down just under the top of my panties. His hands gripped my hips at the sound. My hands moved of their own accord, weaving through his hair and pulling him closer. The ache between my legs I'd been trying to ignore became persistent as I raised my hips off the couch to give him what we both wanted.

"Are you decent yet?" Chad called out. His voice was like a bucket of ice-cold water being dumped over my head. Even though he was still in his room, I tried to jerk my pants up, but Bentley's face prevented my movement. He looked up, smirking at me.

"Not funny," I muttered, blushing for the millionth time of the evening. I wouldn't have admitted it, but I was glad for the interruption. I wasn't sure how things had escalated so rapidly. A few more unsupervised minutes and I wasn't sure how far we would have gone. When Zach and I did the deed, it had been planned for months. There was nothing spur of the moment about it.

"Very true. It's not funny, but at the moment, short of locking Chad in his room, humor is the only thing keeping me sane," he said, sliding my jeans off my feet. I had gotten so worked up in the moment that I forgot I was lying there with my scar out in the open. I could have turned Bentley away, but it somehow felt wrong after the intensity of what had just happened. His eyes lingered, not on my scarred leg, but on the Wonder Woman panties that barely covered me.

"You're trying to kill me," he muttered.

"Why?"

"Seriously? Forget about the fact that we've been interrupted twice now, but Wonder Woman underwear?"

"Panties," I corrected.

"What?"

"They're panties," I teased.

"Whatever, they're still Wonder Woman," he said, helping me into his pair of sweats. His hands gently cupped my bad leg. I shivered as his fingers moved over my scars. Thankfully, he didn't say anything. I might have embarrassed myself by bawling or something. Besides my doctors and my parents, he was the only one who had seen my scars.

"And that's a good thing?" I asked, bringing my thoughts back to his fascination with my panties.

"Wonder Woman is like a top-of-the-list fantasy chick, so you wearing those seriously adds to the whole image." He pulled the sweats over my hips and into place, ending the game.

I had to laugh at his reasoning. They were just panties, but in light of what had almost happened, I guess it made sense. In spite of him seeing my leg, I was still aching for more than I cared to admit.

"I'm coming out," Chad yelled, officially ending the mood.

"He's like a damn toddler. Now I get why my mom always joked that kids would one day ruin my sex life." He rolled up the leg of the sweats so he could look at my knees.

"Wait. Your mom would tell you that?" I thought I'd misheard him.

"What took so long?" Chad grumbled, sitting next to me on the couch. He grimaced when he spotted my knees, which looked as bad as they felt. Thanks to Bentley's momentary distraction, I'd forgotten about the throbbing abrasions.

"Yeah," Bentley said, answering my question. "My mom was pretty forward about that stuff. I think she was trying to scare me into practicing safe sex. This will feel cool," he added, dabbing at my knees with some kind of antibacterial cleaner.

I flinched but remained quiet while he continued to wipe away the dried blood. "You're lucky," I said. "My parents' stance was just don't do it."

"Trust me. I would have preferred that over my mom's openness. She felt it was her job to lecture my friends, too."

"True story," Chad interrupted. "Remember when she found out I was dating Olivia Bakersfield?"

Bentley winked at me, chuckling.

"What did she do?"

"She handed me a box of condoms in front of the guys and made me practice rolling the condom onto a banana."

"No she didn't," I gasped, covering my mouth.

"I shit you not," Chad grumbled.

"You're neglecting to tell her the whole story," Bentley pointed out. "Like, for whatever dumb-ass reason you said you couldn't wait to 'tap that' when you were talking about Olivia?"

"You said that in front of his mom?"

"That's right." Chad chuckled. "I did say that, didn't I? Still, I should have bet money on it because it happened."

"Like anyone would have taken that sucker bet. Who didn't have a shot at Olivia? All you had to do was ask," Bentley joked, bandaging my right knee before turning to the other one.

"Ha, ain't that the truth." Chad agreed as they high-fived, proud of themselves until my disgusted look brought them back to reality.

"So, did you ask?" I asked Bentley, who had suddenly felt the need to concentrate on bandaging my other leg.

"*No comprendo*," he said, not looking up.

"Yeah, right. Maybe I'll be the next person to do the punching."

Both of them burst out laughing.

"What's so funny?" I asked, looking back and forth at them as they roared with laughter.

"You couldn't hurt a fly," Chad said, squeezing my bicep.

"Hey, I'm tougher than I look."

"We know," Bentley said to pacify me. "We both think you *could* hurt a fly."

Chad laughed again.

"You're both assholes," I complained, sinking back against the couch cushions as Bentley pulled the sweats I'd borrowed down over my bandaged knees. The sweats were huge on me, but I liked them.

"Yeah, and you're adorable," Bentley answered, leaning in to give me a kiss on the head.

"Again with the adorable. Keep it up and I'm going to take my adorable cane and shove it somewhere."

"Damn," Chad said, mockingly covering his ass with his hand.

Bentley finished up the first-aid service by taking care of my hands, and we decided to relax and watch TV. After fighting over the remote, he and Chad finally settled on an old science fiction movie about aliens. I didn't know how to break it to them that I didn't like science fiction, but just like *Ferris Bueller*, they claimed it was a classic, so I kept my mouth closed and resigned myself to a two-hour torture fest. If all else failed, I could take a nap or play on my phone.

As it turned out, the movie wasn't all that bad. It was intense and had me gripping Bentley's knee more times than I should have, not to mention making me jump several times.

Chad had a bad habit of talking throughout the movie. Bentley shushed him on more than one occasion, telling him he was ruining the movie for me, but I didn't mind. It was a bittersweet moment. In a way, Chad reminded me of Dan. As he talked, it made me feel at peace. It was nice to be included and not treated like the victim.

By the time the movie ended, I was yawning. It was later than I thought and I was ready to crawl into bed. Bentley offered me the use of his bed, claiming he could take the couch, but I declined the tempting offer. I had an early class and I wasn't ready for Bentley to see what I looked like in the morning.

Saying a sleepy good night to Chad, I burrowed back in Bentley's arms as he carried me from the apartment and down the stairs. He was spoiling me and I should have protested, but his arms felt so good. I almost dozed off by the time we reached the car. I yawned big, apologizing.

"You could have stayed at my apartment," he said, reaching over to grab my hand as we drove.

"Too soon," I answered honestly as he pulled in front of my dorm building.

"I told you I would have slept on the couch."

"I know. It just feels too soon for that. It's really only been a couple weeks that we've known each other. We have to take it slow," I said, flushing when I remembered the scene from his apartment earlier. That definitely hadn't been slow. I wondered if he would call me on it. Call me a tease. It's not like I had any real experience with guys other than Zach, but I knew no one liked to feel like they were being led on.

"I can do slow." He climbed from the car to help me out, but I refused to let him carry me into the building. It was late, but there was no telling who would still be sitting in the common room inside. There was no way I was going to open that can of worms.

Our progress was annoyingly slow. I hadn't noticed in all the time sitting on Bentley's couch, but now that I was walking around, I was pretty sore from my fall earlier. My movements were a mix of stiff hobbling and shuffling.

"I had fun tonight," I said when we finally reached the entrance.

"You sure? You look like you're in pain just walking around."

"Well, I'm not going to lie. I'm a bit sore, but the game was fun and the after was, uh—"

"Better than a party?" he offered, placing his hands on my hips.

"Definitely better." I dragged my bottom lip into my mouth, which had become a nervous habit anytime we were this close.

"You know, when you do that, it makes the whole *going slow* thing tougher." His lips left a hot trail across my cheek. I didn't need to ask what he was talking about. It was pretty clear when his mouth found my bottom lip and dragged it in. He sucked on it for a moment before moving to the rest of my mouth.

I clenched his shirt tightly into my fists, holding on as my head swam. Pressing myself as close to him as our standing positions would allow, I wished with everything inside me that I would have taken him up on his offer to stay over. Even though it was my idea, taking it slow was as hard for me as it was for him.

He pulled his lips from mine and gazed down at me. "Kissing is allowed, though, right?"

I gave a shaky laugh before answering. "Definitely," I said, reaching for the handle of the door behind me. Pulling it open, I stepped backward into the building.

"Can we meet for lunch tomorrow?" he asked before I could disappear into the building.

"I have class until twelve thirty, and my class after that starts at two."

"That's fine. We can meet between your classes," he said, naming a central location for us to meet up.

I agreed before letting the door swing closed behind me. Despite being dead on my feet, and the fact that my knees were currently cussing me out, a goofy smile spread across my face as I shuffled to my room. Tracey would have said I was falling for his "smexy" charms if she was still alive, but she would have liked him. I wish she could have met him. It was at times like this that I missed her the most. My smile slipped for a moment as the familiar sense of loneliness and loss threatened to take hold. Bentley's image came to mind, reminding me I was no longer completely alone.

Reaching my room, my smile returned. Maybe not as wide as before, but it was there. I was no longer alone.

"Where have you been, young lady?" Trina teased as I pushed our dorm room door open. "Oh, Lord. Judging by that sex kitten grin on your face, you were doing something. Do tell." She tossed the book she was reading to the side. "And what, for God's sake, are you wearing?"

My smile widened even farther as I sat down on my bed. I was not alone at all. I hugged my pillow to my chest as I filled Trina in on my evening. It had been so long since I had talked boys with anyone. It was well after two in the morning by the time I finished filling her in.

. . .

The next few weeks passed in a happy blur as my new friends showed me what I had been missing keeping myself closed off for the last year and a half. Bentley and I spent every day together that he wasn't working or we weren't in classes. We ate together, studied together, and spent a lot of time perfecting our kissing skills. Taking it slow had become an exercise of pure endurance for both of us. His roommates were our only saving grace. Michael had broken up with his girlfriend, so he was at the apartment as much as Chad. My feelings for Bentley had exceeded what I'd never thought was possible. Thoughts of him consumed me whenever we were apart.

Trina told me it was normal to feel like that. She claimed that's what love did to a person. I halfheartedly argued that I wasn't in love. She razzed me about it, but didn't press me. That was one of the things I liked the most about her. I discovered she was a great friend to have. She still hung out with her old friends and went to parties, but we had made it past our rocky beginning.

I packed my bags into my small VW Bug, preparing to head home for Thanksgiving break. It had been more than a month since I'd seen Mom and Dad, and I missed them. I was excited to finally have something to talk about other than my classes or the case. Bentley planned on driving over on Thanksgiving to meet them and to have dessert. Mom had mentioned on the phone that we would be celebrating Thanksgiving by ourselves this year without anyone else over. We used to spend Thanksgiving with Tracey's family until her dad died years ago. After the accident, Patricia and the boys spent Thanksgiving last year by themselves. I would be lying if I said I wasn't relieved when Mom told me Patricia had decided to take the twins to see their grandparents in Ohio this year. Things would be more bearable.

I pulled into our driveway less than an hour later. Sitting behind the wheel, I studied my childhood home, which was filled with so many memories. The front yard was shaded by the big oak tree that Jessica had fallen from when she and Dan had decided to see who could get to the highest branches first. Jessica broke her arm in two places, but afterward wore her cast like a badge of honor, claiming she had made it to the top first.

Pulling my duffel bag from the backseat, I headed toward the front door, vowing not to let sad memories bog me down this time. I breathed in deeply when I opened the door, inhaling the intoxicating smell of Thanksgiving. It was a mixture of pumpkin, spices, cookies, and Dad's famous Chex Mix, which he had been making for as long as I could remember. This was the essence of the holiday season for me.

"I'm home," I called out, dropping my bag on the white bench by the front door.

"Hey, sweetie." Dad greeted me, coming around the long counter that separated the kitchen from the large great room, which was the "heart of the house," as he liked to put it. He wiped his hands on his apron, which read: *The only thing better than a bottle of wine in the kitchen is a bottle of wine in the hand.*

"Hey, Daddy," I said, giving him a big hug.

He returned the hug and then placed his hands on my shoulders, holding me at arm's length. "Something's different about you," he observed.

"What?" I asked, ducking my head. Could he see the difference that I had begun to see in myself over the last couple weeks? When I looked in the mirror, I didn't cringe at my reflection anymore. The severe straight line that my lips normally wore was gone, along with the somber look that never seemed to leave my eyes.

He tilted my chin as he took the time to study my face. "You look happy," he said, sounding hopeful. "Are you happy, sweet pea?"

"I am, Daddy."

"Well, I'll be damned. I guess talking us into letting you live on campus was a good thing, after all. I'm not going to lie, sweet pea. Your mother and I have been worried about you. It seemed like you were struggling to find your footing at first."

"It was tougher than I thought it was going to be at first," I admitted, sitting on the leather couch. "But I'm making it now."

"Finding your groove," Dad said, sitting on the couch next to me and patting my knee.

"Groove? Dad, no one says that. You're showing your age."

"What are you talking about? *Groove* is classic. Come help your old man in the kitchen," he said, standing up. "I have another batch of Chex Mix in the oven."

seventeen

Bentley

"Bentley, your mom tells me you met a girl," Aunt Judy greeted me loudly. I had just stepped into the foyer of her Victorian house, juggling the turkey Dad had deep-fried that morning. Everyone standing within earshot turned to look at me.

"You did, huh, Mom?" I called over my shoulder. I knew I should have waited until after Thanksgiving to tell her about Mac. I had just told her that morning. Knowing my mom, I wouldn't have been surprised if she'd texted it to Aunt Judy during the drive over. No doubt by now the entire family knew.

"What? You didn't say it was a secret," she reasoned, scooting past me with her arms full of her legendary sweet potato casserole.

"I assumed you wouldn't feel the need to blab it everywhere."

"You know what they say when you assume," Dad chimed in, clapping me on the back as we entered the dining room together.

"No, dear. What do they say?" Gran asked, poking her head out of the kitchen.

"Um, that it's wrong," Dad answered lamely.

"That's what I thought," Gran said, winking at me.

I grinned back. Dad may be in his fifties, but Gran could revert him back to being a kid with a look. She appeared frail, but Gran was all steel beneath her papery skin.

"So, tell us about your girl," Gran said, placing a bowl of corn on the large dining room table. Mom and Aunt Judy chuckled at her question. They were relentless.

"Pass. I see you found your spot, Allie," I said to my sister, who as usual, sat in the corner messing with her phone and choosing not to participate in any sort of conversation. Not that she was shy or anything. Allie was a bit of an emo chick that spent her time maintaining her fifteen-year-old social status. The only time she would say anything was to tell us how clueless we were. Like she and her friends were the only enlightened people in existence. In all likelihood she was currently posting how lame Thanksgiving was.

"Why fight it, man? You know with this family it's inevitable that all the details come out. I was convinced they bugged my car when I was dating Devyn," my cousin Grant added, smiling at his bride of five months.

"That's nothing. I swear Mom followed Chris and me to the movies a couple times," Hannah, my other cousin, chimed in.

"I did not," Aunt Judy denied adamantly. Her denial lost some of its effect when she shot Mom a guilty look. "Let's say hypothetically I did. It's not like it scared Chris off," she said, smiling at Hannah's fiancé across the table.

"Maybe I want my love life to be private," I protested, claiming my seat as Gran and Mom carried the last serving dishes to the overflowing table.

"Better start looking for a new family," Gran said, sitting across from me.

"Gran, I'm hurt. You'd throw your favorite grandchild out of the family just because he wants to keep a few things private?" I asked, clutching my heart dramatically.

"Psh," Allie snorted without looking up from her phone.

"Something to add, Allie?" I asked to mess with her.

"Fine, favorite grandson." Allie chose not to respond further.

"You wish," Grant said. "I'm her favorite, hands down. Especially once she hears our news." He reached over to pat Devyn's flat stomach with a wide grin on his face.

The table silenced at his words. The spoon of green bean casserole Aunt Judy had been about to dump on her plate fell to the tablecloth as she gaped at Grant. My uncle Bob was the first to recover as he scooted his chair backward and pulled a beaming Devyn to her feet. Though the dining room table dominated the room, he still managed to swing her around without knocking anything over.

"A baby?" Aunt Judy whispered, covering her mouth as tears filled her eyes. She rose to her feet and gave Grant, who had also stood, a bone-crushing hug.

"You owe me," Grant mouthed over Aunt Judy's shoulder.

Dinner was momentarily forgotten as everyone took turns hugging and congratulating the happy couple. The octave level in the room reached an all-time high as everyone chattered excitedly about due dates and baby showers. Baby talk dominated the dinner conversation, saving me from being in the line of fire. Grant was right. I owed him big time. Maybe a case of beer on his doorstep. Hell, I'd even add a pink and blue bow on it.

After dinner, the women in the family were still talking about the baby when I called out my good-byes and scooted toward the front door. Dad gave me a knowing wave and returned his attention to the football game.

Stepping outside, I felt triumphant as I headed toward my car. I had made it out by the skin of my teeth. It wasn't like I didn't want to talk about Mac. Hell, my roommates had gotten their share. So much so that Chad and Michael had written *pussy-whipped* on our bathroom mirror with toothpaste the other day. I'd left it up, too happy to care.

Talking with my family about Mac was a different story. Mom and Aunt Judy had a tendency not to give up until they knew everything. My relationship with Mac was too new to be analyzed with a fine-tooth comb. I didn't want them to point out any possible flaws or make me second-guess anything. Not that they were cruel; they just felt it was their job to approve of who we dated. Even though I was twenty-two years old, they still treated me like I was a pimply-faced teenager on some things.

Backing out of the driveway, I turned on my GPS, which I had already entered Mac's address into. She lived about twenty-six miles away. With traffic relatively light because of the holiday, I made it there in just less than thirty minutes.

I climbed from my car after parking behind Mac's VW Bug. Before even getting my hand raised to knock, the door swung open, revealing a stressed-looking Mac.

"Are you ready for an inquisition?"

I stifled a groan. Obviously I hadn't gotten off scot-free. I smiled reassuringly and reached for her hand as she closed the door behind me. Let the grilling begin.

eighteen

Mac

Inviting Bentley over for dessert had been a mistake. To say Mom and Dad were thrilled that I'd met someone was putting it mildly. After several refused setup attempts over the summer with sons of different coworkers, Mom had given up. I didn't and wouldn't apologize for my attitude. She should have known better than to push me into dating when I wasn't ready.

Guiding Bentley to the family room, I felt bad for the onslaught of questions my mom was sure to lay on him. If I really cared about Bentley, I would have turned him around and urged him to make a run for it. My only hope was that Dad would interject, add a little humor, and change the subject so everyone was more comfortable. That was what he did. He was the calm in the storm.

graduation night 2013

"So, what do you think about joining the adult world?" Kat's dad, Dave, asked as we all sat down at one long table in the restaurant. Jessica stifled a snort. Dave was famous for asking random philosophical questions.

"Daddy, seriously?" Kat said, rolling her eyes. She implored him to stop, looking to her mom for help.

"It's a fair question," her mom said, shrugging her shoulders.

Zach, the diplomat in our group, took a stab at answering. "Well, sir, it feels pretty good."

"In what sense?" Dave asked, cutting a piece of bread from one of the four loaves the waitress had just set down.

Jessica kicked me under the table to get my attention. We exchanged amused looks as Kat groaned. "Shoot me now," she muttered to Dan under her breath.

I disguised my snicker with a cough as my dad patted Dave on the back. "Come on, Dave. Maybe we should give the kids one more night before we officially call them adults. Let's put off the roast for another day," he said in his normal jovial manner.

Dad was always a go-with-the-flow type of guy. "Why worry about today when tomorrow is another day?" was his motto. His easy breezy spirit would have driven many women nuts, but Mom took his attitude in stride. She was the more analytical and practical one in our household. She took charge of the finances, making sure the bills were paid and money for retirement and my education were diligently put aside each *month. Dad often joked that he would have to die first because he would be lost without her around. Dad was the dreamer, and she was the planner. She liked to say he was the yin to her yang.*

I laced my fingers with Bentley's, flashing him a weak smile as I led him to the wolves. Mom was sitting at the bay window that overlooked the backyard. It was my favorite spot in the house, especially in the cooler months when I could open the blinds without being baked by the afternoon sun. Dad sat in his recliner, trying to appear casual. I knew he was full of it because he was reading some magazine, which he never did.

"Mom, Dad, this is my—friend, Bentley," I said hesitantly. My introduction sounded lame, even to me. It was obvious by the way I was clutching Bentley's hand that he was more than just a friend. Bentley looked at me like I'd grown two heads.

Dad stood up to shake his hand. "Bentley, it's good to meet you. Our girl here seems to think quite highly of you."

"Dad?" I warned.

"Mac?" he returned.

Bentley squeezed my hand reassuringly as he turned to my mom, who had also risen. "It's a pleasure to meet you both," he answered, shaking my mom's hand. "I think highly of her, too, so we at least have that in common," he said, winking at me.

"That's good to know," Dad said, returning to his recliner while Mom sat back on the edge of the window seat. Bentley followed me to the couch. I sat nervously on the edge of the cushion, waiting for the grilling to begin. Bentley, on the other hand, seemed completely relaxed as he sat back on the couch with his arm stretched across the top cushion. He tugged on my shoulder until I was tucked into the crook of his arm. I noticed Mom and Dad exchange a look at the gesture.

"So, Bentley, what are your plans for the future?" Dad asked in an uncharacteristically stern voice.

"Dad!" I said, shocked at his directness. Nothing like going for the high-dollar questions first.

"Sweet pea, it's not a difficult question."

"Maybe not to you. What do you want to know next, when the wedding's scheduled?" I would have expected a direct question like that from Mom, but Dad had never been the probing type. He'd always been the one to run interference. I thought he would have been my ally in this situation.

Glancing at Mom, I could see by the look on her face that she had also been taken by surprise. She stood smiling and interrupted Dad by announcing it was time for dessert. "John, why don't you come help me cut the pies?"

Dad looked like he wasn't ready to concede, but Mom gave him no choice, grabbing his hand and dragging him to the kitchen.

"Oh Lord," I muttered, dropping my face into my hands. "I'm so sorry." I peeked at Bentley through my fingers.

"It's fine," he said, rubbing my back. "Your dad is just being a parent. He wants to know that his daughter isn't dating some deadbeat."

I lifted my head. "That is not my father."

"What?"

"I mean, my dad never would have grilled someone like that. It's like one of those aliens from that movie you and Chad made me watch has taken over his body."

"Well, we'll know if he clutches his stomach during dessert. I'll save you if something tries to claw its way out."

"You joke, but the way he acted, I wouldn't be surprised. My dad is normally Mr. Laid-Back." Mom and Dad returned to the living room carrying dessert plates and three different pies Dad had baked earlier in the week.

Bentley patted my knee before accepting the plate Mom handed him. Dad handed one to me without looking in my direction, which made my glare pretty ineffective. I never thought I would have said this, but thankfully, Mom steered the conversation during dessert, asking Bentley about his classes and where he was from. Eventually, Bentley satisfied my dad by mentioning his job as an EMT. Dad and Mom both looked surprised. Dad's demeanor changed for whatever reason after that. He seemed genuinely curious about Bentley's work. I hadn't mentioned anything about his job when I first told my parents about him. I had myself convinced it wasn't important, but deep down it was because I didn't know how to tell them Bentley had been there the night of the accident. I wasn't sure if that would be a big deal.

Since it was something that was sure to come up eventually, I told them the whole story. Actually, it was the first time I had really opened up to them about the accident. Mom's eyes filled with tears, which happened anytime the accident was brought up. Dad's jaw clenched several times as I told them how Bentley had basically seen me through that dark night. I knew I was probably sharing a little too much with them, overwhelming them with the details I'd kept buried all this time. Over the past year and a half, my answers about the accident had been short and concise. Tanya, of course, knew all the sordid details, but since she was my therapist, it was easier to share those feelings with her. She was an unbiased ear.

Surprisingly, I didn't cry as I dumped everything on my shell-shocked parents. Even Bentley was hearing things beyond what he knew from the accident. Tanya would have been proud. Maybe I was getting stronger. A bigger part of me knew it was because of the man sitting next to me.

I felt guilt ramming out the words. I had most likely spoiled the holiday by letting my diarrhea of the mouth take over, but once I started, it was like a flood gate had opened and I couldn't stop. Mom got up when I was done talking to give me a tight hug. Her eyes and nose were red from crying, but she managed to give me a watery smile. She gathered our plates and took them to the kitchen, declining my offer of help. Dad reassured me with a smile of his own, telling me she would be okay in a few minutes.

Dad returned to the person I'd always known him to be, engaging Bentley in sports talk while I took emotional stock of how I felt. I'd pretty much laid my guts out, but I honestly never felt lighter. Bentley was the one I really felt bad for. A simple invitation to dessert to meet the parents had been turned into my version of a *Dr. Phil* special. If hearing anything I had said bothered him, he hadn't given any indication.

After a few minutes, Mom joined us, looking much better. The conversation after that took on a much lighter tone as Dad tried out new jokes on us. Bentley not only laughed, but shared a few funny stories about his childhood. As the evening wore on, I could tell Mom and Dad approved wholeheartedly of Bentley. I shouldn't have been surprised. He was easy to like.

"Thank you for tolerating all that," I told him as I walked him to the door later that evening.

"All what?" he asked, placing his hands on my hips.

"Dessert in the nut house."

"Please. That was nothing. Wait till I take you to meet my family, then we'll see who's nuts. As for the accident stuff, I'm happy you let me listen in. Even seeing it firsthand, there was no way to know how you felt going through that. It killed me to hear it, but it reminded me how strong you are."

I blushed slightly. "I'm not nearly as strong as you think."

"Whatever, you're stronger than Mighty Mouse."

I shrugged. I think he was putting me on a pedestal I didn't deserve. So, I'd made it through the accident. That was luck. Besides, I wasn't the only one, and I'd definitely taken the long way to accepting it.

"What time should I pick you up tomorrow?" he asked, pulling me closer.

"What are we doing?"

"I was thinking we could go see a movie with my family if that's okay? It's a tradition for all of us on Black Friday. While everybody else is trying to kill each other over TVs, we go see a movie."

"You want me to go to the movies with your family?" I squeaked out.

"Yes." His lips dropped softly to mine. It took a little persistence to get me to open my mouth. His kisses had a way of muddling my brain and I was beginning to suspect he knew that. After a moment, I found the willpower to maneuver my hands between us, so I could push him back slightly.

"I'm not sure I'm ready to meet your parents."

"I met yours," he returned, tilting up my chin so he could claim my lips.

I allowed the kiss for a moment before pulling back. "True, but you're normal."

"You're normal, too," he said, holding me by the shoulders.

"Yeah, but normal enough to meet new people?" I hated to sound insecure, but it was hard enough to feel comfortable with him, let alone his entire family.

"Trust me. They're going to love you. How could they not?"

"Oh, I don't know. All my baggage?"

He shook my shoulders lightly. "You have to stop kicking yourself, Mac. How can I make you see what we all see?"

His voice was kind, but the words were filled with steel. "It might take some brain surgery," I said. There was a thin line between knowing you had issues and doing something about them, but from my point of view, that line might as well have been the Grand Canyon.

"Well, I'm an EMT, not a surgeon, but I can get a hammer. How about that?" he joked, pretending to pound my head.

"I might just let you do that," I said, resting my head on his chest. I exhaled deeply as I finally conceded. "Look, I'll try. It's just going to take time for me, okay?"

"Good. I'll pick you up by noon." He kissed me deeply. His tongue claimed mine and I pulled him closer, wanting more. Locked in his embrace, I found it easy to forget about everything other than the two of us together. That was one way to get through meeting his family. We could just make out the entire time.

The next day I was in major freak-out mode. My room looked like a cyclone-induced wasteland with discarded clothes strewn everywhere. My door had a full-length mirror hanging on the back and today it seemed someone had secretly replaced it with a funhouse mirror. Nothing I tried on looked good. This had never been an issue for me before. The frustration of facing yet another thing that terrified me had taken its toll.

Mom opened my door after knocking lightly. She found me sitting on the floor in the middle of a large pile of clothes, looking completely disheveled.

"Mac, honey, is everything okay?" she asked carefully.

"Oh, sure. I'm only supposed to meet my boyfriend's family today. I look totally ready, don't I?" An unexpected lump developed in my throat. I swallowed hard, refusing to cry in front of her.

"Oh, sweetie," she said, stepping through the clothes to join me. She plopped down and pulled me against her, rocking back and forth. "You are a wonderful, beautiful girl. You have to know they will see that."

"So I keep hearing, but what if you and Daddy and even Bentley are wearing blinders? What if his family sees through me and they don't approve? What does that mean for Bentley and me? Mom, I didn't expect it to happen, but I really like him. I don't want to lose him now," I said, pouring out my guts.

She pulled back and lifted my head to look in my eyes to make her point. "Mac, honey, there is nothing to see through. Who you are is what they will see, and that will be perfect because that is what you are," she said, rubbing my shoulders. "As for Bentley, based on what I saw yesterday, that is a well-grounded young man. Your heart drew you to him for a reason, so believe in that."

"When did you start sounding like Dad?" I asked, rubbing my eyes, which had attempted to water up at her words.

She hugged me again. "Yes, well, you can't be married to someone for as long as your father and me and not expect something to rub off. Here, let me help you up and we'll pick out something for you to wear."

We selected a cute pair of jeans and one of my favorite sweaters. It was light pink and softer than a baby's blanket. Appropriate since that's what I'd been acting like. I gave Mom another hug before heading to the bathroom to finish getting ready.

When I returned, I was surprised to find that Mom had cleaned up the mess I left behind. All my clothes were either folded neatly or hanging in my closet. Since the accident, I had taken her for granted so much that I'd forgotten how much she had helped me in my recovery. I had spent so much time resenting her for only doing what she thought was best. Grabbing my purse, I exited my room before I could change my mind again, following the smell of coffee and bacon coming from the kitchen.

Mom was sitting at the counter sipping coffee when I entered the pristine kitchen. My mouth drooped with disappointment. It served me right for waiting until after eleven to join the living. At least there was still coffee in the pot. "Don't you look nice," Mom said, winking at me. "Your breakfast is in the microwave."

"Bless you." I opened the microwave and sniffed appreciatively. I put a small piece of bacon into my mouth before closing the door again to reheat the food. While my breakfast warmed up, I grabbed a mug and filled it with coffee.

"How did you sleep, by the way?" Mom asked as I joined her at the counter a few minutes later with my plate and coffee cup in hand.

"Okay, considering what I have in store today. Regardless, it's nice to sleep on my nice queen bed. My bed in the dorms isn't bad, but it's not a pillow top."

"Yeah, I remember hating my bed when I went to college. I think they make them small on purpose. No reason to encourage extracurricular activities," she said, shooting me a knowing look.

"Subtle, Mom. Just when I thought you were sounding too much like Dad, the old Mom I know and love comes back with a vengeance."

"It didn't escape my notice that you and your young man seemed quite serious last night." She sipped her coffee, looking at me over the top of her mug.

"Me and my young man? How old are you again?" I asked, trying to make a joke of the situation.

Mom didn't smile as I nibbled on my bacon. "I'm just saying I want to make sure you two are being safe."

"And the size of my bed has some bearing on us being safe?"

She sighed. "Are you two having sex?" she blurted out, making me choke on a sip of my coffee. She patted me on the back, trying to help clear my airway.

"Um, that's kind of personal," I answered, shoving more bacon in my mouth.

"Too personal for your mom? You're still my little girl."

"Mom, I'm an adult. I can vote. I could defend our country in the military if I wanted. I'm on the verge of being able to legally drink. If I want to have sex, I can do it without discussing it with my mother."

"Are you being safe? That's all I want to know," she pressed.

Now I remembered why we had butted heads so much in the past. Mom didn't know how to back off until she got what she wanted. I silently collected myself, not wanting to ruin the morning by saying something I would regret later. "If Bentley and I chose to do anything, I would take care of it," I told her flatly.

"So you have protection?"

"Mom. We are done discussing this."

"Honey, you can't blame me for wanting to make sure you're being smart."

"Well, I am, so don't worry about it," I said, ending the conversation. I returned to my breakfast, trying not to let myself get in a bad mood. Today would be stressful enough. "Where's Dad?" I asked, changing the subject.

"He went out to get a few things he saw in one of the ads."

I snorted. "Dad went Black Friday shopping? He hates shopping under normal circumstances." I would have loved to be a fly on the wall, watching my dad navigate his way around stores on the worst nightmare of a shopping day of the year. Dad's favorite saying when it came to shopping was "buzz in and buzz out." I shook my head. By the way my parents had been acting the past couple of days, I was even more convinced they had been brainwashed. It was the only explanation for the strange behavior.

She sighed. "I know, but he got suckered in. I'm expecting an SOS call at any time. What do you and Bentley have planned today?"

"Well, meeting his family, of course. Thrilling," I answered, shaking my head. "I think we're going to a movie. Something like that." I grimaced.

"That sounds nice. Just remember to be yourself. You'll be fine," she mused, rising to rinse her coffee cup.

I shrugged but didn't answer.

"Maybe now that you're getting out more, you can visit *other* people," she added, picking up my empty plate and carrying it to the sink.

I rolled my eyes, surprised it took us this long to get here. Normally she started a conversation by pushing me to visit

Tracey's mom and everyone else I'd been avoiding for a year. "Maybe," I said to pacify her.

"When?"

"Soon. Just not this weekend."

"That's fine. Patricia and the boys are gone this weekend anyway, but she'll be back next weekend."

"Maybe," I answered, rinsing my cup. That was the best I could give her. I felt like I'd come a long way in the past few weeks. That didn't mean I was ready to face the flood of bad memories that would come from seeing Patricia.

"Okay." She gave me hug, letting the subject drop. "When is Bentley picking you up?"

"Soon. He should be here at any time as a matter of fact. Did you need anything?"

"No, it's nothing. I just bought a new puzzle and thought we could do it together. Oh, and this, too," she said, holding up the box set of season one of *Gilmore Girls*.

"Oh my God, I've wanted this forever," I said excitedly, reaching for it. "It's been ages since we've watched this." *Gilmore Girls* used to be our thing. Not just Mom and me, but all the girls in our crew. When I was thirteen, Tracey, Jessica, Kat, and I, along with our moms, had become hooked after Jessica's mom gave her the entire series for a Christmas gift. It became a Friday night ritual to binge on episodes and junk food. We all had our favorite characters, but in the end, everyone agreed we wanted more Luke and Lorelai.

"Is it okay?" she asked, watching my face carefully.

"It's perfect. Can we watch it tomorrow?" I handed it over wistfully.

"Sure, we'll make a day of it. We can veg all day and make your father cook us tasty treats."

"Sounds like a plan," I said as the doorbell chimed. "That's Bentley. Wish me luck," I added, grabbing my cane.

"They're going to love you."

"Right," I muttered skeptically. I swung the door open, revealing a completely delectable Bentley. Thanks to the mild temperatures that had moved in the day before, he was wearing a light sweater that wasn't tight, but still defined his chest and arms, making him appear wider than usual. The black in the sweater made his eyes seem darker and his lips somehow lusher. I thought about how pleasant they had felt hours before. Too bad we had to waste all the delectableness on a group of people I'd never met.

"Don't you look pretty in pink," Bentley said, sliding his arms around me.

"Is that supposed to be a joke?" The smirk on his face made me cynical of his sincerity.

"Sorry. You know what a John Hughes fan I am. I couldn't let that one slide." He laughed. "I'm not taking you to an execution, by the way," he added, taking in my expression.

"I'd prefer that." I called out a good-bye to Mom as I left the house reluctantly.

nineteen

Bentley

Mac looked like she wanted to jump from the moving vehicle as she twisted her hands in her lap. It was a little funny at first, but now I was beginning to feel like a dick for asking her to do something she didn't want to do. After dodging a bullet at dinner the day before, I knew this was the best way to get my family off my back. It was like ripping off a Band-Aid. After meeting Mac, they'd see for themselves that I was crazy about her, and it would save me from having to articulate it.

"You sure you wouldn't rather go to a movie by ourselves?" she offered as we drove.

"I definitely would," I said, smiling at her hopeful look. "Just not today."

Her smile dropped. "Besides, we're meeting them for lunch

first." I patted her knee as we turned into the parking lot of the Italian restaurant.

"Oh, shit," she said like I'd told her we were going to the dentist or something.

"Is that okay?"

"Well, yeah. It's just that I ate breakfast kind of late. I'm going to look like an idiot sitting there while everyone else is eating."

"Babe," I laughed, "it's cool. I won't order anything either. I'll say it was my fault, that we just had Starbucks or whatever."

"I wouldn't want you to do that. I'll order a salad."

"It'll be fine. They're loud but harmless. I'll be right there with you," I said to reassure her.

"Maybe you won't find a parking spot." She looked hopeful as I drove down each row without finding a single space open. Unfortunately, luck wasn't on her side. I spotted an older couple backing out their Towncar.

"Crap," she grumbled, slumping back in her seat.

"Ready?" I laughed, pulling into the space and turning my car off.

"I'm hoping for a quick death," she muttered, opening her door.

We were halfway across the parking lot when I noticed that Mac seemed to be putting a great deal of effort into trying not to limp. She held me tightly with one hand while her other hand gripped her cane tight enough to make the knuckles white.

"What are you doing?" I asked, stopping on the sidewalk to face her.

She looked confused. "What do you mean? We're walking inside."

"Why are you trying so hard to hide your limp?"

"I am not." She tried to deny it, but I pointed to her hands.

"Mac, seriously? Look at your knuckles." In her stubbornness, she refused to look down at the irrefutable evidence.

"Whatever. I was doing it for you. Introducing your girlfriend to your family for the first time is awkward enough without me limping around like Quasimodo."

I sighed at her words. Was it really worth it for me to put her through this much stress? If she wasn't ready to meet my family, I'd only make things worse by forcing her. "Let's go," I said, tugging her back toward the car. I would call Mom later and tell her we got hung up.

"What?"

"Let's go somewhere else. I can get us out of this," I told her, tugging at her again. She wouldn't budge as she dug her feet in.

"No," she said, straightening her spine. "I'm whining, but I can do this," she added, turning back toward the entrance. "I have to do this."

She started walking, still clutching my hand tightly. At least she wasn't trying so hard to hide her limp now. Her nerves were starting to rub off on me, and even I was beginning to worry. I knew my family would love Mac, but I was now afraid of how they would react to her cane. They wouldn't say anything stupid, but I was more afraid of the initial looks. I should have been less of an evasive asshole the day before and explained things when I had the chance. I didn't need them gawking at her.

As we turned the corner toward the main entrance, I spotted my sister, Allie, standing discreetly outside the restaurant smoking a cigarette. She looked surprised when she saw me, trying to put the cigarette into the receptacle by the door. "Allie?" I greeted her as we approached.

"Hey, Bentley," she answered with smoke exiting her mouth.

"Since when do you smoke?"

"Since whenever. Don't worry about it."

"Do Mom and Dad know?" I asked the question, but I already knew the answer.

"Oh, I'm sure they will now, won't they? I mean, you are the Boy Scout," she hissed. "I'm Allie, by the way," she said to Mac with her fake smile painted on her face. "The bad child."

"It's nice to meet you," Mac answered. The tension between Allie and me didn't make the introduction any easier.

After Allie started middle school, our relationship as brother and sister became dicey at best. We didn't seem to understand each other anymore after that. It didn't help that Mom and Dad were always on her case and expected me to be an example for her.

We followed Allie inside, where everyone was seated at a long table in the far corner of the restaurant. I could tell right away the size of our group overwhelmed Mac. Yet another thing I should have mentioned. I was obviously trying for asshole of the year.

Mom stepped in, automatically sensing Mac's discomfort. I guess you'd call that motherly instincts maybe? Her eyes never once moved to Mac's cane. I should have known. Taking Mac under her wing, Mom took charge of introducing her to the family like they were old friends. Watching the scene from Mac's perspective, I could see how our loud and boisterous behavior could be intimidating. Growing up with it had obviously made me immune.

Mac and I sat next to each other through the meal. No one noticed that she barely ate her salad, or at least if they did, no one commented. After a while, she began to feel more comfortable and was able to answer the many questions being fired at her. I intervened anytime they got too personal.

"So, what's with the cane?" Allie blurted out, silencing everyone at the table. I couldn't believe she had gone there. Mac looked to the floor, completely unprepared for the ambush.

"Allie James, that is personal and none of your concern," Mom scolded her. Allie remained unfazed as she looked at me ominously before turning back to Mac.

"I mean, if it's a trendy thing you're going for, it works. Especially with the limp. Do you spend a lot of time practicing that?"

I jumped from my chair, ready to wring her neck. Dad grabbed my arm to stop me. "Allie, you can wait in the car," he said, pointing toward the door.

"Of course!" she snapped. "Because Bentley is perfect, right? He brings his crippled girlfriend to lunch and we're all supposed to fall all over her and feel sorry for her."

"Allie, get the fuck out!" I yelled, attracting the attention of the rest of the restaurant, including the manager, who came over. I couldn't help myself. Allie had pushed me over the edge. She left the table with her phone at her ear, having accomplished what she wanted. Mac, who looked like she had been dropped in a tank of ice-cold water, stood up and left as quickly as her limp would allow. My mom tried to call after her, but it was too late.

I went after her, not even sure what I would say. This was my fault for dragging Mac here. I should have listened in the first place instead of thinking I knew what was best for her.

I stepped outside to see Mac's retreating backside making a beeline for the car. Allie was standing next to a bench on the sidewalk, talking on her phone and smiling with satisfaction as she watched Mac walk away. Still pissed, I snatched the phone from her hand and smashed it against the asphalt, scaring the shit out of some poor old couple approaching the door.

"You asshole!" Allie yelled, seeing her phone in pieces on the ground. She stormed back into the restaurant while I raced after Mac.

"Mac, I don't even know what to say," I said, rushing to her side. I couldn't get a read on her expression. She didn't look mad or happy or anything in between. Her face was blank.

"Can you just get me out of here, please?" She backed away from the car so I could open the door for her. She lowered herself quickly into the seat and closed the door, not even caring that I was still in the way.

I climbed into the driver's seat and started the car, but hesitated before backing out. "Mac, I—"

"Bentley, just drive," she interrupted.

"Sure," I answered, gripping the steering wheel tightly. I drove toward her house wondering if this would be it for us. I wanted to make a case for myself, but at the moment it seemed pointless. Mac stared directly ahead with her arms crossed across her chest.

"So, your family was nice," she said, breaking the silence. She caught me off guard and I wasn't sure I had heard her correctly. "Well, except your sister. Don't take this the wrong way, but fuck her."

I wanted to laugh, but I couldn't tell if she was being facetious or if she was serious. "Hey, no offense taken. That was pretty much my sentiment, too. So, are you okay, or do you, you know, want to talk about it?"

"To tell you the truth, I'm not mad like I thought I would be. I think getting the hell out of the restaurant was more of a reflex action, but after thinking about it for a few minutes, I kind of realized that this is my life."

"I'm not sure I understand," I said.

"People are always going to stare and look at me differently. There's nothing I can do about it. For the rest of my life, I'll just have to put up with it."

"Mac. There's no way I'd ever tell you how to feel, but no one in there was looking at you differently. As for my idiot sister, that was more an attack on me than you. Trust me. My parents will make her pay. Even more than I did."

"What do you mean, more than you did?"

"Let's put it this way, my dad's still probably helping her find the broken pieces of her phone."

"You didn't," she said, shaking her head. "Bentley, you shouldn't have done that."

"What?" I asked incredulously. "I did it for you, to defend your honor or whatever."

"I didn't ask you to smash your sister's phone. Believe me, if I can't handle an insult from a bratty teenager, what hope do I have?"

"Well, shit. I don't even know what to say. I mean, you sound okay, I guess?"

"Whether I am or not, it's not your job to come to my rescue every time you think I need saving, or fix me if you think I'm broken."

"It's in my nature. Hell, it's what I do for a living. I have to help," I said, trying to justify my actions.

"Well, if we are going to be together, then you'll have to get over it. Just be there. That's it."

"So, we're good then?" I asked. I was at least happy to hear her describe us as "together" still.

"Sure. I've gotten used to being carried around, so you're stuck now."

"What about all that talk about not saving you or fixing you? Now you still expect me to carry you?" I teased.

"Why do you think I said 'just be there'? I need your muscle." She smiled.

"Well, it's nice to be needed in some way, I guess."

"I did like your mom and your cousin. What was his name again?"

"Grant. Yeah, he's cool. We were thick growing up even though he's a couple years older than me. I do remember being jealous, though, because he got to do all the cool stuff before me. Eventually I realized the benefits of having an older cousin," I said, flashing a wicked grin.

"Meaning?"

"Older chicks and scoring booze before I was old enough. Well, before he was old enough, too, but he had older friends, so it all rolled our way. We got caught so many times that Grant was on my mom's shit list for a long time. Now it's funny to see her singing a different tune since Grant will be popping out a baby."

"Really? I didn't realize your cousin had the equipment to 'pop out' a baby."

"Sorry. I meant his wife, Devyn, will be popping out a baby."

"Word to the wise: I'd refrain from referring to it as 'popping out' when she's around. I'm not sure pregnant women like that phrase. It's kind of gross."

"Good point. In my experience women get a little testy about that kind of stuff when they're about to have a baby."

"Have you had a lot of experience with women in labor?" she asked as I steered the car toward our next destination.

"I've seen a few babies born out on calls, but I haven't actually delivered one myself. It's definitely a life-changing moment."

"That's pretty awesome. I guess I assumed you only handled bad calls."

"Actually, most of them aren't life-or-death situations. For the most part, people just need our assistance, like a grandma who fell and broke a hip, or a kid who tried to fly out of a tree and broke his leg. One time we had a little girl who had an asthma attack and her mom didn't have an inhaler."

"So you really are like a hero," she joked.

"Hell yeah. You're looking at Batman right here," I said, flexing a muscle.

"And so modest. Where are we going, by the way?" She looked out her window, taking in the surroundings as we passed.

"Well, I figured the movie was out. To tell you the truth, for a while I was just driving around without taking you home, hoping I could get you to talk to me. I thought now we could walk on the beach a little. It's such a nice day. It should be pretty pleasant," I said, heading toward my favorite beach spot. It was more of a private beach access, farther down the coastline from the large hotels, so it was hardly ever crowded. "Is that cool?" We approached a secluded parking lot that not many people knew about. I found out about it from a friend who works beach patrol.

"Yeah, it's just been a while since I've been to the beach." She climbed tentatively from the car after I parked. The breeze off the ocean whipped her hair around her face until she gathered it in her hand behind her head. She studied the long expansion of sand that led to the water.

"Are you okay? We can go somewhere else. I figured after everything that happened today, you could use a little space."

"No, this is okay," she said, removing her shoes before stepping onto the sand. Her cane sank slightly as she probed for harder ground. That was why she'd been hesitant about the beach. She didn't know how to tell me I was a dumb-ass. I moved to her side with the intention of scooping her into my arms when she held up a hand to stop me.

"I just need to get to the hard-packed sand. Can you help me get there?" she asked, holding out her free hand.

She stumbled slightly a time or two, but with my firm grip on her hand, we made it out of the soft sand without falling. I expected the proud look she had on her face when she had navigated the stairs at the arena, but instead, she looked troubled and wasn't saying much.

I was dying to know what she was thinking, but Mac was like listening to a foreign language without a translator. I was clueless.

"Did you know we came to the beach graduation night?" she asked, breaking the silence.

I shook my head. Now I understood.

She moved to a dry spot in the sand and I helped her lower herself down so she could watch the waves roll in. I joined her, draping my hoodie over her shoulders when I noticed her shivering slightly in the breeze. She reached down for a handful of sand, letting it drift away in the wind.

"You know what sucks the most? It's going to sound completely selfish and totally bitchy . . ." She paused, grabbing another handful of sand. I waited patiently for her to continue. Despite myself, I was curious about her life before the accident.

"The part that sucks the most is I'm tired of being sad. I'm also fucking sick of all the *firsts*. We used to come to the beach all the time. Especially after Zach got his license. Almost every Saturday or Sunday, we'd load up in that Suburban and stay there all day. It was where we could let loose, you know?" She paused to toss a seashell into the waves that rolled in and out with the tide. "Graduation night we went to the beach to celebrate. It was part of an agenda we'd made months before. Graduation night was supposed to be perfect."

I continued to listen without commenting, placing an arm around her shoulders.

"I'm so damn sick of being sad," she repeated, nestling close to me.

"I know." There were no words that would take away what she was feeling. Grief was a greedy bastard. I felt hopeless listening to her talk. In spite of what she had said in the car earlier, I wanted to protect her from harm, but she was facing a monster I couldn't save her from. Instead, I was forced to sit at her side while it ripped out my guts.

"I'm sorry I brought you here. I didn't mean to bring up painful memories," I whispered after she fell silent.

"I'm not. I've wanted to come for a while. I can't believe it's been over a year. A year of missing the sound of the hard rolling waves during high tide, a year of missing the scent of the briny sea air, the way the cool sand feels after the sun goes down," she said, digging her toes in the sand. "I can't believe it's been over a year," she repeated.

twenty

Mac

had really been caught off guard today. Not only by Allie during lunch, but coming here to the beach also. The reason I'd made such an effort over the past year and a half to keep myself away was to avoid these moments. My fear now, having Bentley in my life, was that it seemed he was always seeing me at my worst. I couldn't help wondering if he felt like he was my rebound relationship—the one that put in all the work picking up the pieces, being the shoulder to cry on, listening through every bad memory, only to lose out when the next great guy swooped in and collected the reward.

Of course, I wasn't damaged from a normal breakup. Bentley was seeing the fallout from five lost relationships. My friends and I had been the type of close-knit group that was supposed to endure forever. If Bentley was smart, he'd flee while he could, or at least call the professionals for a straitjacket. Fortunately for me, Bentley was one of the good guys. If he wanted to run, he would have done it already.

We sat side by side with our eyes closed, listening to the incoming waves. My sadness was replaced with contentment. That was what being in Bentley's arms provided. Taking the opportunity to finally look at our surroundings, I noticed that we were the only people around. The spot where we sat was hidden out of sight from the few scattered houses that lined the beach. It was like our own small secluded island.

"Are you warm enough?" he asked when I shifted closer to him.

"Yes. The sun feels good with the breeze," I answered, tilting my face to his. The bright sun shined in my eyes just enough so that it was difficult to make out his features. His hard jawline cast a small shadow on his shoulder. Just beyond that were the dimples that drew me to his face from the instant I first laid eyes on them. He shifted his head to shield my straining eyes from the sun. Using my jeans to brush the sand from my hand, I reached up and ran my fingers through his hair, pulling him closer. He accepted the invitation, pressing his lips softly to mine. The tenderness threatened to turn me to mush, but right now I didn't want softness. I wanted hard and rough. I wanted it to be real, to erase the demons from earlier.

Gripping his hair tightly, I became the aggressor, crushing my lips against his. All I knew was that I wanted so much more. Bentley lowered us down to the sand, our lips never coming apart. I allowed my hands to explore his body, feeling the evidence of his desire that clearly matched my own. The ache between my legs became more insistent with demands I had never experienced before. Zach and I had never reached this level of intensity when we'd gone all the way. It had been painful from the start, and was over with almost as quickly.

Bentley groaned as I shifted against him, trying to get closer. His hands left my face, moving to the curves of my body, which were begging for his attention. He continued to toy with my tongue, caressing it with his mouth. The friction from my jeans rubbing against the dampness in my panties only added to the intense heat. I wanted more, feeling him pressed hard between my legs.

My hips began to move against him, taking over to satisfy the hunger of need. He didn't seem to mind the movement, even as I pulled him tightly against me, practically anchoring him in place. He gripped my hips roughly, accepting my passion.

Needing no further encouragement, my hips continued to surge against him. My mind was filled with a mass of confusion from the feverish hormones running rampant through me. My body knew what it was seeking, taking full control. "Bentley," I exhaled, breathing like I'd run a marathon.

"It's okay, baby." His warm breath moaned against my neck. He kept one hand on my hip, guiding my rhythmic movements while his other hand slid under my sweater. A whimper left my lips as he moved across my bare stomach, along my rib cage. I waited with bated breath, knowing where his exploring hand was headed. The moment his fingers found my hard nipple through my lace bra, my body exploded with a sensation like broken glass shattering into a million delicious pieces. I shuddered against his mouth, which had turned to a knowing smile as I came apart in his arms.

Breaking the kiss, I buried my head in his neck, completely overwhelmed. I'd been on a cloud and had now come back to earth as my breathing returned to normal. I wasn't exactly sure what had just happened, but I felt too mortified to look at him.

"Mac," Bentley said, breaking through my inner turmoil. He stroked my back for a second before tilting my face up so he could look at me. "There's nothing to be embarrassed about."

I didn't comment, but I'm sure my flushed cheeks said everything for me. He was a fine one to talk. He wasn't the one who'd just had his first orgasm. The worst part was I could still feel the evidence that he hadn't finished pressed against me. I'd selfishly made sure my own needs were satisfied without giving his a second thought in the process. Maybe I was damned to be an eternal tease.

"What are you thinking?" he asked, stroking a thumb across my bottom lip.

I shook my head, not even sure how to articulate the mixed emotions currently treating my body like a pinball machine.

"Mac?"

I shrugged, trying to move off him, but he anchored me into place.

"Come on. Let me in," he urged me.

I wanted to keep my mouth shut, but knew I wouldn't be able to deter him. "I'm thinking I'm a selfish person," I admitted.

"What the hell are you talking about?" His dark eyes bore into mine.

Exasperated, I finally answered, figuring he'd let me up once I connected the dots for him. "It's embarrassing. That was the first time, I'd—you know, and it wasn't even from actually doing anything. On top of that, I leave you with this." I pointed to the still apparent bulge in his pants. "You should be running right now, Bentley. I already drove another guy away in the past. With everything you've seen lately, how could you possibly still want anything to do with me?" I said in a huff that turned to aggravation when he started laughing. "What's so funny?" I demanded.

"You. You're so ador—" I slapped my hand over his mouth to halt his words.

"If you say *adorable*, I swear I'll punch you in the balls."

He mumbled against my hand. I lifted my fingers so he could speak. "Why fight it, babe? I can't help how I feel, no matter how much you try to convince me otherwise. Besides, you think I'm any better than you? I pushed you to meet my family when you weren't ready. I brought you here without asking. What about the basketball game? Shit, I bet I can make a longer list on why you should be dumping me," he said, looking directly at me. "But you know what? Neither of us is going anywhere. You know why?"

I shook my head.

"Because we obviously like each other, Mac. So what if we're hitting some bumps at first? We're just smoothing the path, right? As for using me for my body, if you want to lie back down and give me a few minutes, I'm all in, if you know what I mean," he said, reaching for the button on my jeans.

"I bet you would be." I reached for his hand although part of me wanted to let him continue.

"Kidding. Another time and another place." He dropped another kiss on my neck. Another time was right. The way he was sucking on my neck, I was on the verge of tearing his clothes off, wishing we were back at his apartment.

He jumped to his feet and helped me up, waiting for me to get my balance before he let go of my hand. I brushed the loose sand from my butt. Before I could turn and navigate the soft sand back to the car, he swept me up in his arms, easily trudging forward before I could put up a fight.

"You know I can walk, right?" There wasn't much conviction in my voice since I actually loved it when he carried me. I'm sure my physical therapist would scold me, but what he didn't know wouldn't hurt him.

"You can add this to my list, too, babe. I can't help wanting to carry you."

"Then you have to add it to mine also because I like it," I admitted.

"See, it's a win-win," he said, smiling.

"I guess we do selfish well," I agreed as he set me back on my feet when we reached the sidewalk. "Thanks for bringing me here." I glanced back at the ocean one last time.

"Are you just saying that to make me feel better?" Sliding his arms around my waist from behind, he rested his chin on my shoulder as we watched the waves. The beach would always hold the special memories of my old life, but with Bentley, I was ready to start fresh. I had to admit it was a tad bit embarrassing to think about how he and I had commemorated our first trip to the beach, but it would be a secret we would always have to share. My heart swelled with contentment. Turning in Bentley's arms, I gave him a gentle kiss on the lips I loved so much. "Thank you," I said sincerely.

He didn't ask what I was thanking him for. He knew.

We arrived back at my house sooner than I would have liked. Bentley helped me out of the car, and I was sad our day had to be over because he now had to work the rest of the weekend. Monday seemed far off. I was getting spoiled seeing him every day.

twenty-one

Mac

As promised on Saturday, I spent the day with Mom, watching *Gilmore Girls*. Dad, who wanted no part of what he called our "perfect dystopian show," spent the day hanging Christmas lights on the house and setting up the yard full of blow-up decorations and light-up reindeer. Dad loved Christmas, making our house look like it belonged at the North Pole with Santa. Every year he added something new to his masterpiece. If it were up to him, he'd decorate even sooner, but Mom always insisted he wait until after Thanksgiving.

He'd managed to find some awful-looking decorations over the years. Like the blow-up snow globe that blew fake snow on a snowman that for some reason had a sadistic-looking pair of eyes. He looked like a possessed Frosty. After several years in the Florida humidity, half the Styrofoam pieces stuck to the inside of the globe, partially obstructing the evil-looking snow-man inside. The next year, Dad brought home another god-awful blow-up decoration of a big fat Santa driving a sleigh. The problem was the last reindeer was too close to Santa, so it looked like maybe Santa was doing something inappropriate to the poor reindeer. When Mom pointed it out, Dad acted offended, saying she should get her mind out of the gutter. They both tried to drag me into that debate, but I refused to get involved. Somehow, Dad won and the perverted-looking decoration remained. We'd yet to see what the new addition would be this year, but I suspected our TV-watching marathon was Mom's way of avoiding what was going on outside.

Watching the familiar show with her, I was engulfed in a flood of memories from the previous times we'd watched the show together. It was good to have Mom next to me now as I reminded her of the disastrous time we decided to give each other facials while watching the show. Somehow we goofed it. The green goop on our faces hardened too quickly and had become a mess when we tried to remove it.

Throughout the day we gorged on Thanksgiving leftovers, likening ourselves to the characters on the show, who always seemed to be eating. Halfway into disk number four, Mom, who had been fighting sleepiness since the end of disk three, lost the battle and was snoring quietly on the couch beside me. Covering her with the afghan Nana had crocheted before she passed away, I lowered the volume on the TV and headed for my room.

I lay down on my bed, glancing around my room and taking note of how different it looked versus how it once had. At one time, my room had been cluttered with years' worth of books, pictures, posters, movie ticket stubs, and other knickknacks that defined my time growing up with my friends. After the accident, I couldn't handle the reminders. I purged everything until only my furniture, television, and bed remained. My room now was about as personal as a hotel room, minus some crappy-looking painting hanging on the wall. The more I looked around, the more I suddenly missed my old stuff, so I got up and headed to the garage to see what I could find.

"What's up, buttercup?" Dad greeted me as I entered the kitchen on my way to the garage. He was sitting at the counter eating a turkey sandwich while he watched a movie on his iPad.

"Is that *Christmas Vacation*?" I already knew before I asked, recognizing the music.

"Yep, I felt it was fitting since I finished decorating. Did you see the yard?"

"Uh, not yet," I answered, edging toward the garage door. "I wanted to wait for Mom." It wasn't exactly a lie. I just had something else I wanted to do at the moment.

He smiled, buying my line of bull. I would have to corner Mom so she could fake the same level of enthusiasm. "What's up then?" he asked as I opened the door leading to the garage.

"I just need a few things from the garage."

"Do you need some help?"

I weighed his words for a moment before answering. I'd

planned to go through the boxes in the garage, grabbing what I wanted, but it would be easier if the boxes were in my room. "Would you mind carrying a few boxes to my room?"

He shut off his iPad. "Do you want all of them?" He didn't need to ask what boxes I was hunting for. He was the one who had stored them away after I'd melted down last year. At the time, I'd told him I wanted them thrown out for good, but Mom intervened, telling me not to make any hasty decisions that I would regret. Even though I had disagreed with her then, I was now glad she and Dad had taken matters into their own hands and saved them.

I nodded. "But finish your sandwich first," I said, feeling bad for interrupting his snack.

"Not a problem." He headed for the garage with the rest of his sandwich in hand.

I went back to my room and had just settled myself on the floor when he arrived with the first box. Pulling the flaps open, a small gasp left my lips when I saw my prom dress folded on top. Pulling it out, I smoothed my hand over the wrinkles on the light pink material, recalling all the planning and searching that had gone into finding the perfect dress for senior prom. Knowing that pink was the most flattering color for my complexion, I had searched long and hard until I came up with one that perfectly matched the mental picture in my head. Seeing it now, I realized how silly I had been during that time. Prom had nothing to do with dresses or shoes but everything to do with friends.

Setting the dress to the side, I looked back inside the box, discovering all the stuffed animals that had once graced my bed. I pulled out the bear that Tracey gave me when I had my tonsils out. It was dressed in light green scrubs. She'd bought it for me after I told her how cute the anesthesiologist had been. I hugged the bear tightly, remembering Tracey's mischievous smile when she handed him over. It was the perfect gift. I placed the bear on the foot of my bed for safekeeping as Dad came in with another box.

In the end, he carried five large boxes to my room. I stayed up half the night going through all my stuff. Each of the boxes provided a roller coaster of emotions—from crying to memories of laughter. My entire old life was in those five boxes. As I unpacked them, I felt like I was finally finding the old me I had also packed away.

The pictures were more difficult to deal with. Most of them were of my friends and me back in elementary school since no one had smart phones at that time. Anything more recent would be on my computer hidden away in folders I never clicked open. Sadly, over the last year or so, their images had begun to fade from my mind. Everything, that is, except the night of the accident. Those memories still haunted me. I hated that my mind had decided to betray me that way. I say *betray me* because it wasn't like I had a choice. My mind was my own, and yet, I couldn't force it to remember certain images of my friends and ignore others. Thumbing through the pictures in my hands caused tears to fall hot and fast from my eyes. Each one felt like I was somehow cleansing my soul. We were rarely serious, which meant half the pictures were of us doing something goofy.

Hugging the stack to my chest much like I had the bear, I was thankful Mom had insisted I keep them. I placed them all in a plastic box with great care so they wouldn't get ruined.

I couldn't believe all the movie theater stubs I found. I didn't remember having so many. Those along with any other paper memorabilia were also treated with the appropriate amount of reverence and placed in the keepsake box Zach had given me for Valentine's Day senior year. It was in the shape of a book with the cover of *Ethan Frome*, which we were all forced to read in English class sophomore year. All my friends hated the book except for me. It was the most thoughtful gift I'd been given, and I kissed Zach enthusiastically for it. I remember he had tried to coax more out of me than the kiss, but I had pulled away. I was so naïve then. Zach had always wanted more out of our relationship than I was willing to give. I just refused to face it. I regretted each of those types of moments now.

Most of the stuff I placed back in the boxes for Dad to store in the garage again. I kept out a few of my favorite things—the *Beauty and the Beast* snow globe Tracey had given me the year we saw the Broadway play together and my Harry Potter special edition set of books that all of my friends had pitched in to get me when my English essay was picked to be published in a local magazine. I arranged everything on the shelves of my bookcase.

Three of the five boxes were now empty. I broke them down flat and placed them in the garbage boxes to be taken out in the morning. I was exhausted, but definitely more satisfied than I could remember being in a long time as I climbed into my bed with the stack of yearbooks I had also kept out. I had one from each year of school, including kindergarten. That was also because of Mom, along with making sure they never became damaged over the years.

All of the elementary school books were basically the same except that with each passing year you could see the signatures got slightly better. By middle school everyone began writing silly anecdotes and jokes to each other. In high school the messages became more and more sentimental the closer we got to senior year. That was the book I lingered through the longest, reading each and every message from my Brat Pack more than once. We all knew we were heading in different directions and our time as a group was coming to an end. Reading each passage now, I felt like I was reading their final good-byes. I set the stack of yearbooks on my nightstand table, except for the one from senior year, which stayed in my hands as I closed my eyes. I fell asleep knowing that in the morning I would be facing another challenge.

twenty-two

Mac

I hadn't slept as well as I hoped to, but I still woke Sunday morning feeling charged. I got ready to go with a purpose. I was finally ready to tackle something I had been putting off for too long. Grabbing a small box I had carefully packed with stuff that I felt no longer belonged to me, I headed out of the house.

It took less than five minutes to get to my destination. My heart clenched as I pulled in front of the familiar house. Taking a deep breath, I grabbed my cane, along with the small box, and made my way up the slightly sloped driveway.

Wiping my sweaty palm on my jeans, I knocked, but was unprepared when the door opened so quickly. I nearly choked on my own breath as I stood face to face with Zach's mom, Janet.

"Mackenzie," Janet gasped, dragging me into her arms for a tight hug. "I'm so glad you're here," she whispered in my ear, hugging me tighter. The plastic box in my arms dug into my side, but I paid no attention as I returned her hug.

"Come in." She stepped back, holding the door open. I entered the house, immediately noticing the changes. The interior looked completely different from the remodeling. The thick carpet had been pulled up and replaced with smooth hardwood floors for easy maneuvering. Walls had been knocked down, opening up the house into one large open space where everything was easily accessible. Stepping farther into the room, I noticed that the family room now flowed into the kitchen and dining room. It felt larger and more spacious. I would have expressed my approval over the changes if not for the circumstances surrounding them.

Janet led me into the family room, where the other occupant I had expected to see was sitting. My heart dropped to my knees. He looked exactly the same with the exception of the wheelchair. "Zach, look who came to see you," Janet chirped as Zach turned to stare at me with the same animosity that had been there a year and a half ago.

june 2013

I'm not sure what I had been expecting when I went to Zach's room. I knew he'd been broken up from the accident like me, and yet, I'd still expected him to look the same. Maybe that

223

was some kind of coping mechanism in my head. Nothing about the person propped up on the hospital bed in front of me resembled the Zach I had known for the past fifteen years. His face, unlike mine, was blemish free from the accident, but he no longer wore the same carefree welcoming expression I was used to. He looked angry and bitter.

He didn't look at Mom and me as we entered. His eyes remained fixated on the television even though the sound was turned all the way down. I looked at Janet, who sat in the corner, with confusion. She shook her head slightly before standing to approach Zach.

"Sweetheart, Livia and I are going to get a cup of coffee." She leaned over and kissed his forehead. "Do you need anything?" He didn't acknowledge her, and she didn't seem surprised. His eyes never left the TV.

Mom and Janet left, closing the door behind them. I placed my hands on the wheels of my chair, maneuvering myself as close to his bed as my broken legs would allow. I focused on his face rather than his legs, which lay motionless in casts. I wanted to smooth my hand across his forehead to erase the harsh lines, but he was out of reach, so I did the next best thing and grasped his hand. His fingers remained slack like a corpse.

"Zach, I'm glad you're going to be okay. I was so scared." The words poured out of me in a rush. I'd missed my friends. The last ten days had been the longest any of us had ever spent apart.

Zach finally pulled his eyes away from the television. He looked at me incredulously. "Okay? Okay? Did you miss my prognosis? Crippled. I'm fucking crippled. I'll never throw a football again. Hell, I'll never fucking walk again, and you're glad I'm going to be okay." His words were like shards of glass, slicing through my soul. He ripped my heart out with razor-sharp teeth, shredding it until it was a bloody pulp. *"And what about Tracey? Are you glad about her, too?"*

Bile rose in my throat. I clenched my fist, wanting to lash out at him. Make him suffer in the same way that his words were hurting me. My eyes blazed as I jerked my hand from his. Tears streamed down his cheeks, taking the wind from my sails. Nothing I could say would cause him any more pain than what he was already feeling.

In spite of his harsh words, I wanted to weep with him. I wanted to rant at whoever was cosmically responsible for all of this, but I did neither. My friends and I didn't deserve this.

"Zach, what can I do?" My voice was thick with unshed tears that refused to come. I didn't know what to do to comfort him. I was an emotionless shell.

"Nothing." His hands clenched into fists. *"Nobody can do anything. My life is over."*

"Zach, it's not over. I know it feels like it is, but it's not. We're going to get through this. I'm going to help you."

"I don't want your help." His voice rose several decibels. As he swiped the tears from his eyes, I saw nothing but hopelessness in them.

"You just need time," I pleaded.

"Get out," he bellowed, reaching for the call button on his bed.

I couldn't respond. Zach never lost his cool. He never held a grudge, and he definitely never raised his voice. His face was a distorted mask of rage as he continued to bellow at me. I tried to reach for him, but he shoved me away.

"GET OUT!" He picked up the glass on his table, threatening to throw it at me.

I was genuinely scared and tried to back my chair away from his bed, bumping into everything in the process. I cursed my plaster-encased legs. I wanted to flee, but I was trapped. Held hostage again by circumstances out of my control.

Zach refused to see me after that. For an entire month I went to his room every day, hoping he would change his mind. Eventually, the constant rejection was too much, and I stopped trying. Just like I had stopped sending e-mails to Kat since she never responded. Only three of my friends had died in that tragic accident, and yet, I had lost all of them; the Brat Pack was no more.

I sat uncomfortably in a chair across from Zach, my hands fidgeting nervously in my lap. "I've spent a lot of time over the past year and a half thinking about what I wanted to say. I know our relationship back then never reached the level you wanted it to. Maybe I was just naïve, but I thought you could handle it. I thought we could handle it. The worst part about finding out about you and Tracey was that you kept it hidden from me."

Zach flinched at the mention of Tracey's name, but his eyes remained fixated on the floor.

"Sure, it would have been tough to handle at first, but if it was over between us, you should have said something. You should have ended it. How do you think it made me feel to find out I had been a roadblock between you and Tracey? I know you thought you were doing the right thing, like maybe you were sparing my feelings or something, but then you had the nerve to get so mad in the hospital and accuse me of being happy that Tracey was gone." I felt a lump in my throat, but I swallowed hard. I promised myself I wouldn't cry today.

"I didn't deserve that. We both lost people we loved that night. Tracey was my best friend. I know you've suffered a great deal. You're facing a life now that you hadn't counted on, but that doesn't mean we abandon each other. Not after everything we've been through together."

I placed my hand on his. He still didn't move, still never looked up from the floor. If any part of the old Zach I once knew still existed, I knew he would understand. "Zach, regardless of everything that has happened, I want you to know I forgive you. And I expect you to forgive me." I squeezed his hand and stood up from my chair. The only acknowledgment he would provide was that he didn't turn away from me when I bent over and hugged him like I had wanted to so many months ago. He didn't return the hug, but I hadn't expected him to. Simply listening was a start. Before I left, I handed him the box I'd brought with me, hoping it would give him a push in the right direction.

Janet hugged me tightly before I left, making me promise I'd visit her again soon. I had no problem making the promise. I would be back for another visit, and another one after that, and another one after that. I let Zach push me away once before, but I would not abandon him. I found a new level of resolve during the visit, facing the evidence of what I did not want to become. Zach was bitter and angry at the world. Today I had taken one more step that would help me finally find closure. The end of my journey was so close that I could practically taste it. In contrast, Zach's defiance indicated he hadn't started his journey yet. He was stuck at the beginning.

twenty-three

Bentley

The holidays seemed to bring out the crazy in everyone. I lost count of how many calls Steve and I took over the weekend. I figured I would have missed all the deep fryer attempts gone wrong by not actually working on Thanksgiving Day, but it seemed people got drunk over the weekend and continued frying more than just turkeys. We treated so many burns I was convinced I'd never get the smell off me. Some of these people were lucky they didn't burn down their houses.

The only good thing about the busy weekend was that I didn't have much time to think about Mac, or more accurately, what had transpired on the beach. It was a good thing since just the mental picture of what we did was enough to give me a case of blue balls, and there was no way I could work like that. Steve would be wondering if something was wrong with me if

I had to go to the restroom too many times to take things into my own hands.

After some arranging and a few threats, I was able to secure the apartment for myself on Monday night. I even managed to bribe Michael and Chad into helping me clean the place. Both grumbled, claiming I was acting like our parents were visiting. They were both smart enough to know what I was hoping tonight would lead to, but that didn't stop them from giving me shit about it all day. They thought they were being hilarious by hiding condoms all over the apartment that Mac was bound to find. Only after I threatened bodily harm to them and Sherman did they collect them all.

The place looked pretty spic and span by the time we were done. I thought I was ready until an unexpected case of nerves hit me as I drove to Mac's dorm. Tonight could go two ways. I could get Mac to my apartment, where she would see the obvious seduction attempt and freak out, demanding I take her home, or it would go my way and lead to an obviously happy ending. I regretted my decision to wait until I picked her up to tell her we had the apartment to ourselves. A little warning would have probably been the smarter course of action. I was acting about as suave as a fourteen-year-old who had just scored his first *Playboy* magazine. Mac certainly wasn't going to be the first girl I'd ever slept with, but she definitely felt like the most important.

twenty-four

Mac

Monday, when I arrived back on campus after the short Thanksgiving break, it felt like the weight of the world had been lifted from my shoulders. Bentley and I had a date planned for that evening, and I found it difficult to focus from the anticipation of seeing him again. I even skipped my last class so I could put in extra time getting ready. I had never seduced anyone, and I didn't want to look like a total amateur.

My decision to wear a dress was the toughest part. As a rule, I never wore anything but pants in order to cover my scars from sight. I knew my leg was unsightly, and figured I was sparing everyone the need to stare. The only problem was I wanted Bentley to see me dressed up. Dresses had a way of making a girl feel pretty. At least they had for me in the past. Trina was a big help in talking me into forgetting what I was seeing in the mirror and trusting that I looked good. She also stepped in when I tried unsuccessfully to do something different with my hair. I was about ready to throw the brush across the room in a fit of frustration when she stopped me. How she did it, I have no idea, but somehow she was able to get my hair pulled up in a sophisticated knot that looked extremely elegant. When my hair was fixed to her satisfaction, she offered to do my makeup.

"Thank you, Trina. I love it," I commented, looking at my reflection in the mirror. "I haven't felt this pretty in a long time." I surprised us both by reaching out to hug her, which she happily accepted.

"You're this pretty all the time. I should hate anyone who can look so good with such little effort," she joked, winking at my reflection.

"Shut up. You've obviously been smoking something, because I'd gladly trade everything for those long legs and pouty lips." I hadn't said anything before, but I'd been envious of her since we met.

"Well, give me your boobs and freaking ass any day of the week. Wait. That sounded different in my head. Now it just sounds like I'm hitting on you."

"Well, I suspected you swung from the other side of the monkey bars." I laughed.

"After the last douche I dated, being a lesbian might actually be promising."

"That bad?" I asked, grabbing my purse.

"Just put it this way, he makes guys on some reality shows look good."

"Oh Lord. That's never a good thing."

"Tell me about it. I'm beginning to think all college guys are assholes. At least all the ones at this school."

A sudden idea occurred to me. "I might know a guy. He's definitely not an asshole."

"What does that mean? Is he a freak of nature or something?"

"Well, he does have his quirks." I had Chad in mind, but the more I talked, the less convinced I was that he was right for Trina.

"What quirks?" Some of her enthusiasm drained away.

"He's a bit of a gamer. He is really funny, though, and sweet."

"Yeah, but a gamer? Like video games, or are we talking dice-rolling fantasy geek?"

"No, not dice games. He's big into Xbox. Maybe more than the average guy."

"Um, thanks, but no thanks," she answered disdainfully, flouncing on her bed.

I was tempted to say more. Really I hadn't cast Chad in the best light. I could do better, maybe. Glancing at my phone, though, I realized now was not the time. Throwing her a hurried good-bye, I headed out to meet Bentley.

Bentley pulled up in front of my dorm building just as I walked outside. He acted nervous when he got out of the car, which I found sweet. I had been struggling with my own case of nerves.

"You look breathtaking," he said, sweeping me up in his arms so my feet dangled several inches off the ground. I could tell he approved of my dress, which eased some of my stress over my leg being exposed.

"Why, thank you." I sounded slightly breathless, but the way he held me in his arms stoked my fire. If my plans went off without a hitch, this wouldn't be the last time either of us would be out of breath tonight. "So, what's the plan?" Bentley set me back onto my feet, hesitantly answering the question.

"Well, Chad and Michael are out for the night, so I thought we'd pick up something to eat and take it back to my apartment."

I smiled without offering any objections. Butterflies filled my stomach. Any doubts I may have had about where we stood tonight were put to rest. It was obvious I wasn't the only one who had given the evening some thought. I hoped I wouldn't be a disappointment, but it was too late to start second-guessing things.

"How was your weekend?" he asked once we were in the car.

"Eventful," I answered, smiling at the understatement.

"Even more eventful than Friday?"

"Let's just say it was a different kind of eventful."

"Do you want to talk about it?" His insightfulness was one of the things I liked most about him, but tonight I didn't want to delve into any of the things that would bog us down.

"Not tonight, okay?"

"Whenever you're ready. I was thinking we could pick up

Chinese food. Does that sound good?" He pulled into a shopping plaza near campus.

"Sounds yummy," I answered, climbing out of the vehicle with him.

To pass the time while we waited for our food, I asked him about work. Listening to his stories, I was amazed by how much trouble people could get themselves into during the holidays, especially when alcohol was involved. It reminded me of neighbors we had years ago who tried setting off fireworks in their screened-in porch. They nearly lost their house if not for the quick response of the fire trucks.

Bentley laughed and, of course, had his own stories about the Fourth. "One year, my friend Jacob thought it would be funny to set off an M80 firecracker under a mop bucket. It was so loud, it sounded like a grenade had gone off. My dad was so pissed."

As we pulled into Bentley's apartment complex with our Chinese food, my stomach hurt from laughing at Bentley's impersonation of his dad freaking out on him and his friends.

"You laugh, but I swear my ass still has belt marks on it. I couldn't sit for a week," he complained, helping me up the stairs to his apartment.

"We all got in trouble like that one year, too. Dan came up with the brilliant idea of setting off fireworks from the top of his house one Fourth of July. I forget where his parents were, but they were gone for some reason," I said, searching for details that weren't important to the story. "Anyway, it was Kat's dad who caught us just in time to see one of our fireworks land smack dab in the middle of the grand oak tree in Dan's back-yard. Nothing bad happened. Well, to the tree, I mean. All of us got grounded. I remember Kat was so upset, like her world had ended. Total drama, let me tell you," I chattered away. I stopped myself when I noticed we were standing outside Bent-ley's apartment, but he was waiting for me to finish my story before we went inside. "Sorry. I was babbling there." Truthfully, I think I was trying to distract myself from a bad case of the nerves.

"No, it's not that. I just like hearing you tell stories. You're easy to listen to," he said, pushing the door open to let me enter the apartment first. I could have kissed him for that remark alone, forget about everything else that made me want him. In the month or so that I'd been coming over, I'd never seen the guys' apartment look so good. It even smelled clean, which meant they had put some real effort into it.

"You cleaned," I commented, standing in the middle of the living room. "How did you bribe the guys into helping with this?"

He set the food on the counter before joining me. "I may have threatened Sherman's life, and some money may have switched hands, too." He placed his hands on my hips, turning me to face him. "Is everything okay?" He gently tugged on my lip. I hadn't noticed that I was unconsciously gnawing it. He leaned in, lightly kissing the corner of my mouth. "Are you nervous?" His lips trailed across my cheek until they reached my ear, covering my arms in goose bumps. His warm breath tickled the tendrils of hair on the back of my neck. He pulled me closer so our bodies were pressed together. My anxiety faded as I felt every delicious inch of him pressed against me.

"No," I moaned as he sucked on my neck, making my legs want to collapse.

I wrapped my hands around his face, dragging his mouth up to mine. Feeling bold, I took charge of the kiss by letting my tongue delve into his mouth. He responded by wrapping his arms tightly around my waist.

He pulled his mouth away, reluctantly. "Do you want to eat?"

I knew what he was asking. He was trying to give me more time. I shook my head, taking his lips again. He practically growled his approval, pulling me closer by cupping my butt tightly. His hands moved under my dress. The feel of his touch on the small of my back made me shudder with pleasure in his arms.

Without breaking the kiss, Bentley lifted me off my feet and carried me from the living room to his bedroom. My fingers worked at the buttons of his shirt, exposing the chest I'd been waiting to see up close and personally. It was the first time I'd touched him like this. I couldn't resist running my tongue along his collarbone. This time it was his turn to shudder.

"Do you like that?" I asked boldly as he lowered me to the bed. My hands slid along his rib cage beneath his shirt. His skin was smooth and practically begged to be kissed.

"You tell me," he said, pressing his body against mine. My dress hiked to my waist as my knees fell apart. Wanting to feel more of him, I pulled at his shirt until he shrugged it off. In the dim light from the hallway, I could see he was as lean as he looked. I ran my fingers over his taut muscles, exploring his chest and chiseled abs. Unable to resist the urge, I lifted my head off the pillow and circled his hard nipple with the tip of my tongue. My body was once again calling the shots, taking what it wanted from him. He responded by grinding against me, which made my toes curl with anticipation. Trying to elicit another reaction from him, I trailed my tongue over his chest until I reached his other nipple. I sucked it into my mouth, grazing my teeth over its tautness. He rocked against me again, running his hands up under my dress. His hands continued to slide upward, taking my dress with it until it lifted over my head.

He gazed down at my lace bra and matching panties that left nothing to the imagination. "You are so fucking beautiful," he murmured, running his hands over my chest before reaching behind me to unclasp my bra. My breasts spilled out into his hands. His thumbs circled my hard nipples, teasing them.

I whimpered, moving restlessly against him. I wanted more, but didn't know how to tell him. I wanted him to take me. He must have sensed my need as he shed his jeans and boxers. Shyness prevented me from looking down, though I could feel him heavy and hard against my thigh. I shifted, trying to give him the access that I desired.

"Wait, not yet," he whispered hotly, lowering his mouth to one of my nipples. He sucked it into his mouth, swirling his tongue around until I arched my back. He chuckled lightly at my response, moving to my other breast, where he elicited the same response. "I guess you like that?" he asked, running his mouth slowly down my abdomen. My hips responded by lifting off the mattress as his tongue circled my belly button before moving lower. His hands gripped my hips, supporting me as he placed his mouth intimately on me. I nearly came undone, feeling his wet mouth through my panties.

My breathing became ragged as my hips jerked. "Bentley, please," I begged, unable to handle the pressure that was building inside me. Sensing I was past the point of no return, he peeled off my panties and dropped them to the floor before pulling a condom from the nightstand near the bed. He moved between my legs, and I braced myself for the inevitable pain. It had been a while since Zach and I had gone all the way, but that part of it I remembered.

With Bentley, I wasn't scared. I didn't care how much it hurt. I wanted him too much. I felt him slowly slide into me as he coaxed his tongue into my mouth. My hands clutched his butt, trying to tug him closer. His movements were careful and hesitant, but slower than what my body wanted. Unconsciously, I lifted my hips so that he was buried all the way inside me. He groaned into my mouth as I wrapped a leg around him, locking him into place. His face moved to my neck as he began to move inside me, more forcibly this time. The same pressure I had felt on Friday began to build. I pulled him closer, gripping him hard on his back.

"God, yes," I called out as my release ripped through me. Bentley increased his pace, thrusting deep and fast. I raised myself on my elbows, sucking his neck as he rocked hard inside me. The sensation was mind numbing. I'd never experienced the kind of feeling that had me unsure if I could continue to take the intensity, while at the same time wishing it would never stop. Bentley moaned with pleasure one last time before collapsing on me.

With his face buried in my neck, he whispered something that I could barely make out. "What?" I asked as my body relaxed.

He raised himself so he could look at me, tucking a lock of hair behind my ear before cupping my cheek. "I love you." He looked like he was expecting me to bolt for the door. For a moment, I was tempted to. Did sex automatically put us in a position where we had to declare ourselves? Was he trying to pressure me into saying something I wasn't sure of, or even capable of in the future? I was moving on from my past, but still had serious doubts as to whether love would ever be in the cards for me. I turned my head so I wouldn't have to see the disappointment in his eyes, or worse yet, anger when I didn't return the sentiment.

His hand moved my face so I had to look at him. "Does that scare you?" he asked, running a thumb over my bottom lip.

I nodded my head.

"Why?"

"I'm afraid I'm going to lose you," I answered honestly.

"I'm not going anywhere."

"Maybe not now, but what if I'm not capable of love?" I whispered, voicing my biggest fear.

"You just need time. I know that. I just wanted you to know

how I felt. This isn't a 'you either tell me you love me or I'm gone' moment. It's just another step in our journey, that's all," he said. "There's no rush, okay?" He kissed me so gently I could have wept.

I nodded my head even though I felt I was doing him an injustice by misleading him. I'd been down this road before. Love was nothing but an illusion. I could have ruined the evening by obsessing over it all night, but Bentley distracted me, urging our fingers to explore each other's naked bodies. Eventually, he strolled out to the kitchen to retrieve our cold dinner. Not that I cared. Cold Chinese food versus what we had done was a more than fair trade-off. We ate in his bed, watching an old movie on TV. Any more talk about his declared feelings or my lack thereof was left unsaid.

twenty-five

Mac

Trina rolled over in her bed, pulling the pillow over her face at the sound of the alarm on my cell phone. I didn't mean to wake her since I knew she didn't have an early class today, but I had no choice. Today was physical therapy day for me. "Sorry," I whispered, grabbing the clothes I had laid out on my desk chair. I had already showered the night before to save time, so I basically just had to fix my hair and brush my teeth before heading out.

For the first time I was actually excited for my appointment. I had started feeling stronger since dating Bentley. Not only emotionally, but physically. I couldn't wait to see if Jake, my therapist, would notice the difference.

I climbed from my vehicle and headed inside the therapy office with as much pep in my step as my leg would allow.

Mary, the receptionist, greeted me with a smile. "Mac, did you have a nice Thanksgiving?" She scooted the sign-in sheet toward me as I approached the counter.

I returned her smile. "It was nice. I ate too much food, of course, but that's typical, right?"

She looked up at me, surprise coloring her face. "Well, uh, ain't that the truth. I swear I spend the rest of the year trying to dump all the weight I put on during the holidays, and then start over again."

I knew why she was surprised. Since I'd been coming, I had not been the most talkative person. Most of the time I gave one-word answers to her attempts at small talk. "My mom says the same thing. Doesn't look like you have anything to worry about, though." Mary looked to be roughly Mom's age, but even wearing baggy scrubs, she was clearly trim and in shape.

"Bless you. I don't think Jake would keep me around if I needed to be rolled into the office."

I couldn't help laughing in agreement. Jake wasn't some asshole dictator like her joke made it seem. He was just all about fitness. "I'm sure that would never happen."

She laughed, too. "Only because he would be lost if he had to do all the bookkeeping. You can go on back now."

Adjusting my cane, I headed through the door to the large physical therapy room where Jake normally worked on my leg. With all the different machines and contraptions, the wide-open room looked like a combination dance and Pilates studio mixed with a gym. I grimaced looking at the padded tables that lined the far wall. During my last visit, I'd lain there with an electric muscle stimulator attached to my leg. The idea of electronic impulses stimulating my muscles turned out to be less painful than it sounded, but I still found the vibrating, tingling sensation unpleasant. Hopefully, I would be spared that torture treatment today.

"Hi, Mac," one of the other therapists called out as I passed. She was working with an elderly man on the rowing machine.

I waved to her. "Hey, Grace. How are the girls?" I learned a lot about each person that worked in the office by listening, even if I hadn't engaged in much conversation.

"Growing like weeds. Thanks for asking. They're with their dad this week, so the house is pretty quiet."

I set my bag and cane on the long counter on the opposite side of the room. "Is that a good thing or a bad thing?" I asked, going to the mats on the floor where I knew Jake would start me off with stretching.

She laughed. "I never thought I would say it about my babies, but after having them home for Thanksgiving break, the silence is a little nice."

"Nothing wrong with that, honey," the elderly gentleman piped in. "Beth and I love our grandkids, but we thank God Almighty every time we send them home."

"My darling, Mac. How's it going today, girl?" Jake bellowed, entering the room as the three of us laughed. "Did I just walk into the Twilight Zone or something? What's so funny that even my lovely Mac is laughing?" he asked, hunkering down on the mat by my feet. He grasped my bad leg at the ankle and lifted carefully as I lay on my back.

"You know the routine. Take a deep breath and exhale as I lift." I grimaced as he pushed against my leg to stretch my hamstring. "That's good, Mac. And back down. So, what was so funny?"

"Grace was just telling us about how nice and quiet her house is." I gasped slightly as he repeated the stretch on my other leg.

"She was, huh?" He looked at me for a second in the same surprised fashion Mary had. Jake had more success at getting me to talk during our visits, but he hadn't seen me actually engage in conversation with anyone in the office other than him. "Don't let her fool you. By the end of the week, she'll be moping around."

"Not this time. I'm going to binge on *Game of Thrones* and eat all the food the girls normally won't eat," Grace called out.

Jake looked at me, shaking his head. "Sounds like a plan." Grace and her husband had split up during the summer after ten years together. They were still trying to work out the kinks and custody headaches. Being shuttled back and forth every other week between parents didn't sound like an ideal situation to me if I was a kid, but what choice did they have? None, I guess. Thank God Mom and Dad had never put me in that position.

"You seem more sore than usual," Jake commented as I continued to grimace while he twisted and stretched my bad leg. "You overexerting yourself in other ways I need to know about?"

I choked, sucking in a deep breath as an image of what

Bentley and I had done in his apartment the other night flashed in my head. I rolled to my side coughing, while Jake patted my back.

"Whoa. You okay, girl?" He helped me to my feet so we could move to the next exercise.

I cleared my throat, shuffling slowly behind him since walking without my cane took more effort. "I, uh. No. I've just climbed more stairs since I last saw you."

"Really? What is that, two times now?"

"Three. The theater, a basketball game at the arena, and I climbed the stairs at Bentley's apartment the other day."

"Wow. Okay, how was the leg afterwards?" He slid my foot into the harness of one of the leg exercise machines.

"The stairs at the apartment made me pretty sore, but not intolerable. It definitely wasn't as bad as the arena and much better than the theater."

"That's great. I don't want you to overdo it, but it's good that you're pushing yourself. I can tell by the way your calf muscle is developing that your leg must be getting stronger. We'll do some work with the weights to see just how strong."

"Oh joy." I had a hate-loathe relationship with the weights. They hated me and I loathed them.

Jake chuckled. "You're cracking me up today. I like this happier, more talkative Mac. Things must be going good with Bentley."

"Yeah, it's good." Jake kept up a running commentary as he put me through the paces on each machine. By the time we were done, my legs felt like cooked spaghetti.

After confirming my next appointment with Mary, I headed to my car, still sweating profusely. I caught my reflection in the tinted windows. It was never a pretty sight after my therapy sessions. My hair was stuck to the back of my sweaty neck and my face was a red blotchy mess.

If Bentley saw me now, he'd probably rethink the whole *love* thing. Since his bold declaration the other day, he continued to be open about his feelings. He wasn't pressuring me in any way, but I could tell he was disappointed I hadn't returned the sentiment. It wasn't that I didn't have strong feelings for him. I just couldn't bring myself to say it.

twenty-six

Bentley

I checked the clock for about the twentieth time since arriving at work that morning. Not one call had come in for us to handle. I was bored out of my mind. I would have texted Mac, but she was spending the day with her mom. It probably wouldn't be cool to interrupt that. She was home for winter break, so we'd been commuting back and forth the past couple weeks to see each other.

I went home myself for a few days to celebrate Christmas, but Allie still hadn't forgiven me for busting her phone. She basically took the fun out of the visit. Seeing the impact her behavior was having on Mom and Dad, I couldn't help regretting my hasty actions at the restaurant that day. I lost my head and now Allie was making everyone in the family pay for it. It wasn't like they could throw her out. Regardless of what Allie believed, she was still a fifteen-year-old kid. I tried to put myself in her shoes to give her the benefit of the doubt, but half the time I wanted to throttle her for what she was doing. The entire family was walking on eggshells wondering what she would do next.

Ironically, it was Mac who was the most sympathetic toward Allie, claiming the two of them weren't all that different. In spite of my argument, she disagreed, saying she understood the shell Allie seemed to keep herself in. Hearing Mac talk was a glaring indication of how far she'd come in the last few months that we'd been together. It was hard to remember what she had been like that first day in the library.

In the weeks that followed, Mac was forced to spend more time than she wanted dealing with the court case surrounding her accident. Things had become tense, and I could tell how much it bothered her. Mac wanted nothing more than to put the whole thing behind her. The situation made me feel powerless. I couldn't believe how much the trucking company and, worse yet, the insurance companies had dragged this out. Mac never openly complained, but how were people supposed to move on?

Before winter break, Mac was beginning to spend more nights with me than at her dorm. I'd gotten used to having her over, and now it felt weird that she wasn't there. I tried to talk her into staying with me the entire break since Chad and Michael had headed home for Christmas, but she claimed her parents would flip out if she did that. Not that I bought that excuse. I mean, we were both adults. What more could I do?

I'd be a dick if I pressed the issue, especially considering everything else she had going on.

The answer was nothing except sit and watch the clock count down the hours until my shift was over. We'd made plans for her to come over and spend the night on Wednesday since it was New Year's Eve, and we wanted to make the most of our night.

All I had to do was get through this slow-ass shift. Not to play devil's advocate, but I found myself wishing a call would come in so at least we'd have something to do. It was sadistic as hell. I knew that, but after a dozen hands of Go Fish with Steve, I was ready to jump in front of a moving bus myself so there would at least be a trauma to take care of.

Steve had just dealt another hand of cards when a call finally came in. We both jumped like a couple of rookies on day one. Grabbing our gear, we headed for our waiting rig. We got sketchy details over the radio as we drove. The bottom line of the situation was a three-car pileup on I-4 with multiple traumas. Steve flipped on the sirens while I navigated the best route to get to the accident. We worked well together and both knew our jobs. Judging by the numerous calls coming over the radio, we weren't the only ambulance en route.

Traffic was at a standstill on I-4. We were three miles away from the accident scene, and the normal busy highway was like a parking lot. Steve figured out right away the siren and lights weren't getting us anywhere, so he jerked the wheel, maneuvering the ambulance to the grassy shoulder. I braced my hands on the dashboard as we bounced along the thin strip of grass on the side of the highway. We were only going twenty-five miles an hour at best, but since all the cars we passed weren't moving, it gave the illusion that we were moving much faster. Motorists were standing by their cars, rubbernecking to try and get a glimpse at the accident up ahead. Some had even climbed atop their vehicles. People's fascination with gruesome scenes never ceased to amaze me.

"Son of a bitch," Steve swore when we spotted the accident as we approached. I had to agree. It had been more than a year since I'd seen that kind of pileup. Three cars had been involved, but it was the minivan that suffered the most devastation. I braced myself for the worst possible scenario. Minivans had the potential to hold kids, which meant we could be walking into something exceptionally bad.

Steve and I jumped from the emergency vehicle, ready to do what we were trained for. We heard wailing and screaming coming from one of the cars, which I noticed upon approach was crushed in on one side. A few people sat on the grass, bleeding from different wounds, while still more remained trapped in their vehicles. The scene was overwhelming and became louder with each passing second as fire trucks and highway patrol cars rolled on to the scene. It reminded me of Mac's accident, which now seemed so long ago. That time only three had survived. Looking at the mangled carnage in front of me, we would be lucky to save even that many.

twenty-seven

Mac

I drummed my fingers impatiently on the steering wheel. I was a patient, careful driver, but even I hated catching every single damn traffic light like I'd done since leaving home. I was ready to scream. Someone at the traffic control office had to be deliberately screwing with me. It was eleven at night on a Tuesday with virtually no traffic, but every red light wanted to stop me. If I didn't know any better, I would have blamed Mom, who was less than thrilled that I'd decided to head to Bentley's tonight rather than tomorrow like originally planned. After an endless day of bickering over the case, I'd stopped caring what she thought by midafternoon. Even Dad had gotten sick of trying to referee our exchanges and spent the majority of the day hiding out in the garage. Finally, after a tense dinner, I decided we all needed a break from one another.

I started to second-guess my spur-of-the-moment decision as I waited at yet another red light less than a mile from Bentley's apartment. He had given me a key a couple weeks ago and told me to use it anytime. Surprising him by being at his apartment when he got off work had seemed like a romantic idea, especially since Chad and Michael would be back on campus soon, ruining this type of moment again, but now that I was almost there, I worried that I was cramping Bentley's style. He wouldn't be home for several more hours, and for all I knew, he would come home completely exhausted and wouldn't want to do anything but crash.

Pulling into the parking lot, I sat in the car debating my decision. Looking at the staircase, I felt a jumble of nerves in my stomach. For some reason, once he'd declared his feelings, I felt I had to maintain a certain amount of independence. Not because I didn't care for him, but I wasn't ready to act like we were living together yet. I'd hoped to get there, but I wasn't going to force it.

Climbing from the car before I lost my nerve, I headed for the stairs, leaving my overnight bag behind until Bentley got home. I may want my independence, but I knew my limitations.

The stairs were as daunting as they always were. I was breathing heavily by the time I made it to the top, but the familiar feeling of pride and adrenaline from my accomplishment propelled me down the walkway to his apartment.

As soon as I opened the door, I knew I'd made the right decision. It had been a couple days since I'd seen Bentley, and I missed him. Maybe that was saying something. Was it love?

For some reason, I couldn't bring myself to admit that. I'd been ignoring the taunting voice in my head that reminded me Bentley was always on my mind. In the short amount of time we'd been together, he had somehow been able to fill the void inside me. If that was the truth, then why was I trying so hard to deny my true feelings for him?

Regardless of my scrambled brain, I set to work out my whole seduction plan, which involved lighting the few candles Bentley had scattered around that I knew were completely for my benefit. I had teased Chad one day about the holes in his socks when his feet were propped up on the coffee table. I joked about whether they smelled as bad as they looked. Bentley had taken my comment seriously and forced Chad to go take a shower and change his clothes. I felt somewhat bad for making him go to that trouble on my account. I noticed the candles the next time I came over. At least now they would serve my purposes well.

After the candles were lit, I straightened up the man cave a bit. It wasn't all that bad, for the most part. Probably because Chad and Michael hadn't returned from break yet. A week from now, this place was likely to be a disaster.

The busywork of cleaning didn't kill nearly as much time as I thought. Before I knew it, I was left with nothing to pass the remaining hour and a half until Bentley got home. Sinking down on the couch, I picked up the remote, aimlessly flipping through the channels for something to watch. I finally stopped on some cooking reality show, wishing I had thought to stop on the way over and pick up something to eat. My stomach rumbled as I watched the cupcake challenge unfold. I could have definitely gone for a cupcake right at that moment. I could get up and scrounge for something, but based on my experiences coming here on other days, I'd have a better chance of finding Red Bull than something to eat.

My leg made the decision for me anyway with its slight throbbing, so I stayed put on the couch. I massaged my twitching muscles, realizing I'd probably done a little too much running around today. Trying to ease the ache, I shifted positions so that I was lying down with my leg propped up on the arm of the couch. I had found the right spot. Feeling relieved, I turned back to the TV to torture myself with more cupcakes I couldn't have. My new comfortable position reminded me that I was more tired than I thought as I suddenly found myself fighting to keep my eyes open. I yawned heavily and pulled the blanket off the back of the couch after finishing a long, drawn-out stretch. I figured resting my eyes for a few minutes couldn't hurt.

I woke to the room tilting as I was gently lifted off the couch. "Hey," I said, looking sheepishly at Bentley. Obviously, my whole seduction scene had been an epic failure. He didn't answer. I could tell he was upset. Maybe my initial thoughts had been correct and he did have a problem with me being here. He was probably exhausted from work and now felt he needed to take care of me. I squirmed slightly in his arms, letting him know he didn't need to carry me to bed. His hold tightened. Not in a way that was painful, but Bentley was showing me he was in control.

He didn't speak as we entered his darkened room, nor did he flip on the light. He lowered me to the bed, covering my body with his. In the dim light streaming in through the window, I tried to decipher what his silence meant, but his expression offered no clue. I was not used to this side of him. My hand moved to his face to smooth out the tension, but he captured it, pulling my hand to his lips, where he placed a searing kiss on my palm.

He straddled me. Bringing my hands to my side, he held them in place with his, making it impossible to touch him. The intensity of the moment made my heart thump heavily in my chest. "Are you okay?" I asked as he stared deeply at me, practically through me. Whatever this was, it wasn't the normal Bentley. His usual smile was missing.

He nodded, but didn't say anything. Even in the dim light I could tell he was troubled.

"Because you're kind of freaking me ou—" Before I could finish my statement, he covered my mouth with his, cutting off any further talk. His kiss was rough and forceful, but I took it eagerly. The passion that seemed to surface when Bentley and I were intimate flared to life as I moved restlessly beneath his body, responding to the assault of his mouth on mine. In the month that we'd been sleeping together, this was as aggressive as he'd ever been. It was scary and exciting at the same time. I wanted to beg him to tell me what was wrong, but the sensations he had evoked wouldn't allow my mouth to ruin the moment.

We practically tore the clothes from our bodies, tugging and pulling until we were gloriously naked. Bentley buried his head in my shoulder, biting it just enough to sting, but not enough to leave a mark. He reached for the box on his nightstand, throwing it across the room after quickly tearing open the condom package. He entered me in one swift movement, taking my breath away. He filled me completely and was in full control, taking what he wanted. I couldn't help gasping as he moved fast and hard like he was trying to finish a race. My passion became clouded in confusion. Something clearly wasn't right. Knowing he was hurting, I stroked a hand softly down his back, hoping it would calm whatever was hurting him. I may not have spoken the word "love" yet, but it didn't mean I didn't care deeply for him. Seeing Bentley like this was tearing me up inside.

His movements slowed, coming to a halt as my hand continued to gently stroke the length of his back. All the forcefulness left him as he slumped heavily on me. I soothingly massaged his head, which was still buried in my neck. After a moment, he lifted himself onto his elbows, keeping our bodies joined.

"Am I too heavy?" His hand found my face, brushing my hair back before he placed a tender kiss on my temple.

"No," I replied. His loosened body language indicated he was much calmer than he had been seconds ago. Featherlight kisses moved down over my eyelids, which fluttered closed. The difference in his touch was night and day. He kissed me tentatively like he was seeking permission before claiming my mouth. I took him in, running my hands over his back in slow gentle circles.

This time when he started moving again inside me, he was as gentle as his tongue. My desire returned with each thrust.

His free hand continued to stroke my face as my hips matched his pace. We were moving as one. I moaned, feeling myself reaching the point where I needed to go. Bentley increased his tempo, helping me reach the peak. I stiffened under him as I shuddered into what felt like a million pieces. He continued moving until his own release came seconds later.

He collapsed on top of me with us both breathing as if we'd climbed a mountain. Neither of us said a word even though I was dying to know what was wrong. I resumed caressing his back, figuring he'd say something eventually. His breathing evened out, and I wondered if he had fallen asleep until he lifted himself off me and headed to the bathroom to clean up.

I sat up in the bed, watching his retreating backside. The moment felt awkward and I wondered if I should get dressed. Maybe he wanted me to leave. I was still lying in bed confused when he returned. He climbed next to me, dragging me backward until I was spooned in his arms. He left a sweet kiss on my neck, stroking a hand up and down the length of my arm. I wanted to talk to him, but the mood in the room was almost tranquil, and after a few minutes my eyelids began to droop. I tried to stay awake, but my eyes were no longer cooperating. My last conscious thought was of Bentley exhaling deeply, like he'd been holding his breath.

The bed beside me was empty the next morning when I woke up. I saw my bag sitting on the floor, which meant Bentley had gone down to my car to get it. I got up and placed the bag on the bed, pawing through it to find a clean pair of jeans and my favorite pullover sweater. Once I had dressed and cleaned up a little in the bathroom, I walked out to search for Bentley. I found him in the living room watching some sports channel.

"Hey," he greeted me. I eyed him critically for a moment, trying to read his mood.

"Hey," I answered quietly, joining him on the couch.

He switched off the TV before turning to face me. He reached for my hand, lacing our fingers together. I watched as his mouth opened and then closed as if he had reconsidered what he wanted to say. "I'm sorry about last night," he said finally. His voice was slightly hoarse, like he was coming down with something. "I shouldn't have been so rough," he continued, looking me over carefully like he was checking for marks or something.

"It's okay. What happened anyway?"

"Bad day at work." He rubbed his thumb over my knuckles.

"Oh." The single word stuck in my throat. In all my possible scenarios, I neglected to think his mood had something to do with his job. I assumed it had something to do with us.

"Yeah. Big car accident on I-4."

I wanted to tell him to stop or selfishly plug my ears to block him out. I froze, sitting like a statue as he talked. "It was awful. Three cars were involved. One was a minivan." He ran his free hand over his head like he was trying to erase the image from his head. Images of my own accident filled my head. I saw the crushed Suburban clearly as if it happened only yesterday.

"Witnesses said the van flipped several times." His voice shook slightly. I pulled my hand from his, though he didn't notice. I didn't want to hear any more. I couldn't. It was too much. Too hard. Too painful. Too crushing. I made a move to stand up, but his next words sent me whirling out of control. "Everyone in the van died. Both parents and their three little kids. One of them was a goddamn baby. A baby, for Christ's sake." He sounded distressed. The words propelled me off the couch. He watched with bewilderment as I snatched my purse and keys off the coffee table. My bag was in his room, but I didn't even attempt to retrieve it. I needed to leave. Like now.

"Mac, where are you going?" he called after me as I pulled the door open so fiercely I was surprised it didn't come off the hinges. I didn't answer him. My only objective was to leave as quickly as possible.

Bentley followed me, pulling on my arm to stop me. "Mac, what the hell is going on?" I avoided looking at him as I jerked my arm free. I was afraid to answer. Afraid of what would escape from my mouth in my frantic state. He easily kept pace with me as I made my way to the stairs, cursing my leg. I would have given anything at that moment to be able to run away and keep running. Anything to escape, but my leg held me up like it was encased in cement.

"Mackenzie," Bentley pleaded, grabbing my hand and finally bringing me to a stop. It was the first time he'd used my old name. The effect was instantaneous as I ground to a halt to glare at him. "Answer me. Are you mad about last night? Did I hurt you? You have to talk to me. You're ripping out my guts here. I need to know what's going on in your head."

I looked at him, feeling a deep hurt that matched the look on his face. That was my fault. I was responsible for the pain he was feeling. Knowing that did not stop the words that left my mouth. "I can't do this."

"Do what? What can't you do?" His voice softened as he tried to make sense of my words.

"All of this. I can't be the girl you want me to be. I can't love you. I can't support you and I sure as hell can't hear about your job. Do you understand that? I am not a whole person. I'm as broken as the window you found me behind the night of my accident. Listening to you tell me about some accident on I-4 feels like you're reaching into me with a dull spoon and removing the last of my heart. I'm shattered, Bentley." I pulled my hand away. This time he let go willingly. Turning on my heel, I limped away, leaving him behind. Now he would finally see why I had insisted on keeping to myself for so long. I didn't have it in my heart to support anyone other than myself.

I made it to my car without completely breaking down. What had I done? The pain in my heart was so intense I literally couldn't breathe. By now, you would think I could handle this kind of pain. That it would feel normal. It should have been as comfortable as a pair of old shoes, but it was none of those. It was raw and more abrasive than I remembered.

I pulled out of the parking lot, ignoring the checklist of steps I usually had to complete before I felt comfortable enough to drive. With tears streaming down my cheeks, I had no idea where to go. No destination in mind. I just drove. I left the campus behind, driving through a residential area that bled into businesses and stores. Eventually, my tears dried up, but that didn't mean I felt any better.

I looked both ways as I approached a stop sign at a two-way intersection. My eyes focused on two little girls who were skipping along the sidewalk, holding hands. Memories of my best friend flooded me when I noticed that their pinkies were linked.

graduation night 2013

Zach reached over and reassuringly squeezed my hand as he backed out of our parking space. His touch was comforting, but at the same time felt like a good-bye. I glanced in the rearview mirror at Tracey, who looked as troubled as I felt. Releasing Zach's hand, I reached for Tracey, lacing her pinkie with mine like we'd done since we were little. Our Pinkie Connection was something we'd never shared with anyone else. It was our version of holding hands, sealing a deal or making a promise. Her eyes filled with tears, which she quickly wiped away with her free hand. I acknowledged her by squeezing her pinkie with mine. There was no way I could throw away a fifteen-year friendship. Little did I realize it would be the last Pinkie Connection we would ever share. If I had—I would never have let go.

twenty-eight

Mac

A horn blasted behind me, jerking back my attention. Glancing in the rearview mirror, I saw that my tears were flowing again. The pissed-off middle-aged man I was holding up looked like he was about to blow a fuse, so I rolled through the stop sign. I now knew where I needed to go. It was so long past due, and yet, something in me told me I could handle it. Swiping the rest of my tears away, I steered my car toward my own familiar neighborhood.

Because of the daytime traffic, I didn't reach my destination until almost an hour later. Pulling into the driveway, I spotted two bikes left carelessly on the front lawn along with a basketball and baseball bat. Smiling for the first time that day, I climbed from my car and made my way to the red front door.

Tracey and I had always loved her front door. Ever since we

were kids, we had claimed it was magical. I didn't know whether I should ring the bell or knock. There had been a time that neither of those options would have been a consideration. I would have just opened it and strolled in like I belonged there.

I lightly rapped on the door with my knuckles. I could hear laughter and yelling beyond the door, and after a minute passed, I knew my attempt hadn't been heard. I rang the doorbell and waited. I could hear a familiar voice yelling for someone to get the door. My stomach cringed from nerves. The door was pulled open abruptly, startling me to take a half step backward.

"Mackenzie!" two excited voices greeted me before I was wrapped in a bear hug by two preteen boys, who looked much older than I remembered.

"Braxton and Nicholas," I returned, hugging the twins as my cane fell to the ground. "Look at you two. You're almost as tall as me," I mused, getting a good look at Tracey's brothers, who had turned into handsome young men in the last year and a half.

"Who are you kidding? I think we have you beat," Braxton said, puffing out his chest and standing tall.

"Is this yours?" Nicholas asked, picking up my cane.

"Yeah."

"It's u-g-l-y, ugly," Nicholas declared, turning my cane around in his hands. "I mean, it wouldn't make a bad sword," he added, brandishing it at his brother like a pirate. "But it's too ugly for a girl."

"Gee, thanks," I muttered, smiling. I'd forgotten how honest they could be. Glancing down at my cane, I looked at it from their new perspective and saw they were right. It was the one my doctor had issued after I was finally able to dump my crutches for good. At the time, the only thing I'd been able to focus on was that my doctors were telling me I would most likely need my cane for the rest of my life. "You're right. It is pretty ugly," I said, watching as they fought over who got to hold it.

"Boys, what are you doing?" Patricia asked, walking into the living room where the twins were play-fighting with my cane and an umbrella Braxton had snagged by the door. Patricia's eyes widened with surprise when she saw me. "Mac? Oh my God," she gasped, pulling me in for a crushing hug. The fact that she knew to call me Mac surprised me. My arms wrapped around her as my old life came back into focus. I couldn't believe I had ignored the people who had meant so much to me. Just because Kat and Zach had turned their backs on everyone didn't mean I had to.

"I missed you," I whispered as she tightened her hold on me. Patricia may not have been my biological mom, but in many ways she'd been a surrogate mother. I definitely would have called her a friend. She had been the voice of reason anytime Mom and I would butt heads.

"I missed you, too, sweetie. I've been waiting for you to come see me." She led us into the living room and sat down. Glancing around, I saw that the room hadn't changed. Every picture I remembered still hung on the walls, chronicling not only their lives, but mine also. My eyes found each and every one that Tracey and I were in together. I remembered each of those moments fondly.

Turning back to Patricia, I addressed her statement. "I know. I just miss her so much, and I thought it would be too hard. Not for just me, but all of us. I was wrong." I said the words with finality as they took root.

"We're family. There's always going to be reminders, but they don't always have to be painful." She clasped my hands in hers. "I was afraid you were staying away because you were angry at Tracey."

I looked at her with shock. "Why would you think that?"

"For taking someone who belonged to you. For betraying a friendship," she said, looking pointedly for my reaction.

"You knew about her and Zach."

"I did. I wasn't sure you knew until Janet mentioned it last year. Zach said something to her about you knowing. Tracey didn't mean to hurt you."

I nodded. "I know. I just wish she would have told me. We were best friends."

"I know, sweetie. She was going to tell you. She wanted to get graduation over with first. It was eating her up inside. I can tell you she fought her feelings for a long time because she was afraid of hurting you."

Hearing that made me feel terrible for Tracey. I could only imagine how hard everything had been for her. She'd always been the most sensitive one of our group. In the end, it had been my selfishness that had cost Tracey her life. "It's my fault she's gone," I confessed to Patricia, feeling the weight of the burden I'd been carrying. I waited for her reaction, expecting her to jerk her hands away in disgust.

"Mac, why would you say that? It was a tragic accident, but it was not your fault. How could you think that? Is that why you haven't visited before now?"

My eyes filled with tears. She had no idea. It was my fault. She just didn't know. In a rush, I told her every reason why she was wrong. Why it was my fault her daughter was dead. I told her how I had hesitated getting into the Suburban that night. How that hesitation had put us in the truck's path.

"Mac, some things in life are out of our control," she said, trying to make me feel better. I shrugged. She may be right, but it didn't change my other decision that had cost Tracey.

"But if I would have given my seat to Tracey . . . Forget that. I should have given my seat to her. If I would have done that rather than thinking of myself, she would still be here. That night I'd realized the seat no longer belonged to me. I should have insisted she take it. Who cared what the others thought?"

I was blinded by my tears, which were falling so fast I couldn't stop them. It was good that I had gotten my confession out of the way, because I could barely talk after that. My fingers dug into my legs as I tried to regain control. It wasn't my intention to fall apart. She reached over and covered my hands to settle me. "Honey, if you would have traded seats with her, you wouldn't be here," she said softly.

"I know," I sobbed. "Isn't that what you want? You'd have your daughter back."

"Sweetie, I miss my daughter every single day, and probably will until the day I die, but I could never pick her life over yours like that. Do you think Tracey would have wanted that?"

I shook my head, already knowing the answer. Tracey would have never wanted that. It was an impossible situation with someone losing, no matter which way it went. She would have hated knowing I blamed myself. I'd made so many mistakes over the last year. I was still making them. The hurt look on Bentley's face came to mind. I'd given him a chance. Allowed us to become close and then put him in a box to ensure I would never be hurt. In the end, I'd done us both a disservice.

Patricia and I talked for a long time after that. She wanted to know everything going on in my life. She had already gotten many of the details from talking to my mom. I told her about my visit with Zach the previous month and all my unanswered e-mails to Kat. Eventually, the conversation turned to Bentley, and that was when everything poured out of me in a rush. I told her things I couldn't tell Mom. Like she'd always done, Patricia provided the insight of a friend. When I finally stood up to leave, I felt infinitely better knowing what I needed to do. Giving her a kiss on the cheek, I promised I would visit again.

Patricia called the twins to say good-bye before I left. They reappeared with my cane, or at least I thought it was my cane. I could tell Patricia didn't know if she should laugh or yell at them. She looked at me for guidance. I couldn't help laughing as I reached for my cane, which was no longer an unassuming gray color. As a matter of fact, not a speck of the old color was visible, although I wasn't sure if it was any less ugly. Nicholas and Braxton had covered every square inch of the cane with superhero stickers. No matter which way I turned the cane, there was a costumed crime-fighter staring back at me.

"Um, thanks, guys," I said, taking it from them.

"Looks much better, right?" Braxton asked, beaming at me.

"Much," I said, sending an indulgent smile Patricia's way.

With one last hug for the three of them, I left with Patricia trying to explain why it had been wrong to decorate my cane without asking. As I walked to my car, my steps felt lighter. My whole life felt lighter. I shouldn't have waited so long to face this demon. Perhaps if I had come to see Patricia sooner, I could have saved us all a lot of heartache. Now I just needed to right my wrong with Bentley. I could only hope I wasn't too late. I wouldn't blame him if he told me to go to hell. A person could only stomach so much of the type of drama queen I'd been when he and I had met.

I ran several scenarios through my head about how to get Bentley to listen to me as I drove back to his apartment complex. I felt I had an ace in the hole if he'd only give me the opportunity to explain.

I was disappointed to see that Bentley's car was not in its usual spot when I turned into the parking lot of his building. In all my different scenarios, I hadn't considered that he wouldn't be here. I had myself so worked up, I felt like I needed to see him now or I would burst. There were several places he could have gone, aside from simply running to the store or going out for something to eat. He could be at his parents' house, but how desperate would I look if I suddenly showed up at their door?

I could call Chad to see if he'd heard from Bentley, but that was unlikely since he wasn't back in town yet. The obvious thing for me to do would be to bite the bullet and call him. That was the least appealing option. I wanted to talk to him in person to explain things. Hell, beg him if I had to.

I was so wrapped up in my thoughts I didn't notice someone standing at the driver's side of my car until I heard a tap on the window. "Holy shit!" I yelped. If I hadn't been wearing a seat belt, I might have jumped through the roof of the car like I was sitting on an ejector seat. "Bentley," I gasped, climbing from the car when he opened my door. I grabbed my cane as I stood. Bentley's eyes flickered to it instantly, but he didn't comment. There would be a story there if we could get through my apology first.

"What are you doing here, Mac?"

My heart dropped like a stone in a pool, but I had expected some resistance. "I wanted to talk to you," I stammered, trying to poise myself and remember all the things I had thought to say during my drive over. Usually Bentley was the talker. He would have rescued me in this situation and changed the subject by launching into some story. I didn't have that life preserver now. He stood like a statue, waiting in silence for some kind of explanation.

"So, talk," he said when I had done nothing but stare at him like a child.

"Can we go up to your apartment?" I was afraid he'd shoot me down, but I didn't want to do this in a parking lot.

He nodded, heading for the steps without worrying whether

I was keeping up. Not that I didn't try, but my leg would only allow me to go so fast. My limp became more pronounced the closer we got to the steps. I didn't care if it took me three years to climb them. What I needed to say would be worth it.

Climbing the stairs became a nonissue when Bentley swept me up in his arms. I couldn't tell if that was a good or a bad sign. His face gave no indication either way. As a matter of fact, he wouldn't even look at me. I wanted to tell him that he didn't have to carry me, but he seemed dead set on ignoring me as he scaled the steps quickly. I enjoyed the way his arms felt around me. If this was the last time he would hold me, I didn't want it to end.

We reached the second floor all too soon, and he didn't hesitate to deposit me down as soon as we reached the landing. Following behind him, I bit my lip, wondering if he would listen to what I had to say. I imagined he wouldn't have gone to the trouble of carrying me up here if he didn't at least plan on letting me explain.

He had his front door unlocked and pushed open by the time I caught up. He waited, letting me enter first. The apartment looked like it had when I left earlier. His coffee mug still sat on the table half full and the TV played in the background. I wondered where he'd gone that he didn't bother to turn anything off.

As I stood in the middle of his living room, my leg begged me to sit, but I ignored the ache. I needed to be close to the door in case he rejected me. My walk of shame would be easier if I didn't have to stagger up off the couch.

Bentley leaned against the door. His expression was hard to read, and I tried to focus on something other than how handsome he looked standing there. His arms were folded across his chest as he waited for me to start.

Everything I wanted to say, starting with an apology, had lodged in my throat. I gulped hard, trying to clear the way for my words. "I love you," I squeaked out like a complete moron. It wasn't what I had planned on starting the conversation with, but my mind went blank and I panicked.

"What?" He looked like he had been daydreaming and missed what I said.

"I love you," I repeated with more conviction than before. It wasn't a lie. I had just planned on leading up to it by apologizing first. "I've loved you for a while now. I was too much of an asshole to admit it. I thought if I kept you at arm's length, it would prevent you from hurting me." He opened his mouth to say something, but I hurried on. I wanted him to hear everything I had to say first. Then he could agree that I was an asshole.

"I know that was unfair. Hell, I know I've treated you unfairly from the beginning. From day one you accepted me for who I was, despite all my faults. You never got aggravated, and you never gave up on me, no matter how many times I tried to push you away. You changed me, Bentley. I don't know if you know that, but you helped me believe I could live again and be happy. For a long time I didn't think that was possible. And even if it were possible, I thought it would be unfair to the memory of my friends, so I kept throwing up walls. Most of all, I was terrified my heart wouldn't be able to handle another loss. You've made me feel things I'd never felt before."

He moved away from the door to approach me. I continued, trying to get everything out. "I love every single thing about you. I love your dimples. I love your lips. I probably love those a little too much." His lips smirked. "I love that you're funny and caring. I even love that you're a slob and that you're scared of your roommate's iguana. More than anything, I love that you feel everything. I'm sorry I didn't listen to you when you needed me this morning. I was selfish and once again only thinking about myself. I cannot and will not return to the bubble I existed in before I met you. It won't always be easy, but I promise if you forgive me, I'll try harder to pull my weight in this relationship. I'll be there for you this time." I don't think I'd ever given a longer speech in my life. I meant every word. That much I was sure of.

His expression remained unreadable. I was dying inside, wondering what he was thinking. After a moment, he took another step toward to me. My breath hitched as he took a step again. If this was his way of torturing me, I couldn't deny that I deserved it. He closed the remaining distance, bringing our bodies together. His reached for my chin, tilting my face up to look at him. "You love me?" he asked.

Relief filled me as laughter trickled up through my throat. "That's what you got from that whole spiel? Are you telling me I could have stopped after the first sentence?" I asked as his eyes moved to my lips. His thumbs stroked my cheeks.

"Well, you just kept talking. Besides, it was pretty enlightening. Except for the part about Sherman. I am not scared of him. I just don't like that bastard," he said, dropping a kiss on my lips.

I relaxed in his embrace. My body felt ready to collapse from exhaustion. He swept me up in his arms, cradling me against his chest. I broke the kiss, looking up into his eyes. My fingers traced over the planes of his face. "Does that mean you forgive me?"

"Babe, there was never anything to forgive. That's why I went to your parents' house. I owed you an apology for not being more sensitive. I'm a mule sometimes, as my dad likes to remind me."

"You went to my house?"

He nodded. "I had to."

"You shouldn't have to apologize for wanting to talk about your job."

"Can I ask you a question?" He suddenly looked serious.

"Yes," I answered apprehensively.

"What the hell happened to your cane?"

A giggle rippled through me, making me shake in his arms. "It's a long story. One I'll tell you another time. I'd rather be doing something else," I said, pulling his head close, claiming the lips that were mine again.

epilogue

Bentley

"You sure you want this one?" She had to be yanking my chain. Over the last few months I learned Mac loved to play practical jokes. She and Chad had a running contest going on who could pull the best prank.

"Absolutely. It has just enough bling."

"It's definitely eye-catching."

"Does that bother you?" she asked, reaching for it.

"No way. If that's the statement you want to make, who am I to say anything?"

"Whatever, jerk." She slapped me. "I just think it's time to retire my superhero stick. It's way too boyish. This cane screams *girl*."

"It screams, all right," I coughed.

"Careful or I'll buy that one," she said, pointing to the neon orange cane on the rack.

"This one is fine," I choked out, herding her away as she laughed. Her face lit up with happiness. I'd once thought she couldn't possibly get any more beautiful, but over the last few months I'd discovered a new level of confidence in Mac, and she practically radiated from it. "You're sure about this?" I hesitated, handing the blinged-out cane to the cashier.

"You said you'd buy me any present I wanted," she reminded me, taking the cane off the counter while I paid the total. "Are you trying to welch?"

"Not on your life. I'm looking forward to your thank-you later on." I chuckled when her face turned a delicate shade of pink as she glanced at the clerk. She was so damn cute. It was easy to embarrass her.

She changed the subject. "What time is the party?"

"Your mom said six. That means we have time to stop at the beach first. Are you game?" She nodded her head with excitement.

The drive didn't take long, and before I knew it, we were pulling into the small vacant lot near the private stretch of beach we had now deemed "our spot." How could we not, considering the pleasant experience we had shared here previously? Climbing from the vehicle, I hurried to Mac's side to carry her down to the sand. She rolled her eyes, but stood ready, knowing I wouldn't give her a real choice in the matter.

"You know, eventually I won't need you to carry me. Jake

says climbing all those stairs at your apartment is making my leg stronger."

"Well, good for Jake," I muttered. I'm sure Mac's physical therapist was a nice guy, but he was screwing with my happy time.

She laughed. "You'd think you'd be sick of lugging me around."

"Babe, you gotta know by now this is my thing. You wouldn't rob me of a little pleasure, would you?"

"Evidently not."

I set her on her feet when we reached the hard-packed sand. "So, do you feel any older?" I asked, pulling her back against me so she rested against my chest. My arms moved around her stomach, holding her in place. "You're the big two-oh. Almost a real adult."

"Thank God. I haven't felt like a kid in a long time." Her voice didn't carry a trace of sadness. Mac's road to recovery had been a long one. I was glad I was here to walk beside her, and even carry her whenever she let me.

Her relationship with her parents was a lot less rocky now that the case had finally been settled. She and her mom still argued occasionally, but I was smart enough to stay neutral. It was actually her relationship with Patricia that Mac appreciated the most. She was her last real friend from her past since neither Kat nor Zach had come around. In spite of their rejection, Mac refused to give up, reasoning that eventually her friends would be ready to face their demons like she had. I was afraid her friends' silence would drag Mac back into some pit of despair, but if anything, it made her appreciate her happiness even more. She had finally realized how strong she could be.

"I love you, Mac," I whispered in her ear, grinning when I felt her shudder in my arms. She was putty in my hands. Always had been.

She turned in my arms. Her eyes, which had become my favorite feature, practically glowed. They were no longer dull and flat like they had been when we met. They were completely alive.

"I love you, too," she said, tugging her lip into her mouth. That move got me every time. I wasn't naïve enough to think she didn't know what she was doing, but I took advantage of her subtle invitation and placed my lips on hers.

Despite Mac's best efforts to keep going, I reluctantly broke the kiss, not wanting to start something I wasn't sure I could stop before we had to leave to get to her parents' house by six. "Come on, babe. We gotta go." I tried to stand, but Mac pulled at my shirt, tugging my neck closer. "Your dad said he's making lasagna." The words had the desired effect. Mac dropped my shirt and reached for her cane before I could even finish talking.

I laughed. "Wow, remind me to never stand in your way when your dad rings the dinner bell."

"You've never had his lasagna," she threw over her shoulder as she navigated through the sand. "Trust me, they could write sonnets about it."

Following behind her, I closed the distance within seconds and scooped her up into my arms. "Why didn't you say so?" I hoisted her over my shoulder fireman-style, making her giggle as she bounced up and down from the uneven ground. Her laugh was contagious, and by the time I reached the car, we were both breathless.

We brushed the sand off each other as best we could. "Hey, perv. I didn't get any sand on those," Mac said, swiping my hands away from her chest. "Besides, you insisted we had to go."

"Damn, that's right. You sure your dad's lasagna is all that?"

"Damn straight. Now, come on. I'm hungry."

Mac's parents were finishing up dinner preparations by the time we plowed through the door, still laughing at the way she had bounced on my shoulder.

"You should have seen it, Mom. I was flopping around like some rodeo clown on the back of a bull. Hey, that's what I should start calling you—*my bull*." She patted my broad shoulders. We were all laughing at her new nickname for me when the doorbell rang.

Mac's mom had her hands busy tossing a salad and her dad was pulling the lasagna from the oven. "I got it," I volunteered as Mac made a move to climb from her barstool.

"Thanks, Bull," she teased.

"I don't know if I should be offended by that or not," I teased, smiling at the light dancing in her eyes that was too damn hard to resist. She squeezed my hand as I headed toward the front room. The doorbell chimed a second time just before I pulled open the heavy oak door revealing an attractive girl who looked vaguely familiar standing on the porch. She jumped slightly in surprise, looking like she was on the verge of bolting by the way she squeezed her bouquet of flowers in a death grip.

"Is Mackenzie here?" she asked, shifting nervously. Her free hand gripped her purse strap as tightly as the flowers.

"She sure is. Come on in." I moved aside to let her enter, but she remained frozen, looking over my shoulder with obvious uncertainty. Turning around, I saw that Mac had followed me. Her eyes fixated on the girl in front of me like she had seen a ghost. Understanding dawned on me as Mac opened her mouth to speak.

"Hello, Kat."

TURN THE PAGE FOR AN EXCERPT FROM

misunderstandings

a novel in Tiffany King's Woodfalls Girls series

Available now from Berkley Books!

one

The rain was coming down in steady sheets as I stepped from the yellow taxi that had deposited me in front of Columbia Center in Seattle. "Keep the change," I said to the driver as I reached back inside the taxi to pay my fare. I stood momentarily with the rain pelting my face, tilting my head back to see the top of the tallest building in the state of Washington—all seventy-six floors of it. I knew that fact because I looked it up on the Internet. I needed to get an idea of what I would be dealing with. Not that my friend Rob, who I was here to see, worked on the top floor, but it was close. His office was on the fifty-second floor, which meant a long, torturous elevator ride.

Something I wasn't looking forward to at all. Back home in Woodfalls, Maine, the tallest building was the three-story Wells Fargo bank they had built across from Smith's General Store a few years back. I was attending college at the University of Washington at the time, but back in Woodfalls it was big news. My mom, the town's resident busybody, made sure I received daily updates about the construction. Now, as I stood here, the building in front of me made our little bank back home look like a dollhouse.

The rain was beginning to find its way down the generic yellow raincoat I had purchased from the Seattle airport just that morning. The pilot had gleefully informed us before landing that Seattle was having its rainiest September in years. The irony that the rainiest state in the country was having its rainiest year in history was not lost on me. Why wouldn't it be cold, rainy, and miserable? It matched the way I felt about this place. Of course, that wasn't always the case. When I first arrived in Seattle three years ago, I was a greenhorn from my podunk hometown. That was why I had chosen UW. It was as far away from Woodfalls as I could possibly get without applying to the University of Hawaii. Three years ago, I had decided that nine months of rainy weather was a fair trade-off to finally be surrounded by civilization. That and it was hundreds of miles away from my often annoying but well-intentioned mother. The endless array of restaurants, museums, and stores and the music scene had tantalized me, making me vividly realize just how lacking and uncultured Woodfalls was. Everything about Seattle intrigued me, making me never want to leave, but Puget Sound was by far my favorite thing about being there. On the weekends I would haul my laptop and textbooks down to one of the cafés on the waterfront. I would spend hours drinking coffee and working on schoolwork. That is, when people-watching didn't distract me. That trait is something I had obviously inherited from my mom. Still, everything had been going along just the way I had imagined it would. It was liberating to be out from under my mom's thumb and the prying eyes of everyone back home. Here I could be my own person, with my own life. Then everything went to hell. I met Justin Avery—the whirlwind hurricane who left my head spinning and my stomach dropping to my knees like I was on a roller coaster.

My thoughts were broken when a wave of water splashed up from the road, soaking my pants from the knees down. "Terrific," I grumbled, looking down at the ruined pair of strappy sandals I had just bought. This was what I got for abandoning my typical attire of jeans and Converse shoes.

Stepping away from the offending curb before another rogue wave of nasty puddle water could finish the job, I focused on making it into the building without busting my ass or, worse yet, breaking my neck. The fake leather that had seemed so smooth and comfortable when I bought the sandals was now doing a great impersonation of a roller skate. My toes were also threatening mutiny from the cold, only adding insult to injury. This was the gajillionth reason why I had vowed never to return to Seattle. The city and I had bad blood between us.

The only reason I was standing here now was for Melissa and Rob, my two best friends from college, who had demanded that I be here for their engagement party. I'd tried every feasible excuse I could come up with—"I'm sick," "I'm out of the country," "I can't get off work." No excuse seemed to stand up to Melissa's bullshit meter.

"You're one of our best friends. You have to be here," Melissa insisted.

"No. I hate you. I'm not your friend. I never was your friend," I said.

"I wish you could see the world's smallest violin I'm playing for you right now. Come on. Pull on your big-girl panties and stop hiding."

An uncomfortable silence interrupted the conversation before Melissa finally spoke up again. "I'm sorry, Brittni. I'm a bitch for even saying that. I just mean you can't let what happened dictate your life forever," Melissa had reasoned. "Besides, you're my maid of honor. I need you. Just think of this trip as a test, like dipping your toes in water. Chances are you'll hardly see him, and if you do, it's not like you guys even have to talk."

"Maybe," I said. "I'll talk to you later."

"You mean you'll see me lat—" Her words were cut off as I ended the call.

"Maybe" was the best answer I could give at the moment. The only hope I had left was my boss.

"It's a good time to go since I'll need you more next month," Ms. Miller, my principal at Woodfalls Elementary, had stated. "Mary Smith has her wrist surgery scheduled for October and won't be able to return to work until February. I swear, I've never seen someone so damn gleeful over a surgery. I'm sure it has something to do with that god-awful book-reader thingy she got for Christmas. She's always crowing about some new author she's discovered," Ms. Miller added, looking perplexed. "Me, I need an actual book in my hand, not some electronic doodad that will most likely come alive and kill me in my sleep."

"I'm thinking now might be a good time to lay off the science fiction flicks," I had countered dryly as I tried to squish the unease that had settled in the pit of my stomach. That was that. Ms. Miller was the only obstacle left. It seemed fate wanted me in Seattle.

Now, two weeks later, here I was with my shoes squishing across the tile floor of Columbia Center. It was glaringly obvious that nothing good could come from me returning to Seattle. I skirted around a security guard and headed for the women's bathroom so I could survey the damage.

"Holy shit," I muttered when I took in my appearance in the long expanse of mirrors that lined the wall. I looked like a drowned rat. My long hair, which I had painstakingly straightened earlier, had been replaced with my typical corkscrew curls that were the bane of my existence. "Damn," I sighed as I pulled my compact from my purse so I could repair my makeup-streaked face. This was just another sign I shouldn't be here. If my friend Rob hadn't been expecting me for lunch, I would have chalked it up as a lost cause and headed back to my hotel. At the moment, I'd gladly trade my soaked clothing and frozen toes for solitude in my hotel room.

"Get a grip, wimp-ass," I chastised myself out loud, ignoring a startled look from a formfitting-suit-clad woman before she hustled out of the bathroom. "Yeah, keep moving. Nothing to see here but the freako talking to herself in the bathroom," I said, grabbing a handful of paper towels to mop up my feet and legs. Tressa, my best friend back in Woodfalls, would have a field day if she saw what a mess I was, and Ashton, my other friend, would laugh and make a joke about it. I was supposed to be the one who never got frazzled and always held it together. Tressa was the more dramatic one of our trio. She made snap decisions often, never giving any thought to the consequences. Growing up, I was often left holding the short end of the stick in most of her escapades, but I didn't care. I envied her fearless attitude. I could have used an ounce of her fearlessness at the moment. I was the cautious one. The overanalyzing, skeptical, glass-is-half-empty kind of girl. Only once had I thrown caution to the wind, and it had bitten me in the ass. That one mistake was never far from my mind. How could it be? I left town and ran back home because of it. Being back at the scene of my troubles didn't help the situation. I needed to get my act together. Two years was a long time ago. I needed to buck up or whatever shit they say to get someone to stop freaking out.

I pulled my brush from my bag and ran it through my damp blond locks, cringing as it tugged through the tangled curls that had taken over my head. After a futile moment of trying to make my hair look more dignified and less like a refuge for wayward birds, I gave up and threw it in a clip, which at least made it so that I no longer looked like the bride of Frankenstein from those cheesy black-and-white movies. I added a layer of my favorite lipstick and finally felt halfway normal.

"You got this," I said, pivoting around and striding out of the bathroom. I ignored the eruption of laughter from the two giggling girls who were entering as I was leaving. Obviously I would be their comic relief for the day.

I straightened up, finding the backbone that had liquefied and all but disappeared the moment the plane's wheels had touched down on the wet tarmac that morning. "Screw him. He doesn't own the city. I have every right to be here," I told myself as I headed for the long bank of elevators to the right of the bathrooms. A small crowd of people hurried onto one of the elevators as the doors slid open. I declined to join the overflowing box, waiting instead for the next elevator, which would be less crowded. Being closed in with a group of strangers wouldn't cut it for me. I couldn't stand being in confined spaces anyway, but elevators and I had a hate/hate kind of relationship. I hated them, and if the seventh-grade hand-crushing incident was any indication, they hated me too.

"No problem. The doors will open and you will step inside. Nice and easy," I whispered to myself. I knew it would require all my will and strength to remain sane on the elevator as it carried me up fifty-two floors to Rob's office. As is always the case with my luck, he couldn't have been on the first five or so floors, making the stairs a viable option. N-o-o-o-o-o, it had to be practically up in the clouds.

The ding signifying the arrival of the next car prompted me out of my inner whine-fest. I took a deep breath as if I were about to jump into water before cautiously stepping aboard the elevator. I exhaled a sigh of relief as the doors slowly closed and I found myself alone for the impending ride up. This was a good thing in case my hyperventilating, I-wish-I-sucked-my-thumb-or-at-least-had-a-stiff-drink elevator behavior decided to surface.

My relief was short-lived when a hand reached between the closing doors, causing them to reopen.

"You know, sticking your hand in like that can result in serious injury." Personal experience had me pointing that out before the words locked in my throat.

All the air escaped from my lungs and I wheezed out a startled swear word as the elevator doors slid closed, trapping me inside with him. I would have gladly shared the ride with a couple of brain-starved zombies instead of him.

Our eyes locked as all the animosity and hatred from two years ago radiated off him in waves.

"Justin," I squeaked out in a voice that was totally not my own.

"Selfish bitch," he greeted me with venom dripping from each word as he punched the button for the fifty-second floor with the side of his fist.

I cringed as the elevator walls began to close in on me. I knew he hated me. He had all but shouted it in my face the very last time we'd been in the same vicinity. His eyes and words had cut me like razor blades. Every syllable had traveled across the quad until all the students who had been lounging around had turned to stare at us with morbid fascination.

Justin was the love of my life.